THE NEW-OLD QUAKER WOMEN'S CLUB

Susan McCracken

Legacy Book Press, LLC

Camanche, Iowa

This book is dedicated to my daughter, Alisha Jeddeloh; without her constant suggestions and editing of my stories and research, this book would not have been possible.

ACKNOWLEDGEMENTS

I owe a great deal of thanks to the Quakers who have impacted my life, beginning with my parents who made sure our family was at the meeting house several times a week. My Junior Endeavor teacher, Fleda Hadley, started us on our understanding of scripture and where to find the various books included in our Bibles, even suggesting I might want to be a missionary someday.

In addition, there have been many longtime Quaker friends at Indianola Friends, Pleasant Plain Friends, and now West Branch Friends who have shared my spiritual journey with me. I also owe a great deal of gratitude to the many years spent as a camper and later as a counselor at Camp Quaker Heights. Each of these Iowa Quaker experiences impacted my life in positive ways.

My experiences as pastor at Pleasant Plain and West Branch have given me the desire to dig into the history of the Society of Friends. Eventually, as I began exploring new ideas from authors of more progressive theology—Bishop John Shelby Spong, Brian McLaren, Barbara Brown Taylor, Diana Butler Bass, Phyllis Tickle, Marcus Borg, and Quaker Phillip Gulley—my spiritual journey was greatly enriched and set on a slightly new and exciting path.

A special thanks to the readers who shared the book with me as it was being written, offering their comments and suggestions: Mary Ferring, Carolyn Hansen, Gwen Senio, Don Haines, Carol Wells, Shelley Erickson, Kari McCracken and Margaret Kelly. And a special thanks to Karen Bauer and Margaret Amudavi, two current Quaker women who shared their stories of working in Africa to "be the church" and enrich the lives of the Africans in Kenya.

And finally, without the many experiences shared with my parents, my two beautiful sisters, my best friend, and the joy of raising four children on a small Iowa farm, there would not have been the rich colors to share in the stories from my life's journey thus far.

A special thanks to every person who has impacted my desire to do my best to love God and my neighbor as myself.

CONTENTS

PRESENT DAY
HOW DID THIS HAPPEN?
MAPLE GROVE FRIENDS
MEETING HOUSE

The ceiling fan whirred overhead, the only sound in the silent meeting house. Elizabeth Smith—Beth to her family and good friends—shifted in the pew to get comfortable, wincing a little at the creaking of the old wood—and the creaking of her bones. It wasn't easy at the age of seventy-one to sit for so long. But it was the time in Quaker services when all sat in quiet communion with God, waiting for any messages that might stir them to speak, and she cherished this weekly moment of silence.

That didn't mean it was easy for Beth to center herself and quiet her rambling thoughts, though. She thought she might never be able to sit through a silent Meeting for Worship for a whole hour (or two or three!) like the early Friends did, the same type of worship the Conservative Friends still maintained, with no pastor to bring a message. She felt lucky to have an open-minded pastor at Maple Grove Friends, especially since so many of the Quaker Meetings in their Yearly Meeting had pastors whose messages moved Friends too far away from the needed time to sit in silence, a foundational heritage of their faith.

To settle her mind so as to be able to listen for the Spirit if it should enter with a message, she thought about the pastor's sermon this morning, especially the scripture she had closed with, Micah 6:8, "And what doth God require of thee but to do justly, and to love mercy, and to walk humbly with thy God."

Beth thought about how that was the very same verse that led to the first time she felt the Spirit within her bringing a message to share when she was just fifteen. She had been expecting some kind of loud voice in her head, or maybe even trembling like some of the early Friends when they felt the Spirit moving them to speak, giving them the nickname of Quakers. But it wasn't anything like that for her. For her, it was more of a gentle nudging to share the love of God that had moved her to rise and speak that morning. Her voice was shaking so badly that they probably thought there was something wrong with her since she was only a teenager. But when the pastor's message had talked about Micah 6:8 and God's only requirement that they should act justly, love mercy, and walk humbly with God, she knew the only way she would be able to do those things would be through God's love, and that's what she shared.

Beth still agreed with the Society of Friends founder, George Fox, that there were answers to the mystery of God that were not to be found in any one official church or pastor, no matter how profound their messages might be. But the Society of Friends had certainly faced disagreements, including two major splits in the United States in the 1800s over disagreements about the importance of scripture in developing one's faith versus relying on the moving of the Spirit.

Even now there was a lack of agreement on whether people identifying as LGBTQ should be welcomed and accepted, or whether or not scripture should be taken literally, or even the purpose of mission work. Beth thought those beliefs should be explored and questioned and not simply accepted because that's what she was taught. Her life had changed a lot since she was a kid, and so had the answers to many questions that challenged her to read more works by progressive theologians.

As Beth thought about that powerful day so long ago and how far she felt the present-day Quaker Meetings had moved from their roots, she felt that familiar stirring of the Spirit within. This time there were no words, just an inner knowing: it was time for her to do something to truly be the church—to do justly, and to love mercy, and to walk humbly with God.

PERK UP COFFEE SHOP

As she waited for her best friend, Sylvia Wilson, to join her, Beth sat in a comfy chair at Perk Up, the one and only coffee shop in their

Midwestern town of Maple Grove. She had just finished listening to a podcast by a famous agnostic, chuckling at the thought of being able to just tap an app on her phone and hear a woman speaking on the reasons so many Protestant churches were slowly dying—something Beth herself had been wondering about as over the years her own Quaker Meeting had lost almost half of their normal attendees.

Beth thought about what a long spiritual journey she had been on during her seven decades of life, beginning with their 120-year-old Maple Grove Friends Meeting. It was with the Society of Friends where she had begun her spiritual journey and spent so many years worshiping with longtime friends and neighbors.

But Beth had seen too much of a move toward fundamentalism and a growing emphasis on evangelism in their Yearly Meeting, the regional organization of Friends Meetings to which Maple Grove belonged. Even though Maple Grove Friends was more progressive than many of the other Meetings in their Yearly Meeting, she continued to long for fellowship with a group of Meetings that would not insist on a literal interpretation of scripture; Meetings where the worshippers focused on "being the church" rather than pursuing the goal of "saving" people to the exclusion of all else. In other words, she wanted to be part of a group that lived out Micah 6:8, acting justly, loving mercy, and walking humbly with God.

She liked the Friends' tradition of calling their church building a meeting house since it was the worshippers who were the church, and the building was simply where they met. And it was the church—her family and friends who met each week for worship—who needed to be accepting of all who desired to worship with them, including any LGBTQ believers. She also felt strongly that they should care about justice, support laws that would help save the environment, care for the poor, and believe in a God of love.

After feeling nudged in the previous Sunday service to take action to figure out how to be the church, Beth had called Sylvia to meet her at the coffee shop. To tell the truth, ever since she'd retired the year before, her days had become tedious with few challenges. She was used to staying busy. She and her husband had begun farming right after they married in their early twenties, but Bob had lost his life in a farming accident when their kids, Tyler and Kristy, were still in elementary school, and Beth had gone back to school to become a physician's assistant to support her family.

She had loved working with the patients in the only primary care clinic in their area, but by the time she turned seventy, she decided it was time to hang up her coat. Over the past year, though, she'd found she needed something to engage her mind, as well as fill the days since the kids were both married with no grandchildren yet to spoil. She felt she still had contributions to make to society; she just didn't have any idea what those contributions might entail—until now.

Beth and Sylvia had been having thought-provoking conversations on the direction of the Society of Friends for several years, especially the need for Friends to return to the founding Quaker principles of Simplicity, Peace, Integrity, Community, Equality, and Stewardship, fighting against the injustices that were still present in the world.

Beth loved Sylvia, who was the most compassionate person she had ever known. Sylvia had become just as close as the sister she'd never had. Beth's three brothers were pests while growing up, but they had become her protectors and chaperones in high school and beyond, and she enjoyed good relationships with each brother's family. But she had always wished for a sister to share her secrets with, and Sylvia was just such a friend, especially now that they were both retired.

The two women were nearly opposites in both looks and personality. Beth had battled her weight her entire life but had settled for being what her grandmother had called "just a bit plump." She had made peace with enjoying life's tastiest foods on special occasions, no longer becoming obsessed with the latest fad diet. She was an introvert and typically spent her evenings catching up on the day's news online or watching sports on TV. She preferred fine dining, the occasional chick flick, and traveling with a few special friends rather than being a social butterfly, unlike Sylvia.

Sylvia was a farm girl as well and had gone to the same high school as Beth, but she moved to the East Coast after college to use her political science degree. She was extremely smart and quite pretty, with shoulder-length, silver-streaked hair and a body that had remained thin her entire life. Beth had never quite understood why Sylvia had never married.

"I'm too busy working," Sylvia always said when Beth prodded her about the need to find a handsome, reliable husband.

It wasn't until Sylvia had finally tired of chasing after the various candidates in her political party and moved back to the Maple Grove area that she and Beth had become close. Declaring she was politically independent, a mugwump, as she liked to say, on her sixty-fifth birthday, Sylvia had moved back to the home place where she had grown up. Her father was beginning to suffer some dementia, and it was too much for her mother to care for him alone. Sylvia had always felt a deep-seated urge to care for anyone who was suffering, and she returned to the farm to care for her ailing parents because it was what she wanted—and needed—to do. For the most part, she was just there to assist when one of them had a doctor's appointment, plus she helped keep track of their medications, fixed some of their meals, and listened to whatever problems they had navigating their current stage of life.

When it came to their local Quaker Meeting, Sylvia and Beth's efforts to return to the Quaker beliefs of old had been met with enthusiasm by many in their Meeting, but only with basic tolerance by the leaders of their Yearly Meeting. The two women were frustrated that there had never been much support from any of the other local Meetings, and no actions leading to change had ever been forthcoming.

Rushing in, out of breath and apologizing for being late after helping her mom finish washing their breakfast dishes, Sylvia sat in a cozy chair next to Beth and they began their conversation over steaming caramel lattes, which always set the tone for their intense discussions.

Sylvia started with the question that had been on her mind ever since returning to Maple Grove Friends. "Are we wrong about this strong urging that we should focus on following Jesus's teachings to help bring about a kind of heaven on earth like he taught, rather than just getting people saved? Should we just follow the Yearly Meeting superintendent's goal of telling people they're sinners who need to repent and ask Jesus to be their Savior, and then go out to recruit others?" Sylvia asked. "I'm having a hard time thinking there's any good reason to do that when there are so many other problems in the world right now that should be the church's focus."

"No!" Beth said. "I don't think that was the main focus of Jesus's teachings at all. And we both believe we should 'be the church' and everything that being the church should encompass: protecting the environment, caring for the poor, forgiving often, rejecting racism, fighting for the powerless, sharing earthly and spiritual resources, embracing diversity, loving God, and enjoying this life!"

"Well," Sylvia said, "that sounds great. I just don't know how we got so far away from the original ideas of George Fox and the early Quakers."

"I know how I got here, and it's probably been similar to a lot of our experiences growing up in an orthodox Friends church, whether in North Carolina, Indiana, Ohio, or Iowa."

Sylvia nodded. "I agree. But I can't help but believe there's hope for the Society of Friends going forward. That's the thing that keeps me with Quakers and looking for ways to make a difference in how we live out our faith."

"Good luck with that," Beth said. "It seems most Friends are content to dwell in the past, lamenting the declining numbers of members, and the closings of not only many small, rural Meetings but also some of the larger ones."

"Then we must do something. I just don't know where to start," Sylvia declared. Beth nodded slowly, a seed of hope having been planted in her, too.

"How about inviting Lois and Nancy to help us figure out what to do next?" Sylvia suggested. Lois had been coming to Maple Grove with her family since she was in junior high, and Nancy had joined after marrying a local Quaker man over forty years earlier. The four friends had been sharing occasional lunch dates after their careers had wrapped up, discussing a variety of topics, including stimulating though rather depressing thoughts about their own Meeting's decline.

"Yes, great idea!" Beth said. "I'll plan a lunch date so we can ask them to join us in figuring out ways to help Friends return to their original ideals."

Could four retired women—still in good health, and, Beth liked to think, pretty sharp minds—really do something to make a difference, to begin reversing the numbers of declining Meetings and members in the Society of Friends? It was certainly an idea worth exploring.

"What's happened to Maple Grove since you and I were in the youth group when we were kids?" Beth asked. "I think we were trying to learn the basic values our Quaker ancestors thought were important way back then."

"I loved those Sunday evening meetings!" Sylvia said. "Maybe we should go back to the beginning to figure out how we got to where we are today."

Chapter 1

1958

Junior Endeavor

Bethie

Sunday evenings always meant going back to the meeting house, but for Bethie, as her parents often called her, it would have been better if their youth group didn't start at seven, which meant missing the endings of the TV movies that started at six. Living a fifteen-minute drive from their meeting house meant leaving home before finishing the story of Dorothy and the Tin Man with the missing heart, the Scarecrow who wanted a brain, and the Cowardly Lion who needed a big dose of courage to go to the Emerald City to meet the Wizard of Oz. Every year it was the same problem, and Bethie was afraid she might never know if they all got what they needed and if Dorothy made it safely back home to Kansas.

But going to Junior Endeavor with their pastor's wife, Mrs. Hadley, was so much fun. The group was trying to accomplish all the tasks listed for the high schoolers even though they were just the younger group, starting when they were in fourth grade. If they got everything accomplished, they would get an award at the Yearly Meeting banquet in August.

The task they were working on now, much to Bethie's delight, was memorizing the books of the Bible. Competition was a big motivator for her, and she was the best at memorizing each week's group of assigned books. She also adored the Bible Sword Drill, where Mrs. Hadley would call out the name of a book and the chapter and number of a verse, and then they would each race to see who could find it first. Bethie was often the first to wave her hand indicating she had found the sought-after scripture.

The other Junior Endeavor kids were never too excited to play Bible Sword Drill; in fact, Bethie suspected they were happy when she was sick and had to stay home, giving someone else in the group a chance to be first. Even if Bethie was mostly first, though, Mrs. Hadley often waited to call on one of the others who finally found the right verse. Bethie didn't think that was fair, because she had found it first, and besides that, she was a really good reader and never tripped over the hard words. But no matter what Mrs. Hadley had planned for them each week, it was still fun to be with her friends and work for the big award at the end.

When the Yearly Meeting banquet finally arrived that August, it was a disappointment to discover the only award they received was a piece of paper that said they met all the goals. The old guy handing out the certificates did say they were just a junior group, and the hundred-plus Friends sitting around the banquet tables watching the award ceremony had to have been impressed when the group was asked to stand. All that work they did for just a piece of paper, though! They should have at least gotten a trophy for all they had accomplished that year, especially since there hadn't been any real award for their group like the older kids got.

Maybe it will be better when I can be in the high school group, she thought. *At least those groups get to go up front and get a banner to hang in the meeting house.*

But before Bethie was old enough to be in the high school group came the sad news that Mr. and Mrs. Hadley would be leaving in a few months to pastor another Meeting. She was crushed. What would Junior Endeavor be like without her beloved leader?

"Mrs. Hadley," Bethie asked timidly after Pastor Hadley's last Sunday meeting for worship, "will you sign my autograph book?"

Almost everyone in her seventh-grade class had a similar book, and she had asked several of her friends and a few of her cousins to write in hers. She had never asked an adult to sign it, but Mrs. Hadley had been her Junior Endeavor youth group teacher on Sunday evenings ever since she was in fourth grade, and Bethie really wanted to know what this caring woman she so admired would write about her.

"Of course, Bethie!" Mrs. Hadley said warmly. "I'd be happy to sign one of the pages in your special book."

She had hoped Mrs. Hadley would write something nice about her, and not just sign her name. As soon as they were in the car heading home, Bethie opened the book just wide enough to find the long-awaited page while still keeping it closed enough to prevent her three brothers' prying eyes from reading it.

I hope someday I will read where Bethie Smith is going to be a missionary helping reach those in other countries who don't know about Jesus. Love, Mrs. Hadley

A missionary, Bethie read with surprise. *Why would she think I would be a missionary? Could I really go to some foreign country and tell people about Jesus?* She thought of all those slideshows the missionaries gave when they came back to America raising money for their work—those mud houses in Africa and wild animals roaming around didn't seem like any place she would want to live. But, Mrs. Hadley was always telling them that God had a special plan for each of their lives, so she supposed that if God did call her to be a missionary, she would have to go.

CHAPTER 2

MARCH, PRESENT DAY
WHERE DID IT ALL BEGIN?
THE CLUB—BEN'S BURGERS

Beth, Sylvia, and their other two longtime friends, Lois Hansen and Nancy Frazier, had agreed to meet for their monthly lunch together at Ben's Burgers, a family-owned restaurant that served the best salads and sandwiches laced with hummus and avocado.

After catching up on their kids and gushing over the latest grand-kid photos, Beth and Sylvia shared that they had decided it was time to explore how, as Quakers in the twenty-first century, they might somehow preserve the testimonies of the early Friends.

"My Junior Endeavor leader once told me she hoped I'd be a missionary someday. That obviously didn't happen," Beth said with a snort, "but that doesn't mean we can't embark on a different kind of mission. If we're successful, perhaps we might be able to convince some of the more evangelical Meetings around the country to change their focus from recruiting sinners to living out their faith. Shouldn't we all be following Jesus's teachings about bringing a bit of heaven to earth through our actions, like feeding the poor, fighting for justice, and finding ways to save the environment?"

"You're crazy if you think we four old women are going to change anyone's opinions!" was Lois's first reaction. Her tall figure and blonde hair always turned heads when they were together—or was it her boisterous voice? Her friends were never quite sure. She had been a teacher, and even though she wasn't shy about sharing her opinions, her smile and warm personality made her well-liked by everyone. She had maintained her warmth despite a less-than-wonderful marriage and divorce. The divorce had occurred early in the marriage, just after the birth of their first and only child, and it was years before she and her ex-husband had gotten to the point of polite greetings and the occasional brief conversation about their son, Justin. He had chosen to pursue a career in the army, to Lois's dismay. She had wanted him to find a nice local girl to marry and offer her beautiful grandchildren.

"Some of the people I've talked to during Yearly Meeting sessions just say the same old things we've been hearing for years!" she said, laughing. She had served on nearly every committee at Maple Grove Friends, and she had been the clerk of their Monthly Meeting for Business for more years than she liked to remember.

"But how will anything ever change if we don't do something?" Nancy asked.

Nancy always looked put together in color-coordinated outfits and jewelry to match. It was a habit she had learned from her mother, who had never quite understood the other pastors' wives who looked like they shopped at Goodwill and rarely wore makeup. Nancy was the quiet one of the group, but when she did speak, everyone listened. She was the wise one on whom they depended. Nancy had been a pastor's kid, moving with her family throughout her childhood to serve in a variety of Methodist churches. She considered it a blessing that her dad's final pastoral assignment had been in the same town as Maple Grove Friends Meeting. She had been classmates with the other women, but they didn't become close friends until they were adults.

After earning a college degree in accounting, Nancy had married a man whose family had been longtime members of Maple Grove Friends. When Nancy returned from college and fell in love with Allan, she also fell in love with the Friends' congregation, and she and Allan had been attending Maple Grove ever since.

By the time Nancy finished college, Allan had already started a successful electrician's business, and he persuaded Nancy that they could be a good team if she wanted to use her degree to manage the financial side. And he was right—when they were ready to retire and sell the business, they were fortunate to be financially solvent with their four boys out of college and established in their chosen careers. So far there were only two grandkids who lived close enough for her to spoil, but Nancy made sure she was always available to "grandparent," as she liked to refer to her times keeping her ten-year-old twin grandsons.

Nancy was less active in the church because of the time she spent with the twins, but she still felt a bit of excitement when Beth and Sylvia shared their passion for "being the church."

"I think I have an idea," Beth began. "What if we look at some of the strong Quaker women throughout history and how they worked to make a difference? We can list all the things they did and the contributions they made to improve the lives of others."

"That does sound intriguing," Lois said. "It's right up my alley as a former teacher! Who are you thinking about?"

"Well, I just did a little research and there are a bunch of them. Of course, one of the first was Margaret Fell Fox, who married the Society of Friends' founder George Fox, plus there's Mary Barrett Dyer, Elizabeth Fry, Lucretia Mott, Sarah Mapps Douglass, the Grimké sisters, Dr. Ann Preston, Harriett Tubman, Elizabeth Comstock, Susan B. Anthony, Alice Paul, and even a couple of current women we might want to include," Beth said, her enthusiasm growing.

"Wow, I've never heard of any of them except Harriet Tubman and Susan B. Anthony," Nancy said.

"That's because you grew up in the Methodist Church," Sylvia said with a laugh. "If you asked me if I knew any famous historical Methodist women, I would have said no. But we're all glad you're now a convinced Friend!"

"Don't worry, Nancy," Lois chimed in. "I've been a Quaker my entire life and I haven't heard of all of these 'famous' women, either. Are you sure it's worth our time researching what all these old Quakers accomplished hundreds of years ago?"

"They aren't all old—well, relatively speaking," Beth countered. "What if we each chose the women we wanted to learn more about and then researched the ways they improved the lives of others? I'm guessing their courage to do the hard work to bring about change could be examples for Quakers today."

"I'm game!" Sylvia said.

"Me, too!" Lois and Nancy said at the same time.

"Maybe we could meet at least once a month and share what we've learned about these brave ancestral Quaker women. Of course, the hard part will be figuring out what we can do to help change the direction of other Friends Meetings!" Beth finished.

"Should we have a name for this exciting project?" Sylvia asked. "I mean, maybe someday we could even write a book with all the research we discover about these women, and then maybe there could be book clubs reading and discussing how they can start 'being the church'!"

"I like it!" Nancy said. "I think we should call ourselves the New–Old Quaker Women's Club."

With that settled, the four friends started planning which famous historical Quakers they would learn about, giving themselves a month to research each woman who had "been the church" and made a difference in people's lives.

CHAPTER 3

1614-1702

MARGARET FELL FOX

ENGLAND

The sun was warm on Margaret Fell's cheeks as she walked the grounds of Swarthmoor Hall, which had been her home in northwestern England for the past twenty years. She had less time to herself now that she was a mother of seven and approaching her fourth decade, but she still tried to enjoy these beautiful woods and hills. *How did I ever get so lucky,* she wondered, *to have married such a kind man as Thomas?* Thomas's family owned the beautiful estate; he was still handsome and so very smart—after all, he was a barrister-at-law, highly respected for the work he did representing those who had been wrongfully punished and imprisoned. Margaret's heart swelled with love as she thought of Thomas, and despite her duties to see to the care of their children, she missed his presence, especially during these long summer days while he was away at work in another part of England.

"Margaret!" her neighbor and good friend, Rebecca, called from her carriage as it pulled in front of the house.

Margaret hurried toward the carriage as Rebecca climbed down and greeted her.

"You simply must invite George Fox to Swarthmoor, my dear! He has been bringing the most amazing messages all over the country-side, and he will be in our area in only a few days!" Rebecca gushed.

"I did hear mention of this man," Margaret replied. "But why should I invite him here? He would only be talking to a few of our friends and my passel of children!"

"We can spread the word of his arrival," Rebecca said, "and I can promise you there will be a crowd. We can rearrange your ballroom and provide a platform on which he can stand so all may hear his message. I have heard he has been called to begin a new gathering of believers who only need to look to Jesus for the answers to life's problems, not the hierarchy in the Church of England!"

Margaret thought about Thomas, his prestigious title and all his hard work as a barrister. What would he think if she arranged such a gathering without his permission? There would be no way to secure his blessing, and if what Rebecca was saying were true, this preacher might cause a lot of trouble for their family.

"I don't think it's a good idea," she finally said, not wanting to offend her friend nor anger her husband.

"But Margaret, what if George Fox is right? Would God want every single person to have to report to a priest and attend the only church of which the government approves? What harm would it do just to listen to what Fox has to say?"

"Well . . ." Margaret began.

"Thanks, my dear friend!" Rebecca said quickly as she climbed back in her carriage. "I'm going to get to work spreading the word that George Fox will be making an appearance at Swarthmoor Hall!"

A few weeks later, Margaret shook her head as she and her servants prepared the ballroom for the gathering she still was not entirely comfortable hosting. But it was too late to cancel the event, and she would do her best to make sure nothing George Fox said would put her family in danger.

As friends and neighbors began to arrive, some in carriages, some on horseback, a few walking from nearby estates, the excitement mounted. When Fox finally entered the room where the crowd was impatiently waiting, Margaret stared at his solemn face. There was a look of sheer determination and passion in his eyes that seemed to affect Margaret in a strange and deep way when he greeted her at the door. Who was this man? Some sort of Messiah to save them from the rigid rules of the Church of England?

Before his sermon, he simply asked, "You will say Christ saith this, and the apostles say this; but what canst thou say?" And then he began to speak from the heart of his conversion on Pendle Hill and how God had revealed to him that God was everywhere, the Light of God within each and every person, and anyone could preach God's word—man or woman. He said peace and simplicity were important, as well as using the language of commoners and being a person of integrity. He said there was no reason to swear an oath when your yes was yes and your no, no; honesty was to be every person's trademark.

Fox's words were well received, with many engaging him in serious conversation and asking questions when he finished speaking. Margaret herself became convinced this was the truest way one could know God—not through the long sermons she had to sit through each week as the priest spoke as if only he knew God.

It wasn't long before Margaret experienced what a breath of fresh air it was to simply sit in the silence and center one's thoughts on God in anticipation of a message from the Holy Spirit to share with the gathering. When Margaret felt the Spirit move within her, she heard that still, small voice encouraging her to share the words she felt from the Spirit's leading. Sometimes a member might rise and begin singing a hymn, and other times it was simply the stillness of the plain, unadorned ballroom, so different from the ornate Anglican cathedrals, that made Margaret feel at peace.

Arriving home a few days later, it took some time for Thomas to accept his wife's newfound religion. Although Margaret knew he wasn't too keen on the ideas Fox preached, at least he let her continue to hold Meetings for Worship on First Days at Swarthmoor.

"I will follow the Light of God, not man," Margaret proclaimed to Rebecca one afternoon as they sat with their tea and crumpets discussing their new beliefs. "In fact, I have received word that King Charles is going to be in London in a fortnight, and I intend to speak to him about the persecution of Friends."

Rebecca gave a somewhat sarcastic laugh. "You cannot be serious, my dear friend! No one will grant you access to the king."

"Then I shall persist until I become such a pest I am granted an audience. And I will write letters to every priest, preacher, and teacher in our country and challenge each one to prove that the Friends' principles and doctrines are false!"

• • •

Now in her eighties, Margaret sat in her prison cell, once again awaiting her release. She smiled as she thought of her dear friend,

Rebecca. Margaret would never have dreamed she would actually be granted an opportunity to implore the king to protect, rather than persecute, the new Society of Friends. She was filled with gratitude for the many times she had been blessed to play such an important role in spreading these beliefs, and especially the joy of marrying its founder at the age of fifty-five after her first glimpse of him when she was only thirty-eight.

I know it must have been God's timing when we were both sent to the same prison for refusing to take an oath in support of the king, Margaret thought, a smile brightening her face. *And then, after Thomas had passed and George proposed marriage, I knew I had been blessed to be given a second wonderful man with whom to spread the good news of God's love.* She and George preached every first day and many in between, so it was fitting that only two days before his body wore out, Margaret was blessed to be present as George preached his last sermon. It had been almost nine years ago now.

Together they sought to follow God's leading, sharing the message of the Light of God within each and every person, and Margaret was at peace with whatever the future might continue to hold for her ministry.

CHAPTER 4

APRIL, PRESENT DAY
THE CLUB—BEN'S BURGERS

"I'm so happy we chose Margaret Fell Fox as our first Quaker woman to learn about. She was a powerful speaker and partner with George Fox, helping spread the new Society of Friends religion," Beth began after the women had finished their lunches and caught up on the latest news.

"We must be going way back in history," Lois murmured. "Wasn't she born a long time ago?

"Of course!" Beth replied. "She was born in 1614."

"That would make her 406 years old," Nancy said, math calculations never leaving her mind for long.

"So what did she do that can help us today?" Sylvia asked.

"Wait," Lois said. "First, I want to know how she managed to hook up with George Fox!"

"I guarantee you'll be amazed," Beth said. "This woman's life was unbelievable. Her courage was something I haven't seen in our day and age."

"So, what did she do that was so amazing?" Sylvia asked again.

Beth began sharing the parts of Margaret's life she had found most interesting: the integrity it took to stand up to those in power, her travels all over the British Isles, and even the amazing fact that Margaret and her first husband, Thomas, had raised nine children! Then after George died, Margaret lived out the rest of her life at Swarthmoor, and in that last decade she was able to publish many of his journals.

"She must have had such a powerful experience with God that she felt she could never give up trying to convince others to follow the new Quaker beliefs," Sylvia mused. "And just think, here we are, four hundred years later, and we're still a part of what Margaret and George began."

"But what can we learn from her life?" Nancy asked. "What ideals can we live by and help people rethink their purpose nearly four centuries later?"

A look of doubt crossed Lois's face, too. "I'm beginning to wonder about that myself. From all you've shared with us, especially how Margaret came to be known as the Mother of Quakerism, she was still a type of evangelist, going around the British Isles talking about a new way to follow Jesus. Isn't that just like some of the terrible stuff we endured growing up when we were forced to go to revival meetings every year?"

"You're right," Beth agreed. "Revival meetings were torture for us when we were kids! But isn't that what we're trying to get to-day's Quakers to understand? That there are more important things we should be doing beyond trying to get people saved so they go to heaven when they die? Why can't we focus on all the things we can do to make a difference for those who are struggling here and now? Shouldn't we be looking for ways to encourage our Meetings to be more inclusive, such as for LGBTQ people being condemned as sinners? And what about caring for people in need, doing what we can to save the environment—you know, all the ways we said we should 'be the church'?

"Is it possible for us to capture Margaret's passion for sharing the Light of God within each of us, and focus our own passion on ways to move beyond some of those harmful ideas from our past, like revival meetings?" Beth finished.

"This is going to be a lot harder than I thought, but if I never have to sit through another revival, that will be a blessing!" Lois said.

"Then I would like to suggest we take seriously this task of pre-senting ways to move beyond the evangelical focus of the various Monthly Meetings in our Yearly Meeting," Nancy said quietly. "Each Quaker woman's life we examine has to still have meaning for us today in order to bring about change in the twenty-first century."

They all agreed that the task before them was somewhat daunting, but there was also a sense of excitement and hope for change—and a determination to work hard to make it happen.

CHAPTER 5

1969

REVIVAL MEETINGS

LOIS

"This is a timeline of Biblical history, beginning with the Garden of Eden and ending with the Rapture when Jesus comes to take his followers out of this sinful, fallen world!" the traveling evangelist said with fervor, gesturing toward a long piece of white paper stretched out across the stage. It began with God creating the world and then traveled through human history all the way to Rapture, an unknown time in the future when Jesus would come back to earth and take believers to heaven with Him.

Lois was a freshman in college, home for spring break, and coerced by her parents to attend the latest traveling evangelist's messages every night of the week. She had decided during her sophomore year of high school that she wasn't even sure there was this God she had learned about in years of Sunday School and more sermons than she could count. She couldn't even remember anything from those boring messages from the pastors who had come and gone at their Maple Grove Friends Meeting.

As she stood, gripping the back of the wooden pew in front of her and singing yet another verse of "Just As I Am," Lois fought with the emotions churning in her doubting mind. Why was she feeling so much pressure to join the others who were making their way to the altar to pray as the balding, overweight man begged every one of the remaining "lost sinners" to join them? *No,* she thought resolutely, *this is just this one man's idea, and he is being paid to scare all of us poor Maple Grove congregants into admitting we are sinners bound for hell. I'm not going to hell, and I don't believe in hellfire and brimstone.*

There had been many times in the past three years when "Doubting Lois Kay Hansen," as her parents called her when they were displeased with whatever rule she had broken, had wanted to believe in what she'd been taught. She wanted to believe that Jesus died on a wooden cross to save all human beings from sin so God would forgive them, and that heaven would be waiting for them when they died. But it just didn't make sense that a loving God would demand a bloody sacrifice to save the ones He had created in the first place.

Unfortunately, there was always a nagging thought in the back of her mind: *What if it is true? What if I die and there's a hell and I will burn for all eternity? What kind of incredible, horrible pain would that be? And what if there really is a heaven where no one is sick or ever dies, with streets paved with gold?*

Lois remembered a previous weeklong revival—and of course her family insisted they never miss a long, mind numbing, passionate plea to change one's sinful ways—when she had honestly believed she needed to go kneel at the wooden altar in the front of the sanctuary and pray to be a better person. When she was six or seven, she had prayed and asked Jesus to come into her heart one night at her mom's insistence, but it hadn't made her a different person. So maybe she needed to try again to be more like what God—if He even existed—would want her to be. No more fighting with her sisters, no more talking back to her parents, no more doubts about burning in hell.

But later that night as she lay in bed, away from the swelling music and impassioned calls to come to the altar and get saved, Lois decided she certainly shouldn't give in to the preacher's almost threatening pleas. All her prayers had never made any real difference in the past, and it wouldn't make any difference during this particular revival, either.

She had spent many a dark night with questions swirling in her mind about God's existence. She still wasn't convinced that people hadn't created this whole idea of an invisible being somewhere up in the sky who would answer prayers some of the time yet let a person like her wonderful grandma die on the operating table during her cancer surgery.

No, Lois seemed to have far more questions than answers about what it meant to believe all the things she had been taught growing up. She hoped her college classes, especially the Old Testament class she had signed up for in the next semester, would give her some of those elusive answers about God and Christianity.

CHAPTER 6

1611-1660
MARY BARRETT DYER
NEW ENGLAND

Lovingly and gently stroking the growing child within her, Mary smiled, wondering if it were a beautiful little girl or strapping young boy who moved within her. *William and I have longed for a child to join our family,* she thought, *and soon our hope will become a reality.* It was high time a woman of nearly twenty-six years of age and her husband should have a child to love and nurture.

It was only two days later that the labor pains began, and Mary knew it would not be long before she would be holding her first born. But as her beloved friend and midwife, Anne Hutchinson, held the blue and lifeless form that had failed to utter a single cry after leaving her body, she knew there was something terribly wrong.

"What is it? Please, Anne, hand me my baby!"

It was then that she knew the pain of not only childbirth, but also child death.

"I'm so sorry, Mary!" Anne said. "Your baby . . . your baby . . ." and when Anne started sobbing, Mary knew something grievous had happened.

"Please tell me!" Mary begged. "What is wrong with my baby?"

Reaching out to grasp Mary's hand, Anne began to describe the child. "Your baby has a beautiful face, but sadly, most of the head is missing. The limbs are not where they should be, and for whatever reason, God did not intend for this baby to live, for the child would have been the source of cruelty from other children—and, I fear, even by the church."

"No, that can't be! I felt the movement of arms and legs, and this child was created in love. Surely God would not allow such a thing to happen to William and me!"

"I am so sorry," Anne said again. "And I fear what might happen if the church leaders learn of this deformed child. You know such a child is viewed as evidence of the heresies and errors of Antinomianism the belief that Christians are freed from the bounds of Mosaic law by God's grace."

"Then what are we to do? I love this child! Please let me see it!"

It was only as Mary held this child of God who had been a part of her that her heart broke.

"Mary," Anne said gently, "we must privately arrange to bury the child before his birth becomes public."

"I know thee is correct, Anne, but please, let William and me spend a few moments alone with the child, and then we will make arrangements for a burial."

If Mary had known what would take place when somehow the authorities did, indeed, learn of the lifeless and misshapen child born and buried in a secret place, she might never have returned to Boston!

• • •

Twenty-three years later as she sat in a Boston prison awaiting her execution, Mary Dyer only briefly questioned her firmly rooted belief that the theocratic law of the Massachusetts Bay Colony went against the freedom of religion that had brought her and her beloved husband William from London to New England so many years ago. Their Puritan religion had been unable to purify the Church of England, and they had believed their journey to this new world was their only hope for the freedom to worship as they felt God desired. But what had happened to them and their sought-after freedoms?

What events and acts during her adult life would suggest she die for her newly found beliefs that differed from some of the Puritan ideals? Was it her precious stillborn baby, so deformed it broke her heart? This precious child she had carried for nine months who was never the monster Governor Winthrop and all the Puritan ministers and magistrates believed was surely due to her different religious opinions?

Was the source of her imprisonment because she and Anne Hutchinson had set about organizing anyone willing to join them to study the Bible in their homes, albeit in contravention to the theocratic law of the Massachusetts Bay Colony? What kind of land had this become when religious freedom only meant believing what the Puritan ministers were preaching?

Or was their banishment from Boston simply due to Governor Winthrop's desperate plan to reject the beliefs she, Anne, and William shared: the idea that God speaks directly to individuals rather than through paid clergy, and that God's grace is free, not something for which good works are required? Being forced to leave their friends and families and move to Rhode Island to join Roger Williams turned out to be a blessing, though, for it had offered them protection against the religious persecution they had been experiencing in Boston. It just seemed like unjustified punishment for simply exploring their differing beliefs.

And then, when it had seemed there was little hope of changing the aspects of the Puritan religion they could not support, Mary had joined William, Roger, and John Clarke in the decision to return to England. Mary still believed it was the best decision they could have made at the time. The very first time she had heard George Fox preach to a large gathering of Friends, she knew they agreed with the ideas they had shared with Anne when they were gathering in homes and discussing their disagreements with the beliefs the Puritan leaders were expounding. Mary had been so moved by Fox's passion, as well as later when she had heard Margaret Fell Fox speak, that she had wanted to go out and spread the word that everyone could be in direct communication with God. People all over England had been hungry to hear such messages freeing them from the Church of England's demands.

After five years living back in their homeland, though, Mary felt strongly that God was calling her and William to return to the New Country despite the opposition they would surely face there. And she had known she must try again to share with those in Boston her newly confirmed Quaker beliefs, regardless of what the consequences might have been.

Mary had soon learned her fears were not unfounded. After only a short time back on Massachusetts's rocky shores, she was arrested and expelled once again for simply pressuring the government leaders to do away with the laws forbidding the Quaker teachings.

Never one to give up easily, as soon as she had been free to travel, Mary had made as many trips as possible up and down the New England coastline preaching Quakerism, eventually arriving in New Haven, Connecticut. But once again, her preaching had been met unfavorably, and she was arrested and then forced to leave yet another colony.

I'm still not certain what it was that seemed so frightening to the colonists and the Puritan hierarchy, Mary thought once again. *They treated us in the same unjust manner we had experienced in England, and wasn't that the very reason we all fled to America? To be able to worship God in a more personal way, as the Society of Friends believed?*

But Mary had felt in her bones that God was calling her to return to Boston and fight against the laws forbidding Quakers to share their beliefs. Again, Mary was arrested, only this time she was sentenced to death. Standing firm in her faith, Mary had known she was more than willing to die for her beliefs, refusing to repent and disavow her Quaker understandings. But Mary's dear husband, against her wishes, had been able to draw upon his friendship with Governor Winthrop to save her from certain death. It had saddened Mary that two other Quakers were hanged that day while she was set free and forced to again leave the colony.

At that point Mary had known she had two choices—rejoice in her freedom and give up preaching to any and all who were eager to hear these new beliefs or continue doing what she felt God had been leading her to do. For Mary, it was no choice at all, and she had vowed to carry on with vigor.

Eventually Mary's conscience led her back to Massachusetts one more time to defy the anti-Quaker laws. Despite her husband's and children's pleas, she had refused to renounce her faith.

Thus here I sit, she thought, *waiting for what will most certainly be my death this time. I will hang from the gallows knowing I have done my best to spread my beliefs with so many in both my native country as well as this new land where we came in hopes of religious freedom. In obedience to the will of the Lord God I came, and in His will I abide faithful to the death.*

Mary had no doubt their message was so strong that more and more Quakers would follow in the footsteps of their growing group of believers who would courageously not be silenced. She prayed that never again would men and women be persecuted simply for their differing beliefs.

CHAPTER 7

MAY, PRESENT DAY
THE CLUB—NANCY'S HOME

Quaker Club friends: Let's meet at my house this month to share about the next awesome Quaker woman from our list, Nancy texted. *I'll pick up a couple of take-and-bake pizzas so we can save a bit of money. I'm feeling like the Quaker value of simplicity might mean thinking about ways to cut back on spending, and restaurants aren't cheap. Plus Jack and Jace are staying here this week while their parents are on a work trip, and you know how much kids like pizza. They'll scarf down any leftovers when they get back from school. I know we could have postponed our gathering until next week, but I couldn't wait to tell you about Mary Dyer!*

Nancy was still reeling from what she had learned about the Quaker woman who had come to the colonies for religious freedom only to be hanged at the young age of forty-nine. How had such a strong, brave woman not made it into their Quaker history curriculum at Maple Grove Friends? Mary Dyer's desire to spread her newfound faith was considerably more powerful than anything Nancy had heard in any of the thousands of sermons she'd heard in her lifetime.

As the F/friends arrived one by one, their chatter centered on their family lives while the aromas of baking pizzas made more than one stomach growl. Nancy hoped there would be a few slices left for Jack and Jace to feed their growing boys' stomachs when they got back later in the afternoon.

Once a good portion of the pizza was devoured, followed by the rich nutty chocolate brownies Nancy had made that morning, Sylvia was the first to ask what was so fascinating about Mary Dyer.

"Well," Nancy began, "first of all, she was a martyr, willing to die for her beliefs."

"Wait," Lois interrupted. "I thought she was an American. You're telling us she died here—in the land of the free—just because of her Quaker beliefs? I taught my second graders the story of the Pilgrims every Thanksgiving and how they came to America for religious freedom!"

"Yes," Nancy said, "that's probably what we were all taught. But it wasn't freedom in the beginning unless you were of the Puritan faith. The governors of some of the first states were Puritans, and they certainly mixed religion and law."

Nancy went on to describe the many times Dyer was arrested and imprisoned for speaking out against the Puritan leaders, and how she heard George Fox when she went back to England and became convinced to join the Quaker movement.

"So was she killed in England or in Massachusetts?" Beth asked.

"Mary felt a strong need to return to the new country and try to persuade the authorities that it was wrong to make laws against the peace-loving Quakers," Nancy said, "so her last three years were spent sharing her new beliefs in Connecticut, Rhode Island, New York, and finally in Boston. It was there that she refused to repent and give up her Quaker beliefs, and she was sentenced to death by hanging."

"And we're supposed to find something about her life to help us be the church today?" Lois asked. "I hate to break it to you, but I'm not going to be put to death for being a Quaker! We have a constitution and laws meant to protect our religious freedom."

"But what if something happened to our government and some-how a president became a dictator and said we all had to believe in some other religion or face death?" Sylvia mused. "Are you saying you wouldn't stand up for our beliefs?"

"That's not going to happen!" Lois argued. "This is a democracy."

"So was Germany before Hitler, and a lot of other countries even now in other parts of the world," Beth said. "And can any of us predict the future? It seems like everyone in this country is taking sides and not working together! It really scares me to think about what might happen here someday."

"I don't think it helps to speculate about the future," Nancy said. "Let's talk about what we can learn from Mary Dyer's courage. Which of our long-held testimonies did she uphold?"

Beth thought back to her Junior Endeavor days with Mrs. Hadley and how they had talked about being a person of integrity. As a kid, she hadn't had any real understanding of the word and how to apply it to her life. But now, considering all that was happening in the Friends Meetings in their Yearly Meeting alone, an idea began to take shape that might push toward their goal of creating a paradigm shift in long-held beliefs.

"Okay, friend," Sylvia said, looking intently at Beth. "I see the wheels turning in that pretty head of yours. What are you thinking?"

"I'm thinking it's important for us to remember the purpose of this club—the need to stand up to the current beliefs in our Yearly Meeting and not be afraid of being dismissed for our different ways of viewing scripture and how we believe we are called to 'be the church.' Mary Dyer was a person of integrity. She never compromised her beliefs or the desire to share them with anyone who might be looking for a new way to view God. So if we are going to be women of integrity, we need to stand up for what we believe and not back down."

A questioner by nature, Lois looked skeptical. "So exactly what do you think we should be doing that we aren't already?"

Sylvia was quick to take up Beth's idea. "Let's start by focusing on one of those ideals we talked about before we started this project: protecting the environment, caring for the poor, forgiving often, rejecting racism, fighting for the powerless, sharing earthly and spiritual resources, embracing diversity—especially LGBTQ and transgender rights—loving God, and enjoying this life."

"Caring for the poor might be the easiest one to start with. What are some of your ideas?" Beth asked.

"What if we volunteered to help at the food pantry?" Nancy suggested. "I know I could work a few days a week."

"And what if we spent a day canvassing businesses to donate food and even contacted some companies to see if they might be willing to chip in with funds or products?" Sylvia added. "Paper goods and things like toilet paper are always needed, and corporations seem to like improving their images with good deeds."

"Okay, ladies, I think you're onto something," Lois finally admitted. "I have a cousin who has what seems like a pretty important job at Procter and Gamble. Maybe he could get them to donate some Charmin for us."

As the ideas began to flow and each woman made a list of actions she might take, Beth had another idea.

"You know, my good friends," she mused as they began to wrap up their discussion, "I really enjoyed just meeting in your home, Nancy, rather than at a restaurant or at the coffee shop. Maybe we could take turns hosting our club meetings. We could have them in the morning and the person hosting would furnish coffee or tea and a simple snack—fresh fruit, muffins, cookies—whatever each of us chooses."

"It's a no-brainer," Lois said emphatically. "I'll host next month, and then each week we can decide whose schedule works best to host the following month."

"Yes, I agree," Sylvia added.

"It's official! Maybe we should call it 'The New–Old Quaker Women's Home Club,'" Nancy joked.

Their future meeting plans in place, it was with a sense of accomplishment that they wrapped up their afternoon session just as the twins arrived from school. There was nothing like ten-year-old boys to liven up any gathering—and scarf down leftover pizza!

CHAPTER 8
1971
CHARISMATIC GATHERINGS
NANCY

"This is so exciting!" Nancy thought as she arrived at the home of one of her Green Chapel friends. Green Chapel was a non-denominational country church that had closed and then been resurrected to host Saturday evening services geared toward young people in the area. A few were so inspired by the services that they had begun meeting on Friday evenings in each other's homes to explore the gifts of the Spirit.

Nancy had just moved home after graduating with her finance degree and was enjoying the chance to explore the next steps in her life and career. She was fairly certain she had no interest in helping people with their income taxes, but she hoped there was a local business that would have a position she was interested in, perhaps as a business manager or payroll clerk.

Although she wasn't sure what she wanted to do, one thing was certain: she hoped Allan, her high school boyfriend, would be part of it. After graduation, they had not made any future plans because she was going to college four hours away. But they had shared occasional letters, and Nancy had continued to hope he might wait for her to be in his future when she graduated. Now he had started his electrical business in their hometown, and she was hoping to reconnect.

"Hey, there!" Allan greeted as he came through the door, a wide grin on his face. "When did you get back?"

"Just last night! When Jenny called and said our Green Chapel friends were gathering this evening, I was anxious to see everyone. I was hoping you might be here," she added, her cheeks burning a little. "But I didn't remember seeing you at Green Chapel when I was home on break, so I wasn't sure you were part of this group. But I'm really happy to see you."

"I'm sorry I haven't written lately," Allan said. "I've been really busy getting the business started, studying for the test to get my journeyman's license, and trying to visit lots of neighbors to see if they might need some electrical work done. But my friend, John, invited me to come tonight, and I have to admit," he said with a faint blush, "I was hoping you might show up, too. John said you had graduated and were back in the area."

"I'm just glad you're getting your own business started!" Nancy said warmly, hoping her smile reminded Allan why none of the other girls he had dated during the four years since high school graduation had captured his heart.

"Shall we get started?" Jenny said, interrupting the beginning chatter. "I'm happy to see Nancy back from school, and Allan, I think this is your first time, so welcome. Shall we begin with prayer?"

As the group gathered in a circle and joined hands, one person after another offered prayers for the sick, for those in need, and for the country. Suddenly, a boy Nancy knew from their high school class began to raise his head, eyes closed, lips moving in a quiet whisper. Then suddenly he started speaking loudly in what sounded like a foreign language. Nancy quickly glanced at Allan, hoping he wasn't wondering if she had gotten involved in some sort of cult!

When Jenny closed the prayer, Nancy made sure to sit next to Allan for the following discussion of a Bible passage from First Corinthians that talked about speaking in tongues, interpretation of tongues, and several other gifts of the Spirit. Everyone seemed to be excited at the prospect of using this new kind of prayer language for healing, saving souls, and, as one person noted, "praying when no words are adequate." She continued sneaking glances at Allan, but she couldn't tell from his expression what he was thinking.

The gathering only lasted an hour, with Jenny reminding everyone that Green Chapel would be holding services every Saturday evening for any young people from any church in the area. She said lots of young people were attending the services, and, looking directly at Allan, she said she hoped to see them all on Saturday evening.

As they were leaving, Allan grabbed Nancy's hand and suggested they get ice cream at the Dairy Bar. "We can sit outside at one of the picnic tables and catch up on what's been going on in your life," Allan said, a hint of worry in his voice.

"I'm always good for a hot fudge sundae—if you're sure you can afford it!" she teased.

When Nancy's last bite of sundae was gone and Allan had finished his chocolate malt, he cleared his throat. "So, I'm kind of curious about this group. What exactly is going on with that weird prayer?"

"It's a new thing that's happening everywhere!" Nancy said. "It's called a charismatic group, and we're following Paul's teachings in chapters twelve to fifteen in First Corinthians, where Paul talks about the gifts of the Spirit and how they're to be used in worship. Speaking in tongues is what you heard tonight, but there also needs to be someone who can interpret the message, so everyone knows what the language means. That's what John was doing after the prayer."

"I don't know, Nancy. That kind of sounds like a cult to me," Allan ventured.

"It's happening in Catholic churches, and lots of Protestant churches, too—Baptist, Methodist, Presbyterian, and all the Pentecostal churches," Nancy added. "It's not a cult. We're just following teachings in the Bible."

"I guess the question I have to ask," Allan said slowly, "is if you have spoken in tongues?"

Nancy paused, not sure how to explain what had happened to her when she had been home on spring break. Finally she took a deep breath and began to describe the cool March night that had changed her life.

"Do you remember my Aunt Jerry? She's the one who goes to the Assembly of God church. She invited me, my sister, and my friend, Beth, to come to a revival at her church. A traveling speaker gave a message about how he had been a drunken sailor and had 'done all kinds of sins,' as he put it, and how he had become a Christian. He talked about the baptism of the Holy Spirit and how it had changed him. Then he had an altar call."

"But Quakers believe there is only one baptism Jesus came to offer, the baptism of the Holy Spirit. So what was the preacher saying that was so different?"

"He said after a person was a Christian for a while, they needed a baptism by the Holy Spirit to move to the next level of being a follower of Jesus."

"So what exactly happened that night?" Allan wanted to know. "And what does that have to do with getting involved with this charismatic group?"

"Well," Nancy said slowly, "we were all standing there while my cousin played the piano nonstop, and several people had gone to the front of the church and knelt to pray. Before long the preacher pointed his finger right at me and asked me if I didn't want to come down and pray.

"So I went forward, and a lady came over and asked me what I wanted Jesus to do for me. I said I didn't know, and she asked if I knew Jesus, and I said yes, and then she asked if I wanted the baptism of the Holy Spirit. I agreed because I just wanted to be able to go back to my seat."

"So what happened?"

Encouraged by Allan's increasing curiosity, Nancy continued. "I closed my eyes and raised my hands like the lady suggested, and then something did happen, Allan. I started just repeating the name 'Jesus' and it was like the whole rest of the church wasn't there, and then these strange words came out of my mouth. It probably sounds crazy, but I know it was a real Spirit thing, and I have to tell you, even with all my doubts about God's existence that I've had ever since we were in high school, after this experience, I knew God was real."

"Huh," Allan said. "And have you ever had those strange words come again?"

"Yes, sometimes when I'm praying," Nancy admitted. "I just hope you won't think I'm imagining these things. I don't think there are a lot of traditional Protestant churches where the gift of tongues with the gift of interpretation—or any of the other gifts Paul lists in those chapters—are ever really talked about."

"No, I don't think you're imagining what happened to you. But I also don't think any of this is probably for me," he said.

"That's okay! But will you come with me Saturday night to the Green Chapel service? There won't be any speaking in tongues, just a good message and then a gathering at the pastor's house afterward for all of us young people."

"I'll give it some thought," Allan said. "And I'm also going to give us some thought! I've missed you so much these past four years, and I'm really glad you decided to come back to Maple Grove. I was hoping you hadn't come back engaged or with a serious boyfriend. Maybe we can go see a movie Friday if you're free."

Nancy continued smiling long after they made plans for their Friday night date and she was back at her parents' home. Life in Maple Grove had just gotten a lot better. If Allan came back to their charismatic gathering again, fine; if not, that was okay, too. And since she had never heard of the gifts of the Spirit in the Methodist Churches she had attended, she was fairly certain from the few times she had been to worship services at Maple Grove Meeting with a couple of high school friends, the Quakers would probably not be in favor of speaking in tongues with interpretations, either.

Once again Nancy wondered if Allan's family, who had been Quakers their entire lives, would accept a Methodist pastor's daughter who was now part of this charismatic group—especially if she and Allan might have a future together.

CHAPTER 9

1780-1845
ELIZABETH GURNEY FRY
ENGLAND

Elizabeth took a deep breath, stared at the imposing stone fortress in front of her, and shivered. Why had she said she would visit this foreboding place? She was only forty-three years of age, a mother of eleven with several of her brood still at home and in need of her care. Would it not be foolish to enter a prison and risk her life, leaving her children motherless? Surely her husband, Joseph, would not be able to care for all of them, especially with his attention focused on his nearly bankrupt business. And there had to be many others who were wiser and better trained to work with women prisoners.

I don't belong here, she thought. Her father and mother both came from well-to-do banking families in Norwich, though her life took a turn when her mother died when she was only twelve, leaving her to care for her eleven younger siblings. Her family had been faithful members of the Society of Friends, and she had chosen the way of the "plain Friends" as a young adult, choosing to observe the strict "set apart" belief of many in their meeting, which meant no dancing or singing. Marrying banker Joseph Fry at age twenty meant a prosperous lifestyle, which included entertaining important businessmen and then raising their eleven children.

Yet when Quaker missionary Stephen Grellet presented the desperate need within the walls of Newgate Prison, she had felt a stirring within, remembering Jesus telling his disciples that when they visited those in prison, they were doing it as to God. Now here she was.

Clasping her hands to hide their trembling, Elizabeth took another deep breath and entered the iron gates, where a guard led her to a dirty, dark room. Immediately she was horrified at what she saw—women and children everywhere with no beds, no bathrooms, and no lights or fans. There had to be several hundred women crowded in the room, and there were so many children staring at her with scowls on their faces, dirty clothes, unkempt hair, and hopelessness in their eyes.

As several women started moving menacingly toward her, Elizabeth quickly turned toward the guard to let her out—this was a mistake! It had to be! But only the closed door was behind her, no guard in sight.

Remember, she told herself, *the Lord has brought you here.* Saying a quick prayer, she smiled at the woman closest to her. Clinging to the woman's side was a young child, perhaps the same age as Elizabeth's youngest, with nothing but a thin cloth meant to cover part of his body. As a mother, Elizabeth knew the way to acceptance from the women would be through their children, so she smiled at the youngster and spoke softly to the mother.

"How old is thy child? What is the name?"

Immediately the woman softened as she smiled at her offspring. "He is three years old, but he has been sickly and needs my care."

As she chatted with the woman, some of the other mothers joined them. Elizabeth hoped they sensed there was kindness in her manner, not the cruelty of some of their other visitors or the guards. She wondered if this might be the beginning of a way to help these women. Some were accused of serious crimes, even murder, but many were awaiting trial for simple crimes of need—stealing food to feed their families, using counterfeit coins, or being in debt. Was there any way to offer hope to these women, to help them once again become free citizens with a purpose in life? The task seemed nearly impossible, and truly overwhelming!

• • •

For the rest of her life, Elizabeth never forgot that first day at the prison. Now in her sixties with her eyesight beginning to fail, reading had become more difficult, but her past prison visits were a source of many of her fondest memories, most often giving her hope for a better future for all incarcerated women. *What would have happened if I had turned away and not followed God's leading?* she asked herself. *It was my visit to Newgate that fateful day that led to my lifelong calling to improve the lives of the women prisoners.*

Elizabeth remembered the lessons she gave the children, helping them learn to read and write, then encouraging other Friends to set up classes to teach the prisoners skills such as quilting and needlepoint they could use when they were freed. This new treatment had been so successful that eventually she was asked to tour prisons all over England to share the success stories of her work with the Newgate women and children.

One of Elizabeth's most meaningful memories was the time she was asked to speak at both Houses of Parliament about the conditions in the prisons. She had shared how they had provided clothing, instruction, and employment for the women and introduced them to the Holy Scriptures. Elizabeth still firmly believed these new methods helped transform the women into successful members of society upon their release.

Elizabeth was still in awe at everything God had helped her accomplish in her lifetime, taking her to many parts of Europe and even beyond. What a thrill it had been to even work with the government in Australia when some of the English criminals were not being properly cared for after transportation to the penal colonies there.

And then there was God's calling to work beyond prison reform after she had found that young homeless boy frozen on the streets of London. It still caused her such deep sorrow to think how any child of God could be left to die in the street. That calling had led her to organize other like-minded believers to establish a night shelter for the homeless.

Her life had not always been easy, and when Joseph went bankrupt, she had had to curtail some of her own work. But she had stood firm in knowing she would never give up her work as a Quaker believer, encouraging other Friends to focus on helping those in need. *God was with me through it all,* she thought with gratitude, *especially that first day when my choice had been to turn away or enter Newgate's walls. And as long as my health allows, I will continue to be a voice for those who cannot speak for themselves, just as Jesus had taught his disciples.*

CHAPTER 10

JUNE, PRESENT DAY
THE CLUB—LOIS'S CONDO

Lois wasn't certain she was all that excited about meeting in each other's homes, especially since she lived in a condo now that her son was in the Army, and she was on her own. It wasn't that her condo was shabby or in a rundown part of town; it was nestled on a lovely tree-lined street, and she had plenty of room for her friends to sit around her grandmother's round oak table. But she had to admit she considered herself to be in the "restaurant stage of life" and thoroughly enjoyed eating out! These morning gatherings around coffee, tea, and pastries had worked well, though, so she decided there was no reason to push for restaurant lunches, even if it meant she would have to take a turn hosting the club.

As she pulled the Trader Joe's almond croissants out of the oven, the decadent aroma made Lois want to eat hers on the spot! Exhibiting great patience, she set the pastries in her toaster oven to keep them warm while she finished setting the table. Lois was excited about her valiant Quaker woman, Elizabeth Fry, and was anxious to tell the others all the amazing things this woman had done with her life long ago.

For once, Nancy was the first to arrive, buzzing the intercom for Lois to let her into the condo building. "What is that yummy treat I inhaled as soon as I walked in the door?" she asked excitedly.

"Trader Joe's Almond Croissants! Have you ever tried them?"

"There isn't a Trader Joe's anywhere around here, so no, I've never had the pleasure. Where did you find them?"

"I get them when I go to the city to pick up Justin at the airport when he's home on leave. My sister is the one who got me hooked on them."

"Am I the first one here?" Nancy looked around in surprise. She was often the last one to arrive after dropping the twins off at school before their club meetings.

"Yes," Lois said, grinning. "What happened with the boys today?"

"Allan had some errands to run this morning, so he's dropping them off."

"Do you have them every day?" Lois asked. She didn't say what she was thinking—that no retired person should be saddled with grandkids every single day during the week!

"No, just the days Steph has to work."

The door buzzed again. This time it was Beth and Sylvia, who had shared a ride.

"It's about time you got here." Lois softened her chiding with a smile. "You're five minutes late."

"Lois, you know we said any time between 8:30 and 9:00!" Beth shot back. "So please bring us whatever delightful treat you've been baking that smells so good, and then we can get started!"

As the women enjoyed their croissants, oohing and aahing over the almond centers, their conversation soon turned to Elizabeth Fry and her prison work.

"I'm not sure I would ever have the courage to walk into one of today's prisons, and I know for certain I probably could not have entered that scary, dungeon-like Newgate place!" Nancy said after Lois had described Elizabeth Fry's work. "Would any of you be willing to do that?"

"If we're following Jesus's teachings," Sylvia said thoughtfully, "there is that verse about visiting prisons, and how things like visiting prisoners, feeding the poor, and taking care of the sick are all actions that demonstrate our love for God. It's really for God that we do these things to help others."

"Well," Lois began, not sure of the response her next idea would generate, "I've been thinking about this a lot since learning about Elizabeth Fry's work, and I have an idea." She paused, trying to gauge the expressions on the others' faces. "One of my teacher friends was telling me about a Wednesday evening church group in the women's prison over in Cedar Lou, and they're always looking for volunteers to help with the services. What if we signed up to help with one of those some Wednesday evening?"

"I don't know," Beth said. "What would we say that might help? I bet some of them are there because of drugs or child abuse—or even worse!"

Nancy already had her phone out, looking up their state statistics. "It says there are currently over five hundred women incarcerated, and most of them are from poor families, with a higher percentage of Hispanic and Black women. This article also says that some of the main reasons they've been sent to prisons are due to bad experiences living in poverty, substance abuse, and physical, emotional, or sexual abuse."

"And here we sit, four retired White women, all who have had good jobs and retirement funds," Beth said, shaking her head. "How would any message we might share be relatable?"

"But Beth," Sylvia said, "you know what it's like to lose a loved one, and these women have lost the privilege of seeing their loved ones every day, especially those who have children."

"That's true," Beth said, "but I'm no good talking to people I don't really know. I wouldn't have any idea what to say!"

"Yes, you would," Sylvia said, looking directly into Beth's eyes, "because you have a way with words and connecting them with people's lives. Remember the message you brought when Pastor Deborah was on vacation, and how many people spoke to you afterward about how meaningful your message was to them? Or what about the kids you talked to when you were a Sunday School teacher and how well they listened to you? Not to mention all the patients you dealt with in your career," she added. "I'm pretty sure you would figure out what to say to these women that would help them have hope for a better life once they're released. What if you talked about some of the Quaker testimonies, or about Jesus's teachings that everyone is loved by God regardless of their past?"

"Well, maybe," Beth said, still not crazy about the idea. "But you would all have to come with me so I could at least see your three smiling faces!"

"I'll contact the prison chaplain and see what it might take for us to help with a service there, assuming we all agree to do this ministry. It certainly will be a lot easier than the work Elizabeth Fry did," Lois said excitedly. "And really, it can't be that hard. Cedar Lou is nothing like Newgate Prison. Maybe we can even do one service a month if the women accept us."

"That's great, Lois. But let's just start with one service and see how it goes," Sylvia said. "You with us, Beth? Nancy?"

Nancy nodded while Beth said, "Okay, I'll do my best, but I'm only going to promise to go one time and see if I can figure out what to say that would be Light for these women. And Lois, you're the expert teacher, so you'd better chime in once in a while!"

Soon Lois had a pen and pad out, writing down a list of topics they thought might engage some of the women. By the end, excitement had begun to build at the thought of this new way of "being the church," the same way Elizabeth Fry had summoned the courage to do her work hundreds of years ago.

CHAPTER 11

1965

TWIN PINES QUAKER CAMP

SYLVIA

"Do I really have to go to camp again?" Sylvia asked for the tenth time. "I've been going every year since I was ten, and I know everything they're going to say in chapel. And it's sooooo boring! I'll be a junior this year, and none of my Maple Grove friends have to go."

Sylvia knew it was a losing battle, though. She'd forgotten to put away her journal, and her mother, Ruth, had found her entry talking about her new belief that God didn't exist, that He was just a made-up character, like Santa Claus and the Easter Bunny, to get kids to behave. Her mom thought that going to camp was the only way to help her disbelieving daughter get back on track with her faith. Even worse, Sylvia had to ride with her mother's friend, Jenny, since she was the only kid from the area going to camp; and Jenny was going to be a counselor—and her mother's spy, Sylvia was sure.

"I'm sorry, but it's non-negotiable, honey," Ruth said. "Jenny will be here in half an hour, so please hurry and finish your packing."

The two-hour ride to camp wasn't as bad as she feared. Jenny just asked questions about school, her friends, if she had a boyfriend— typical stuff adults tended to ask teenagers. But things started going downhill fast when they entered the lodge to register and Sylvia discovered she had been assigned to cabin 0, the one no girl ever wanted to stay in. *Can this week get any worse?* she wondered.

Twin Pines was nestled deep in a wooded area. Half of the small cabins were for girls and half were for boys, with common restrooms and shower houses for each gender. Cabin 0 was the newest girls' cabin, built in a clearing far away from the other six cabins. Now her only hope was that she would have a fun, young counselor. One year she had been stuck in a cabin with an old woman named Priscilla who had to have been in her eighties! She had told them it was a sin to use slang words like "gosh" and "darn" because it was just like swearing. When Sylvia had demanded to know what they should say when they were upset, Priscilla had told them that saying, "oh, pickles," would be acceptable. But the next year Sylvia's cabin had gotten a college student for their counselor who let them go cabin raiding at night to cover the boys' cabins with toilet paper. That had been so much fun!

When Sylvia finally dragged her luggage all the way to cabin 0, she found the counselor wasn't ancient, but she wasn't young, either. Linda was a pastor's wife from another Friends Meeting, and she and her husband had no kids. That was a deal breaker as far as Sylvia was concerned. She wasn't about to share her doubts about God and salvation with a woman who had no idea what teenagers were dealing with.

Every day was pretty much the same boring schedule: wake-up bell, breakfast, devotions with your cabin mates, then two or three classes, usually one involving crafts. Next came lunch, rest time in the cabin, the half-mile hike to the lake to swim, supper, a vespers service in the woods, and finally evening singing and a sermon in the chapel. It was the evening service that Sylvia dreaded the most because it always involved an altar call.

The speaker for the week spent way too much time begging kids to come down front and ask Jesus into their hearts. No way in hell ("hell" being a swear word Sylvia had begun using around her friends) was she going to go forward. And why in the world did kids feel pressured to return to the altar night after night with tears, confessions, and repeated pleas for Jesus to come into their hearts? Did He leave during the day and need to be invited back every night?

But the evening services weren't the worst things that happened that week.

On one of the final days of camp, when Sylvia had just about decided she would survive the week, Linda took each of her campers aside individually to see if they needed to get saved—at least, that's what Sylvia suspected was the reason for these sessions. She had no choice but to agree when Linda asked her to join her on the grassy slope behind their cabin 0 for "the talk."

"So, what can I help you with on your spiritual journey?" Linda asked softly.

"Nothing," Sylvia said, unwilling to play along and give the answers she knew Linda probably wanted. "I don't believe in God."

Sylvia was sure Linda was shocked at her admission, but Linda kept her cool and simply asked another question. "What about the Bible? Do you believe the scriptures that say we are to confess our sins and ask forgiveness, then ask Jesus to become a part of our lives?"

"No," Sylvia said again, "I don't believe in the Bible, either."

"What about these verses in Romans that give us the steps we need to take to become a Christian and secure our place in heaven?" Linda opened her Bible and started reading the verses Sylvia knew had been labeled "The Roman Road to Salvation."

When Sylvia didn't answer, Linda sat quietly for a while, probably contemplating Sylvia's poor lost sinful soul. Finally she asked Sylvia if she could pray for her over the coming weeks and months. Sylvia did feel kind of bad that she had been so brutally honest sharing all her doubts, so she consented to Linda's request.

"I'll be praying for you," Linda said as she rose to leave, reaching over to hug her reluctant camper.

And then it was over. Finally! On the way home, Jenny kept asking Sylvia about her experiences, especially if she had learned anything in the classes and if her faith had grown. Sylvia faked it this time, saying the services had been good and she had had a good spiritual talk with her counselor. She knew if she said anything about her real discussion with Linda, Jenny would be sure to tell her mother.

Sylvia was determined to find a full-time job the next summer so church camp would be out of the question. No camp, no pressure to repent, no religion crammed down her throat!

CHAPTER 12

1793-1880
LUCRETIA MOTT
NANTUCKET TO PHILADELPHIA

As Lucretia stood on the deck of the ship carrying her to London, she thought of the fateful day in her twelfth year when the Holy Spirit stirred within her. She had been learning about the horrors of the African slave trade in her Nantucket school, even though Nantucket had been declared free of slavery by the Quakers who had settled there. She had read about the capture of Africans on the Guinea coast, the separation of families, and the packing of slaves into the holds of the slave ships, where many died from lack of adequate air, water, food, and exercise. It had all been so horrifying, and she couldn't stop thinking about them.

I will never forget sitting in the silence during the Meeting for Worship that day and feeling an overwhelming presence within me reveal one of God's truths: that He loves all of God's creation, not just White Americans and Europeans, Lucretia told herself as she stared into the misty horizon. An elder in the Meeting that day had explained to her that stirring meant the Holy Spirit had revealed a spiritual insight that would guide her in living her life with God's purpose.

That stirring had led her as an adult to take a stand against the injustice of enslaving other human beings, which had led her on this trip to London to the 1840 World Anti-Slavery Convention. *I must continue to listen to the Light within that has impressed upon me the need to fight against the abomination of slavery. I must be brave like Mary Dyer, who was hanged on Boston Common rather than forsake her Quaker beliefs,* Lucretia told herself firmly. Ending this blight on the world would continue to require all the courage she could muster as she, her husband, James, and their fellow Quakers traveled across the Atlantic to the convention, where they would adopt a resolution declaring the need to end slavery once and for all.

Lucretia was grateful for others in the Philadelphia Delegation, Friends who had financially supported their trip, as well as the other committed Quakers who had helped make the journey's rolling seas much more tolerable. But as the London docks rose on the horizon, she forgot her fear in the excitement of gathering with others supporting their cause.

Lucretia was especially hopeful she would be able to meet Elizabeth Cady Stanton, who was not a Quaker but a strong woman who acted on her convictions. Lucretia remembered reading how Stanton had insisted the word "obey" be removed from her wedding vows. *This is a woman I must get to know,* Lucretia vowed.

Her enthusiasm was immediately dampened, however. The first order of business at the convention had been a defeated motion to accept women as delegates. Even though several esteemed men, both American and British, spoke in favor of the women's acceptance, the majority were opposed. Their arguments arose from Biblical references of women being submissive to men. *I should just cease my presence,* Lucretia thought, but she let a few British Friends persuade her to remain.

Although women were forced to sit in a separate section and were not allowed to speak as delegates at the convention, Lucretia knew the long journey and her disappointments were worth it when she was able to finally meet Elizabeth Cady Stanton.

"I'm so pleased to meet thee," Lucretia greeted the younger woman. "We must not only work for the abolition of slavery but also for the equal treatment of women! I have read of your fight for our God-given rights, and I must hope that somehow together we might use our voices and our actions to create equality for all."

"Yes, we must!" Elizabeth agreed, linking arms with Lucretia.

"Just look at how we are being treated at this convention," Lucretia said angrily. She had been fighting against slavery as a part of the American Anti-Slavery Society for several years, thanks in part to William Lloyd Garrison's abolitionist newspaper, *The Liberator,* and his continued efforts to persuade her to join the cause. As a Quaker, her religious belief in equality was an underpinning of her work for freedom, which had been the impetus for helping found the Philadelphia Female Anti-Slavery Society in 1833. So why were she and Elizabeth being silenced at the convention and banished to the visitor's gallery?

"I am sick of this man-worship," she continued. "It is crushing millions in this land as in other lands. But if I were to rise to speak though forbidden to do so, it would mean sacrificing peace, and I am not led by the Spirit to do so."

"I agree," Elizabeth replied, her eyes aflame with injustice. "You, my good Quaker Friend, have inspired me to do more for this cause. Perhaps when we return to America, we shall be able to organize a gathering of all those concerned for our freedoms as women. It has long been my heartfelt desire to work to allow women to cast their votes for our government leaders. Why should only men's issues be our officials' concerns?"

"What would be the purpose of this event?" Lucretia asked, thinking she had some ideas of her own—like inserting the word "woman" into the Declaration of Independence.

"I believe there are a number of demands we must make," Elizabeth said. "Obviously we should be granted the right to vote, but also to divorce a man for good cause, to have custody of our own children, to be able to own property—"

"In other words," Lucretia interrupted, "we should have all the rights of men!"

"Exactly!"

"We Quakers believe women, Negroes, and Natives who were in America before any Europeans—in other words, all humans—are equal in all ways. So I am ready to work with thee to make this happen!" Lucretia assented.

"Let us make a plan, then, to meet when we return," Elizabeth said.

"Yes!" Lucretia agreed, enthused at the prospect of a future where women no longer accepted that their only lot in life was to submit to a husband and raise their children.

• • •

Lucretia knew her life held few remaining days. After several decades of boldly speaking of equality before any group willing to listen to her impassioned messages, especially in Quaker Yearly Meeting Sessions in the Midwest, she wondered if she would live to see her eighty-seventh year. Her recent trip to her childhood island of birth, Nantucket, had been a marvelous blessing, and she would always be grateful that her granddaughter, Anna, had arranged it.

Secluded in her room, Lucretia thought back to those first times she had felt compelled to fight to end the horrors of slavery. Learning that Negro men, women, and children were bought and sold like cattle, forced to do hard labor for no pay, and accept the cruelty of their masters had been her first calling to step out and make a difference. Then there was that important meeting with Elizabeth in London. What a pair they had become!

If I hadn't met Elizabeth, Lucretia reminisced, *we might never have organized the Seneca Falls Convention* held in 1848 along with her sister, Martha Coffin White, and fellow Quakers Mary Ann M'Clintock and Jane Hunt. As soon as they announced the intent of the gathering, word spread like wildfire, and over three hundred had poured into the Wesleyan Chapel in Seneca Falls, New York, to begin the crusade for equality for women.

She would never forget Elizabeth's opening statement that first day, when only women had been allowed: "We are assembled to protest against a form of government, existing without the consent of the governed—to declare our right to be free in the same manner that men are free. Women deserve to be represented in the government which we are taxed to support, and to strike down such disgraceful laws that give a man the power to chastise and imprison his wife, to take the wages which she earns, the property which she inherits, and, in case of separation, the children of her love."

The eleven Declarations of Sentiments for women's rights they had painstakingly written and presented for approval at the convention had been the beginning of long years of work toward receiving some of the many benefits men had always had, especially the all-important right to vote.

I wonder if I can remember all eleven resolutions, she thought. *I know I'll never forget the way it began, "We hold these truths to be self-evident; that all men and women are created equal."* She and her fellow organizers knew women's equality would never be guaranteed by the Constitution, which was why it was so important to add the words "and women" to their resolutions. Gathering support for a constitutional amendment that would grant women full equality was the most important work they would do for all women.

The resolutions called on Americans to regard any laws that placed women in inferior positions to men as having "no force or authority." They resolved for women to have equal rights within the church and equal access to jobs. Of course, the ninth resolution was the most controversial, as it called for women "to secure to themselves their sacred right to the elective franchise"—in other words, the right to vote. In the following days of the convention, men who were supportive of the cause were also allowed to vote on the resolutions, and they were all passed.

Lucretia wondered what future women would think when they realized that for centuries women were not allowed to enjoy the education of their choice, hold important positions in most religious bodies other than in Quaker Meetings, or experience any of the other rights enjoyed by all men regardless of their character or position.

Even now, despite the years of their many continued conventions and gatherings, women still did not have the right to vote, a human right that should be guaranteed for all. But Lucretia knew her life had had purpose, and she had upheld the Quaker belief of equality for all. Wasn't that part of what had led her to help establish Swarthmore College, ensuring it would be open for both men and women? *Yes,* Lucretia thought, *I believe I have done God's work to bring a bit of heaven to earth for the Negro, for women, and for all who seek the freedoms this country was founded on.*

If only I could live long enough to see a new amendment to the Constitution granting women the same voting rights as men! But even though it has not yet happened in my lifetime, I know it will happen someday because other women will continue to fight for their rights as God's children.

CHAPTER 13

JULY, PRESENT DAY
THE CLUB—
SYLVIA'S FAMILY HOME

After pouring Beth a cup of steaming hot coffee, Sylvia noticed Beth's eyes soaking in the charm of the sun-streamed kitchen in the farmhouse where Sylvia had grown up and now lived with her elderly parents. Sylvia knew Beth was anxious to get her honest opinion of the group's work thus far, so they had agreed to meet an hour before the others were scheduled to arrive. Her parents were keeping themselves busy in another part of the house, knowing their daughter was entertaining her women's group that morning.

Sylvia's mother had always had a knack for decorating, and Sylvia knew Beth seemed enamored with the collection of ceramic roosters, hens, and eggs around the kitchen, the pictures of farm scenes, and the antiques high on a shelf, including a hand-cranked butter churn, a wooden coffee grinder, and various old-fashioned glass canning jars. Sylvia saw Beth's glance continue down the hall to the living room where she had hung the sketch of the Capitol Building she had been in numerous times while working in D.C. And Beth seemed to always enjoy the soft glow and cinnamon scent of the candles Sylvia had lit in the dining room. *I love this woman so much,* Sylvia mused wistfully.

After declining Beth's offer to help, she finished the final preparations for their club meeting, putting out the cups and saucers, cream and sugar servers, a variety of tea bags, and blueberry lemon muffins she had made, hurrying to finish so she and Beth could assess their group's progress.

"I'm sorry we don't have much time left before the others arrive," Sylvia said, sounding a bit exhausted. "I thought I'd have everything ready before you got here, but an old D.C. friend called and wanted to fill me in on the latest with the Jones' campaign, so I'm running a bit behind."

"It's fine," Beth assured her. "I was a little early anyway. I'm anxious to get your thoughts on our club's work so far. But I need to ask—this old friend wouldn't perhaps be a gentleman, by any chance?"

"Beth, it was Peter, my longtime friend, who also happens to be gay. Remember him? He came for dinner when you were visiting me that one summer."

"Oh, yeah, I remember him—tall, dark hair, dark eyes, gorgeous smile?"

"Yes, that's the one. And Beth? I need to ask a favor of you," Sylvia said softly but firmly.

"Sure—name it."

"Do you suppose you could stop asking me about men in my life, and about marriage in general? You know, how you're always suggesting maybe there's something romantic going on between me and any eligible man between the ages of fifty and one hundred?"

Beth looked surprised, but quickly apologized. "I'm sorry, Sylvia. I didn't mean to offend you or be obnoxious."

"I'm not offended, and you could never be obnoxious, silly!" Sylvia said with a shy smile. "But it makes me feel like there's something wrong with me when you're always teasing me about not being married. It's just not in my future plans."

"Okay, I'll try to quit bringing it up. But give me a kick under the table if I start again," was Beth's smiling reply. Sylvia thanked her, and quickly got to the purpose of the early meeting.

"So, what about the group?" Sylvia asked, finally finished with the kitchen tasks and sitting down with her second cup of coffee. "Do you think we're making progress finding clues from these ancestral Quaker women that can help us change the focus of local Friends Meetings away from the current evangelicalism?"

"I think we're off to a good start," Beth said, "but I'm not sure anything we've learned so far will do much to steer us in a different direction. Maple Grove Friends is working hard to 'be the church,' like we've been imagining.

"We are open and accepting of all LGBTQ who want to worship with us, and we've been having gatherings around the peace pole with all the messages of peace in multiple languages for several years now. Remember when we had that first Peace Sunday around the pole in front of the meeting house? Peace has always been one of the Quaker testimonies our Meeting has worked to uphold. It's been really moving to see others in our community gather with some of us on Tuesday evenings to advocate for racial justice and to support the Black Lives Matter movement.

"In fact," Beth continued, laughing, "I've even heard rumors that Maple Grove has been called the black sheep of the Yearly Meeting because we aren't trying to recruit disciples who believe their sole purpose is to find lost sinners needing to be saved so they can go to heaven, while ignoring all the injustices and suffering going on right here on earth."

Sylvia couldn't help but chuckle, too, as she thought about their Maple Grove Meeting being called a black sheep. But she did appreciate the challenges that lay ahead of them if any major changes were going to take place. "I do hope each of our chosen Quaker women can bring into light what it might truly mean to be followers of Jesus's teachings," she said.

The doorbell surprised both women; it seemed like they had just begun seriously analyzing their work. As Sylvia hustled to answer the door, Lois's boisterous voice carried into the room.

"Now, ladies! You didn't think you could start without me, did you?" Lois said with a laugh. "Where's Nancy?"

"She'll be here shortly," Sylvia answered. "She had to drop the boys off at school again before she could join us."

"Sure seems like she has them at her house a lot," Lois huffed. "I thought she was supposed to be retired and free to do whatever she wanted."

"Maybe when you have grandkids, you'll know how much joy it is to help out when needed and the importance of spending time with them," Sylvia said.

"How would you know?" Lois retorted. "And it's hard to have grandkids when your only single son is in the Army and certainly not getting any younger!"

Just then Nancy walked in. "Finally," Lois mumbled, but disapproving looks from both Beth and Sylvia softened her tone. "I mean, I'm just excited that we're going to be talking about a Quaker woman in more modern times."

"I wouldn't call Lucretia Mott's life exactly 'modern times,'" Sylvia said with a laugh. "She was born in the late 1700s and died in 1880!"

"That's better than the 1600s!" Lois shot back. "So what did she do?"

"I can see you're all anxious to hear what I learned, so bring your drinks and muffins to the table, and I'll fill you in while you have your snack," Sylvia said, motioning to the kitchen counter where the muffins and mugs sat.

"For starters," she began, "it's obvious to me that without Lucretia Mott's activism, none of us would have some of the same privileges that White men have always enjoyed." She then went into detail about Mott's work to advocate for the end of slavery and to fight for women's rights.

When she finished, Lois posed another question. "Well, now we have laws against slavery, laws giving us the right to vote, and laws to cover just about any of the other sources of injustice. What causes are left for us to work on?"

"Since I knew this would be an important part of our discussion, I did some research on gender equality in the workplace, plus the racial justice issues," Sylvia began, getting out her notes.

"First, women's equality. I was surprised to discover that men still earn more than women who are doing the exact same jobs—even entry-level jobs have men earning four percent more than women for the exact same work. And it gets really unfair when you see that in the highest-level jobs, seventy-nine percent are held by men, but only twenty-one percent by women! Not only that, but women are also not promoted at the same rate as men, job evaluations often favor men more than women, and one in four women believes her gender played a role in missing out on a raise, promotion, or chance to get ahead."

"Wow!" Nancy said, shaking her head. "I suppose I was fortunate to have worked with Allan all those years where we shared everything, because this is just not fair at all!"

"But what about all the issues around racial justice?" Beth asked.

"Oh, you guys, you won't believe all the inequalities that exist for both people of color as well as the Indigenous. Let me find everything about the issue in my notes. Okay, first, have you read about the levels on which racism exists?"

"No, but I have a feeling you've done your research on the subject!" Beth said admiringly.

"So, there are four levels of racism: First is systemic, which has to do with on-going racial inequalities that are maintained by our society. Just listen to these facts about jobs! While Black or African American, Asian, and Hispanic or Latino people comprise only 36% of the overall U.S. workforce, they constitute 58% of miscellaneous agricultural workers, 70% of maids and housekeeping cleaners, and 74% of baggage porters, bellhops, and concierges. And other things, too, like Black males being twenty-one times more likely to be shot and killed than their White male peers.

"Second is institutional racism which involves discriminatory policies and practices within organizations and institutions. Things like the unemployment rate for African Americans being more than double that of Whites caused by things like someone with a Black-sounding name on a resume having a 50% less chance of being called for an interview.

"The third level of racism is interpersonal, which involves things like bigotry and biases shown between individuals through words and actions. An example of that is a leader excluding people of color from a team because they 'just aren't a good fit with the team dynamic.'

"And finally, internalized race-based beliefs and feelings within us! When we think our way of doing things is better than our colleagues of color."

"These sound pretty serious, so what can we do on both fronts—discrimination of both women and people of color and Indigenous people?" Nancy asked.

"I've been thinking of angles we might use to approach these issues, wondering where to even start!" Sylvia said. "But what if first we all write to our senators and representatives at both the state and national levels, urging them to consider laws banning unequal pay and discrimination of both women and BIPOC individuals—that's a new term from my research that I've started using that stands for Black, Indigenous, People of Color. And by writing, I mean handwritten letters, not those form letters you get on the Internet. When I was working for the senator, I was the first one to read the letters people sent, and I always passed the hand-written ones directly to the senator since I figured anyone willing to spend time writing a personal note probably had some really good things to say!"

"Are you sure this will make any difference?" Lois asked. "It seems to me that the last couple of years our elected officials have just been following the party line. If it's a bill the Republicans support, only our elected Republicans will vote that way, and the same thing happens with the Democrats."

"What about checking with the Friends Committee on National Legislation and seeing what they would suggest?" Beth asked.

"That's a great idea, Beth! I keep forgetting about our Quaker lobbying group," Nancy said. "Remember the sessions we had at Maple Grove to prioritize causes we felt important for FCNL to consider? We could take a look at those, too."

"And one more idea," Sylvia said hesitantly.

"Seriously?" Lois asked skeptically. "Isn't this already enough for us to tackle this month?"

Once more, Sylvia urged action from her friends. "I think it's also important to see if there aren't some smaller, more personal actions we can take that would help us work toward ending racism. I found a long list that I can email each of you that has over forty things we might try to be a part of, and if there's anything that looks possible, maybe we could each try one or two of the things on the list."

"Like what?" Beth asked.

Pulling up the list, Sylvia read, "We might find out if we have a neighborhood association we could join, and we could also donate to one of the agencies in our county that works to eradicate racism and White supremacy, and even work to increase the local minimum wage. And there are lots more to choose from."

"Ok, ladies, I think that's about all the information my brain can handle for one day, but I'm willing to do my best," Nancy said, and Sylvia was pleased to see Beth and Lois nod in agreement.

Sylvia hoped everyone had felt a sense of accomplishment and responsibility as they headed home, all believing they had some important work to do to fight for the Quaker testimony of equality for all. She knew they'd have to draw on their courage to follow their inner leadings, persuading others to work for justice for all, just as Lucretia Mott had once done for the slaves and women in her day.

CHAPTER 14

1972

HEALING SERVICE

BETH

"Are you getting excited?" Nancy asked Beth as they drove to what they hoped would be a service they would never forget. "My Charismatic group is all going to go, too, even though we're from different churches."

"I'm just not sure what to expect," Beth said. "You know I haven't been a part of your group because Tyler is still a baby, and Bob is often either working late in the field or doing chores when your group meets. I had to use all my persuasive powers just to convince him he could take care of Tyler while I was gone. And I'm a skeptic about anyone claiming they can heal people."

"But you read the Hunters' latest book, *How to Heal the Sick,* didn't you? It sounds like they've been successfully healing all kinds of ailments in these services they've been having."

"Yeah, but healing a headache isn't quite the same as helping Ann with her arm!"

Ann was a member of Maple Grove who had been born with one arm considerably shorter than the other. When word spread around the Yearly Meeting that Charles and Frances Hunter were coming to the Midwest and bringing their evangelistic healing service to one of the larger Friends Meetings in the state, Ann announced she was going to attend the service in case she might be healed. Her unequal arms had made many things in life more difficult for her, like picking up her toddler, playing the piano, and even hanging her clothes to dry on the outside line.

It was a two-hour drive from Maple Grove, and the girls chatted about the recent happenings in their lives. Nancy was still figuring out how she wanted to use her accounting degree and whether or not Allan might eventually be part of her decision. Beth and Bob had been married for two years, but Bob said he had absolutely no interest in going when Beth had mentioned the healing service.

Like most Quaker meeting houses, this one had a back area serving as a library, rows of simple pews in the main sanctuary, and a raised platform with a pulpit and two wooden armchairs in the front. Beth was surprised to see the room was nearly full even though the service wasn't scheduled to start for another thirty minutes. The crowd seemed to buzz with anticipation of what might take place. Beth scanned the room to see if she recognized anyone, waving as she saw Ann and her family on the other side of the semicircle of wooden pews.

The service began like most other church services, with prayer and several hymns, and then Charles Hunter began to preach. He was fired up with his belief that God wanted healing for anyone requesting a healing touch. He quoted several Bible verses and said he and Frances had seen many, many miracles of healing during their traveling ministry.

But it was the last part of the service that had the biggest impact. Beth watched as Ann went forward to have Charles pray over her arm. Beth couldn't see that anything miraculous was happening, but then Charles touched Ann's forehead with his finger. She immediately fell backward and was caught and gently placed on the floor by one of the members who had volunteered to help with this part of the service. Charles had told the crowd that when there was a powerful prayer for healing, the recipient might experience something he called being "slain in the Spirit."

From a distance, Beth tried to see Ann's arm as she rose and went back to her pew. It looked to still be the same length as before, but Beth would wait until she had a chance to see her after the service to draw any conclusions about the healing.

Next there were a couple of people who went forward to have prayer for healing: one man who had a leg that was shorter than the other, followed by a lady in a wheelchair who wanted to walk again. Frances was the one who talked and prayed for the woman, even getting her to stand up while Charles held her for a moment, but just as Beth had suspected, the woman immediately fell back into her chair.

"I don't think anyone is really being healed," Beth whispered to Nancy.

"Let's go down, okay?" Nancy asked. "I've always wanted to experience being slain in the Spirit."

With a look of credulity, Beth shook her head. She was sure it was all fake—or maybe people were just fainting because it had gotten so hot in the crowded sanctuary.

"Please?" Nancy begged. "I don't want to go by myself."

Beth hated the "slain in the Spirit" idea, not believing there was really any Spirit involved, but she also wanted to be a good friend, so she reluctantly rose with Nancy and headed to the altar. Several people were babbling something that sounded like gibberish to Beth, but she remembered Nancy telling her about speaking in tongues, so perhaps that was what was happening. *Not for me,* Beth thought. It all seemed like a made-up experience, something the human mind had created rather than the Holy Spirit.

The area had become quite crowded, so one of the helpers took Beth over to the side and asked if she'd like to be slain in the Spirit. Beth was skeptical, but she nodded. She bowed her head and closed her eyes as the woman started praying, and then when she touched Beth's forehead the same way Charles had done with Ann, Beth felt herself falling backward. Fortunately the wall was behind her, giving her a way to slide to the floor.

In a matter of seconds Beth opened her eyes. *If that was supposed to be a Spirit slaying, it was more like losing your balance when your eyes are closed and someone is pushing you over,* she thought. She quickly returned to her seat to wait for Nancy. By now there were so many people in the front of the sanctuary that it was hard to locate her friend, but before long Nancy was heading toward her with a glazed look in her eyes.

Beth wasn't sure what to say, so she didn't say anything to Nancy until the two-hour service was finally over and they were back in the car heading down the highway.

"That was such a wonderful experience!" Nancy gushed. "Didn't you feel the Spirit overwhelm you?"

Beth didn't answer right away, pretending to focus on her driving. Finally she said, "Well, I guess I was 'slain in the Spirit,' but to be honest, I didn't really feel anything special."

Nancy looked at her friend with disappointment. "Would you ever be able to get away and come with me to one of our Charismatic meetings?" she asked hopefully, clearly longing for Beth to experience the same gifts of the Spirit she had been able to enjoy. "Our next one's going to be at Allan's place; he's not really convinced that this new kind of prayer and worship is real, but he likes the pizza we usually order afterwards, and he can talk sports with the guys, which makes me happy since I don't know a single thing about football except when a team scores a touchdown!"

"I'll think about it," Beth said, "but I'll have to see if Bob's free, and I'm not sure I'm cut out for this new kind of religion."

"You'll get into it when you meet our group," Nancy insisted. "I know the first time you experience the baptism of the Holy Spirit, it will change your life!"

Beth didn't answer. As the fields flashed by along the highway, she wondered if anything out of the ordinary would ever happen for her. Her Quaker membership classes had often talked about waiting in the silence for the movement of the Spirit, but the lessons never talked about the gifts of the Spirit. *But maybe I'll see if it works out to go with Nancy when the group meets at Allan's,* she thought. It was always good to keep an open mind, even if that mind was full of doubts!

CHAPTER 15

1806-1882

SARAH MAPPS DOUGLASS

NEW YORK CITY

Why had I thought it would be better to be a teacher in New York City than in my hometown of Philadelphia? Sarah wondered, hot tears searing her cheeks as she left the Quaker meeting house. Once again, she had been required to sit on a bench at the back reserved for Black people only, and no one had spoken to her upon her arrival. And that hadn't even been the most hurtful part of the morning. No, nothing had been as heartbreaking as being asked by a Friend on her way to meeting for worship if she was someone the woman might hire to clean her house!

Sarah thought over her long history with the Religious Society of Friends, going all the way back to her grandfather, Cyrus, who had been born to a slave owned by a New Jersey lawyer. Her parents had often told his story to Sarah and her seven siblings, how his life had changed when he was sold to a Quaker baker who taught him the trade and then freed him. He had set up his own baking business and even baked bread for the soldiers in the American Army during the Revolutionary War.

Sarah remembered going with her mother to the Philadelphia Friends North Meeting as a child and how there, too, they had been forced to sit alone on the bench designated for Blacks only. There was even a day when a White person had asked to join them and had been forbidden by one of the elders.

Friends can talk about their belief in equality all they want, Sarah thought, *but their actions speak much louder than their words.* She had puzzled over her observation that most Friends, as well as members of other religious groups, did not see the inconsistency in providing schools for Blacks, working against slavery, and hiding escaped slaves through the Underground Railroad while at the same time discriminating against them socially. Blacks were rarely entertained in the homes of White Friends, and while White people thought it important to provide an education for Black children, these same children were not allowed to attend White-only schools.

It was only when quietly sitting in the silence of Quaker worship meetings that Sarah felt peaceful, reveling in the beauty of simply being humble and heartbroken to wait for the gentle influence of the Holy Spirit to fill her soul. But now, even when Friends were enlarging Arch Street Meeting House, the so-called Great Meeting House, they were still planning to allot some suitable—but separate—places for the Negroes to sit in the common meetings.

Would this separation of Negroes and Whites never end?

Here she was, a twenty-seven-year-old educator who believed it was important to teach children not only the basics but also art and music. She loved writing poetry and essays, and some of her works had even been published in the "Ladies' Department" of *The Liberator,* as well as in *The Colored American* and the Anglo-African magazines under her pseudonym, Zillah. Yet nothing had changed since she had been a child worshipping with her mother in Friends Meetings.

I must do something to raise awareness of this injustice, Sarah thought. *But what? Who would want to read something about the abolition of slavery and the welfare of Blacks from a spinster Negro schoolteacher?*

Then she remembered something abolitionist William Lloyd Garrison had written in his first article in *The Liberator:* "I am in earnest—I will not equivocate—I will not excuse—I will not retreat a single inch—AND I WILL BE HEARD." Would this passionate White abolitionist be interested in the Female Literary Association she had helped organize? Their goal was to encourage Black middle-class women to combine their literary pursuits with support for the antislavery movement. *Yes,* Sarah thought, *I will write to Mr. Garrison and ask him to review the constitution we have created for our association. We will need influential White men to join our cause in putting an end to the horrific pain of slavery once and for all.*

• • •

As Sarah sat in the silence on First Day in her Philadelphia Friends Meeting House, reflecting on everything that had transpired during the prior seventy years of her life, her only regret was how her rheumatism made it difficult to carry on with the work she had begun so many years ago. It was a privilege to have been such an influential teacher up until the day her health required her to cease her fight for equality. *Have I done all I can to be a voice not only against slavery but also against the separation of Blacks and Whites in the Friends Meetings? I know I helped many pupils in the schools I started.* And, of course, marrying the widowed William Douglass and helping raise his nine children had been a blessing as well.

Sarah felt lucky to have been of strong mind in her mid-fifties when her husband had died. As soon as she had learned of the Female Medical College of Pennsylvania, the first such organization a group of Quakers had started, she had begun taking courses in physiology and anatomy. She remembered how she had wanted to share this knowledge with Black women who badly needed to know how to care for and control their own bodies. She had been especially impressed by the lectures given by Dr. Ann Preston, a Quaker abolitionist who herself had recently graduated from the Female Medical College. Sarah remembered fondly that with her new knowledge, she had been asked to lecture at a number of colleges and institutes, even continuing to give lectures in her home during the last years of her more sedentary life.

Some of Sarah's fondest memories were of the Quaker women she had had the privilege of calling friends, women who had shared their common goals of ending slavery and empowering women. There was Lucretia Mott, and her good friends, Rebecca White and Hannah White Richardson, philanthropists who supported schools and colleges for Black children. And then there were those delightful Grimké sisters, Sarah and Angelina, and the passion they felt to work for justice and equality, as well as the many organizations of which they had all been a part.

But it continued to grieve Sarah to think that in many Quaker Meetings, Blacks were still being separated from Whites. Why had Quakers been so slow to realize that their faith's testimony of equality did not include the Negro worshiper? *One must never lose hope,*

Sarah vowed, *and I shall continue to pray for those who have not yet been moved by the Spirit to stop separating Black men and women from Whites when worshiping the very same God.*

CHAPTER 16

AUGUST, PRESENT DAY
THE CLUB—BETH'S HOME

The August heat meant that walking first thing in the morning was the only way Beth could get her three miles in each day, so she had to hustle to get ready for the club meeting after she finished. But she had showered and managed to whip up a batch of monkey bread, filling the whole farmhouse with the enticing aroma of baking bread and cinnamon.

Beth had remained on the farm after Bob's accident, raising Tyler and Kristy there, taking classes for her physician assistant's degree at the university an hour north of their farm, and then she worked full time at the Maple Grove Clinic. Beth would never forget that dreadful day, the day her life was turned upside down. She and the kids had returned from Yearly Meeting sessions to find the farmhouse swarming with cars and pickups. Bob's tractor and hay bailer had overturned on a curve on their gravel road, and he had been pinned beneath and killed instantly. Yes, death had a way of upending one's life, but Beth's acceptance of losing her husband and her eventual peace rested in her belief that Bob had been a believer in God and was now in heaven.

Beth loved the quietness and open fields that surrounded their home. Other than remodeling the kitchen with granite countertops and newer appliances, buying a few pieces of furniture, and replacing the carpet when the kids were both in college, the home had remained much the same as when she and Bob were first married. She felt content there and was looking forward to opening her home to the club this month.

Beth was just grinding the coffee beans when Sylvia drove up—an hour early! What was going on? Sylvia had the best manners of anyone Beth knew, and it was not like her to come unannounced. But as she looked out the window, to her relief she saw Sylvia coming up the front walk with a bounce in her step and a smile on her face. *Nothing too terrible must have happened to either of her aging parents,* Beth thought.

Beth headed toward the door as Sylvia burst in, excitement written all over her face. "Whoa, girl!" Beth exclaimed as Sylvia threw her arms around her and gave a tight squeeze. "What's got you so wound up this morning?"

"You'll never guess what happened at the Ministry and Counsel meeting last night," Sylvia said. "We may be on the verge of some big changes at Maple Grove Friends!"

"What's the big news? Tell me!" Beth said, unable to think what it could possibly be.

"Do you remember me telling you that Ministry and Counsel has been having some discussions about Maple Grove's place in the Yearly Meeting?" Sylvia asked.

"Yeah, but I also know how slowly the Quaker process works. Our members are nothing if not thorough in making any decisions that might affect all our members, especially important ones affecting all the Meetings in our Yearly Meeting. Those take a very long time!" Beth said with a laugh.

"Well, you also know that for over a year we've been having those pre-worship discussion groups once a month, and we've been examining some of the statements in the Yearly Meeting Discipline—our basic Friends beliefs and rules of conduct. There are some really archaic beliefs we're expected to follow, especially the one about homosexuality being listed as a sin right next to murder."

"Those were some pretty eye-opening discussions," Beth agreed.

"So, remember the chart we made at the last pre-worship meeting where we listed all the reasons to remain a part of the Yearly Meeting and then considerations for leaving?"

"Oh yeah! It was definitely a good way to summarize all the things we had been discussing."

"At our M and C meeting last night, every member agreed that it's time to compose a letter that states the areas in which we find disagreement with the Yearly Meeting, and then present our findings at the next business meeting for all members to consider, and hopefully find consensus to move forward with the letter," Sylvia said. "Isn't that great?"

"Is that really a good idea?" Beth said slowly. "I mean, I've been going to the annual Yearly Meeting sessions almost my entire life, and I have a lot of good friends from some of the other Meetings. Is ditching the Yearly Meeting necessary, even if we don't agree with a lot of their beliefs?"

Sylvia was crestfallen. "But Beth . . . homosexuality the same as murder? Seriously? How can we go along with that if we say we are an open and accepting Meeting?"

"I agree that adding 'homosexuality' to the list of sins was a terrible decision, and I spoke against adding it back in the eighties at that spring Yearly Meeting representatives business meeting. Sadly, we were unable to reach a consensus because most of the representatives thought it would be good to include it. They read the Bible literally and believe the thoughts of those writers thousands of years ago should be interpreted in the same way today. What if we all wrote letters to our Yearly Meeting leaders and told them we think the Discipline should be changed and that word taken out?" Beth asked.

"Beth!" Sylvia almost shouted. "You know nothing will happen with writing letters stating our opinions. I already did that, and I got a letter back from the superintendent saying that's what the Bible says, and that's the belief of the Yearly Meeting."

"Oh," Beth said a little sheepishly, "you're right. I forgot all about that."

"So you'll be at our next Monthly Meeting for business, won't you? And you'll support our need to find another umbrella organization that we better align with?" Sylvia begged.

Beth looked at the longing in Sylvia's expression, and she couldn't deny her friend this request. But was there more to her desire for this change than the need to abandon a literal translation of scripture? She had always wondered why Sylvia had never been interested in men and marriage. Was it possible her long-time friend was a lesbian?

Just then Lois and Nancy knocked on the door, bringing the conversation with Sylvia to an abrupt halt.

"What's going on with you two? I can tell by the looks on your faces that you've been in some kind of deep discussion," came Lois's typical brash greeting.

Nancy looked from Lois to Beth and Sylvia. "Did we interrupt something important?"

"We were just talking about equality," Beth said, hoping Sylvia would follow her thinking. "It was something this month's 'old' Quaker, Sarah Mapps Douglass, was passionate about. Grab a plate and I'll serve the monkey bread. You can help yourselves to the coffee, and the hot water for tea is in the kettle on the stove. You've all been here before, so just help yourselves."

As the women settled in with their refreshments, Beth shared about Sarah Douglass and her work for equality for Black people, particularly in the Friends Meetings she had attended throughout her life. The other three were impressed and wondered what they might glean from her work that would help them "be the church" now.

"I'm thinking about how gay people and lesbians are still excluded in so many churches right now, like that Baptist preacher in Kansas who calls them sinners going to hell, and the work that still needs to be done for equality in our Friends Meetings even now," Beth said. She desperately wanted to look at Sylvia but was afraid her eyes might betray her new questioning thoughts about her friend. It didn't matter to her if Sylvia was gay, but why hadn't she trusted her best friend enough to tell her the truth? Were there other signs she had missed through the years?

"Another thing we need to address," Nancy added, "is the need to speak out against the mistreatment of Blacks by the police. We joined in the marches in support of Black Lives Matter, but I know I haven't done much since then other than the work you assigned us last month, Sylvia. Would Sarah Douglass believe that since slavery is illegal now that everything is okay? I don't think so!"

"And I was just sharing with Beth that at our Ministry and Counsel meeting last night, we came to the conclusion that it was time to compose a list of areas where we are not in alignment with our Yearly Meeting and then take it to our next Monthly Meeting to be approved," Sylvia added.

"You mean leave the Yearly Meeting?" Lois asked in surprise. "Why would we do that?"

"Because taking the Bible literally means believing ideas from the holiness code in the book of Leviticus and from the patriarchal society of Paul's day, ideas that just aren't valid with what we now know from scientific discoveries and human physiology. Being gay, lesbian, transgendered, or any other non-heterosexual orientation is not a sin!" Sylvia said emphatically. "Do any of you disagree?"

When no one offered their opinion, Beth knew it was time she stood up for her friend. "I definitely agree!" she said. "And I think we should start contacting other Meetings and getting their thoughts on some of the beliefs in the Discipline that aren't compatible with Jesus's teachings."

Nancy joined in agreement. "Since you're on Ministry and Counsel, Sylvia, do you want to help us get started on this project? I bet Sarah Douglass wouldn't have just accepted the things so many Quakers today are saying about LGBTQ members any more than she accepted the discrimination against Blacks in the Friends' meeting houses in her lifetime."

"I'm willing to give it some serious thought, Sylvia," Lois said.

"I'll come up with a list of Meetings we can contact," Sylvia said. "If you're all willing to help, we can make phone calls, and even offer to personally meet with any Meeting who might allow us to share our work on equality."

"Here's one more interesting thing I learned from my research on Sarah Mapps Douglass," Beth added. "It seems that British Friends were consistently critical of American Friends and their treatment of Black meeting attendees. When one of the traveling ministers, Thomas Shillitoe, came to the United States in the 1840s, he was disheartened to hear how a "Negro" applicant was denied membership in Mount Holly Meeting. He was also told how John Woolman tried to persuade the members to accept this Black man. When that failed, Woolman predicted the Meeting would dwindle as a result of their denial. And it did. Does that story remind you of our Yearly Meeting and its dwindling membership?"

"Absolutely," Sylvia concurred. "Every year when they read the statistical reports, there are more and more Meetings being laid down, and total membership numbers are continually declining. I can't help but think a part of it is their condemnation of gay marriage and all LGBTQ folks. So we've got our work cut out for us!"

"Got any more of that monkey bread left?" Lois asked. "With all this deep discussion, I'm feeling the need for more gooey, cinnamony, buttery bread."

"It must be nice," Beth lamented. "Why couldn't I have gotten your genetics that let you eat anything anytime you want?"

"Oops," Lois said. "I'm sorry, Beth. I shouldn't have asked for another piece. Just forget it."

"Nope," Beth said with a grin. "What's another pound or two? I gave up any desire to be thin years ago! I can't change the fact that you're almost six feet tall and I'm five four with the metabolism of a snail. I'll cut another piece for myself, too. Anyone else want to join us?"

As the women each took another small serving of monkey bread, they talked about the next assignment and who would host. But Beth only half listened as she kept thinking about her best friend, the one she turned to whenever she needed a listening ear, a supportive hug, a whispered secret. *Was Sylvia really gay? Had she ever had relationships with other women all those years she was in DC? And if so, why hasn't she ever shared that part of her life with me? Sylvia knows my son Tyler is gay and that I fully accepted him when he came out to his friends and Kristy and me in his twenties. And she knows he's happily married to Patrick, and that I can't wait until the adoption of my two future adorable grandchildren is finalized!*

I feel terrible that she hasn't felt free to share her full self with me. Things have changed so much, but I remember how hard it was for Tyler to come out to his family even ten years ago. And I remember how homophobic people were in the past—and still are today. Why are churches some of the last places where LGBTQ individuals feel welcomed? Does Sylvia not feel welcome at Maple Grove?

Questions continued to swirl in Beth's mind after everyone had wandered out to their cars. Should she talk to Sylvia about it? But she didn't want her relationship with Sylvia to change. That would be devastating, and Beth vowed to learn more about Sylvia's understanding of those few condemning scriptures still being used to deny homosexuals and transgender humans a place of acceptance in their Meetings.

CHAPTER 17

1973

FOUR SPIRITUAL LAWS RETREAT

LOIS

"I'm sure you're wondering why I told you all to meet me out here under the oak tree as soon as the benediction was over," Lois said as Beth, Sylvia, and Nancy looked at each other with curiosity. "I couldn't wait to talk to you three as soon they made the announcement this morning about the Four Spiritual Laws Retreat. Please, let's all go! It doesn't cost much to participate, and since most of us have jobs now, I'm sure we can afford it."

"Lois, this doesn't really seem like something you would be interested in," Sylvia said. "You do know it's kind of like a missionary project where we'll have to go knock on doors to present those four steps for salvation, right?"

"Who else from Maple Grove is going, do you know?" Nancy asked.

"I think a couple of the other young adults are going," Lois admitted.

"And would Mark happen to be one of those 'young adults'?" Beth teased.

"I don't know if Mark's going or not," Lois said defensively. She knew Beth didn't understand what she could possibly see in Mark, aside from his good looks, of course, with that adorable curly dark brown hair and those deep blue eyes. But Mark was often the troublemaker in their group with some of the pranks he liked to pull, especially on the elders.

A smile crossed her face as she thought of the Sunday Mark had snuck a transistor radio in his pocket and then accidentally pulled the headphone cord out in the middle of the pastor's sermon. That blast of music had more than one of the elders turning around with accusatory stares at all the kids sitting in the back row. It was all they could do to hide their smiles and try not to laugh.

Lois knew some of the others thought Mark was a bully, but she liked how he wasn't afraid to do whatever he wanted. And since she was a little like that herself, Lois was planning to go on this conference mission trip so she could spend more time with him—if he might be persuaded to join them. She would do whatever she could to encourage Mark to go with the guys and then get at least one of her girlfriends to go with her.

"So, Lois, you didn't answer Beth's question. Would a certain guy by the name of Mark be one of the young adults going?" Sylvia asked with a sly grin.

"How should I know?" Lois shot back, but she could feel a tomato-red flush spreading from her cheeks all the way down her long neck.

"I'm sorry, girls, but I have a date with Allan next weekend, so I'm out. But you other three should go. Maybe it'll be fun," Nancy said.

"I'm out, too," Sylvia said. "I'm heading to D.C. with my parents to look for an apartment. I start my new job in two weeks, and I have a ton of stuff to do before then."

"Okay, Beth, then you have to go with me! I can't do that door-to-door stuff by myself," Lois said.

"Maybe you could go with Mark," Beth said smugly.

"Please, please, please! Go with me!" Lois begged.

"Well," Beth said with a slight frown, "that will be my weekend off at the hospital, and since I was only hired a few weeks ago, I was hoping I might be able to take an extra shift for one of the other nurses. But I suppose I can go with you if you really think you need someone, although it doesn't exactly sound like anything I'm going to feel very comfortable doing."

"Great! Thank you," Lois gushed just as Mark, Bob, and a couple of others walked over to their group.

It wasn't long before they learned that Mark and Bob were both planning to go on the retreat. Lois tried to hide the excitement she was sure was written all over her face, and before long they had arranged to carpool. *How on earth am I going to be able to wait for the retreat to arrive?* Lois wondered.

Somehow Lois made it to the next weekend, and it was time to put her plan into action. Once they arrived at the Sugar Creek Friends Meeting House, she figured that if she got Mark talking about football and his favorite teams while they were all gathered in the fellowship hall for coffee cake and fruit before the first session began, she could follow him into the sanctuary and sit by him. He was smiling at her a lot, so she didn't think he would mind. She did feel a little guilty abandoning Beth, but Beth had found a girl she had been to church camp with when they were in junior high and was reconnecting with her. *This is all working out beautifully,* Lois thought.

Once they were all settled in the pews, the conference leader, Pastor Paul, began passing out packets of pamphlets in rubber-banded stacks titled *The Four Spiritual Laws. Yikes,* Lois thought, *do they actually think we'll hand all these out to strangers?*

"Just like there are physical laws," Pastor Paul began, "there are spiritual laws that govern our relationship with God. Please take one of the pamphlets and read along with me as we go through the important steps to salvation.

"The first law is 'God loves you and has a wonderful plan for your life.' When you are talking with the unsaved, it's important to stress this plan for life. Most people have no idea that they can have a personal relationship with a God who has something important for them to do with their lives.

"After each law, we share the scriptures that the law is based on. The first law comes from John 3:16: 'God so loved the world that He gave His one and only Son, that whoever believes in Him shall not perish but have eternal life.' Then share this verse where Jesus says, 'I came that they might have life, and might have it abundantly,' which you can explain means that God sent Jesus so our lives could be full and meaningful. We follow that up with this question: 'Why is it that most people are not experiencing abundant life?'"

Lois immediately raised her hand. "But we don't know anything about these people. We've never met them before, so doesn't it seem a little presumptuous to suggest we know God has a unique plan for them?" If there was anything she had learned from her college classes in education methods, it was that you began by asking the students to tell you what they already knew.

"I think if you wait until we've gone through all four of the laws, it will be a little easier to understand the entire process," the pastor said stiffly.

"Okay, sorry," Lois said, hoping Mark wasn't disappointed in her outspokenness.

Pastor Paul was probably in his fifties, Lois guessed, and she was pretty sure he thought he had the answers to any and all religious questions. He didn't seem angry, just disappointed that someone would wonder about the laws.

All four laws were presented in the same format—the law, the scripture, and the personal question to ask. As Pastor Paul read the second law, "Man is sinful and separated from God. Therefore he cannot know God's love and plan for his life," Lois gave a quiet snort, deciding that since the language only used the word "man," then women must be exempt from the laws.

After the second law, there was a diagram showing God on one side of a divide and humans on the other, leading to the third law, "Jesus Christ is God's only provision for man's sin. Through Him you can know and experience God's love and plan for your life." Following the law was a diagram of a cross with Jesus's name on it acting as a bridge between God and man. *There it is again, "man,"* Lois thought with disgust.

After more scripture and more droning on, Pastor Paul presented the fourth law: "We must individually receive Jesus Christ as Savior and Lord; then we can know and experience God's love and plan for our lives."

"It's a wonderful plan," he said, "and we have the task of spreading this gospel to the unsaved, of whom there are many in this day and age. Tomorrow you will go out in pairs and begin knocking on doors, asking if you might share this Good News with the household. If they allow you to enter and go through the laws with them, then the final step is to offer to pray with them this prayer on the last page of the booklet: Lord Jesus, I need You. Thank You for dying on the cross for my sins. I open the door of my life and receive You as my Savior and Lord. Thank You for forgiving my sins and giving me eternal life. Take control of the throne of my life. Make me the kind of person You want me to be. Then you say, 'Does this prayer express the desire of your heart?' And if anyone says yes, you ask the person to repeat the prayer's phrases after you. Are there any questions?"

Lois wanted to comment on the use of male-only language, and how it might be embarrassing to go into strangers' homes and tell them they were sinners, but she decided there was probably no point in once again challenging Pastor Paul.

After several other attendees asked questions—the main one being what to do if doors were slammed in their faces—Pastor Paul announced it was time for lunch. Then they would spend the afternoon practicing with each other until they knew the laws and scriptures by heart. Lois thought the practice was totally unnecessary since they all had those little booklets to hand out to people when they went through the steps, but she decided to focus on Mark and do everything she could to make sure he was her partner for both the practice and the real work the next day.

The early September morning was cool but with plenty of sunshine. Pastor Paul had relented and allowed the "missionaries" to go in groups of four after several had worried they still might not know how to answer all the questions people might ask if there were only two of them. Lois was grateful for the change because Mark had wanted to go with Bob, and Lois had reluctantly said she'd go with Beth when Beth had reminded her that she'd only agreed to attend the conference as a favor to Lois.

As the four set out on the mid-sized town's residential streets, they tried to calm each other's anxiety about the task ahead.

"I say we skip this part and go to the donut shop I saw when we drove into town," Mark suggested. "This is a dumb idea if you ask me. I'm not sure how you talked me into this, Bob!"

"It wasn't hard, buddy—you wanted to get out of cleaning the hog pens, plus there's that certain girl you were anxious to be with."

Mark punched Bob's arm as they continued to walk. "You know you're a pain in the butt sometimes, Bob!" Mark complained, but there was a bit of a smile on his face.

"Did you hear that?" Lois gushed in a whisper to Beth. "I really think Mark likes me!"

"Time will tell," Beth agreed, "but he does seem to look at you a lot."

"It seems to me that Bob does the same with you!" Lois added with a grin. "Why haven't you ever dated him? He's farming with his dad, and I know he went to junior college for diesel mechanics, so he's got a good career going."

"I don't know," Beth admitted. "He was always a grade ahead of us and just hung out with the guys. He's hardly ever even talked to me."

"Then this is the perfect time to get to know him—and get him to notice you," Lois said with confidence as they approached the first house where they would attempt to offer the four spiritual laws for salvation.

After knocking on two houses with no success—one of the doors was slammed in response to their request to share the good news, and at the other, no one came to the door—the third door was opened by a young couple, with a kid running around and a small barking dog chasing him in the room behind them. The couple not only greeted them warmly but actually invited them to come in. Each of the four young adults took one law to explain, and then Bob asked the couple if they would like to pray the prayer of salvation. And they did! *Maybe God does have a plan for this mission after all,* Lois thought.

As soon as they were back on the sidewalk, Mark declared, "Okay, ladies and gentleman, I say we've done our job and it's time for a treat. The donut shop is only a couple of blocks from here, and I'm buying!"

"Do you really think we should do that?" Beth asked. "I'm pretty sure Pastor Paul is expecting us to spend the entire morning going to as many houses as possible."

"Who's going to know?" Mark said. "You're with me, aren't you, Lois?"

"Sure," she said eagerly, almost hoping Bob and Beth would decide to go on by themselves.

"Fine by me," Bob agreed. "Maybe we can debrief our missionary experience over coffee and donuts and then take our sweet time heading back to the meeting house."

As the four ate their frosted long johns and drank coffee that tasted as if it had sat in the pot for several hours, they talked about their experiences.

"I think what someone believes about God and Jesus is a personal matter, and we shouldn't be pushing this stuff down their throats," Mark said.

"That's not being fair," Beth countered. "If we don't at least tell people about God's plan for their lives and how they need to accept Jesus as their savior, they won't have a chance to go to heaven. They'll be separated from God for eternity."

"You don't actually believe in heaven and hell, do you?" Mark countered. "Those are just some ideas the ancient priests dreamed up to keep people in line. It's a fear tactic."

"That's an interesting thought," Lois said. "But don't you want the hope of heaven?"

"And it's what the Bible says," Beth said. "The Bible has survived for centuries and has been the foundation of our faith," she added, looking to Bob in hope of his support.

"Beth's right," Bob added, smiling at Beth. "Don't we all want the hope of an eternal life when we die? I know I do."

"Nope, not going there. And I'm done with this conversation," Mark said, pushing his chair back and picking up their trash. "Let's go back and brag about how we got people saved," he said sarcastically.

As they left the shop, to Lois's delight, Mark grabbed her hand. He began whistling, so instead of trying to make conversation, she simply enjoyed the novel feeling of her hand in his.

Lois didn't think Bob and Beth fully agreed with Mark's suggestion to ditch the rest of their mission, but she was secretly thankful they weren't doing any more door knocking. She was also pleased that Beth and Bob seemed to be getting along well. She could hear Beth telling Bob about her RN work with the hospital patients, and then at some point in the conversation, Vietnam and the year Bob had spent in the war after being drafted came up.

Yes, the retreat was turning out to be exactly what Lois had hoped for—getting Mark to notice her, and then the added bonus of Beth being able to get to know Bob. *We make a pretty good foursome, if I do say so myself,* Lois thought triumphantly. *I'm sure great things are in the future for all of us.*

CHAPTER 18
1792-1879
GRIMKÉ SISTERS
SARAH AND ANGELINA

"Father," Sarah said firmly, "I know you are seeking a remedy for your failing health, but you are in no condition to travel all the way to Philadelphia alone. Since there is no other family member available to accompany you, you must allow me to go with you on this trip and be your nursemaid. I insist on it."

Sarah was thankful that her father's work as a judge in the highest court of South Carolina had allowed her to think about justice and how she might best make a difference in the lives of the less fortunate. But she was angry that her mother and father refused to allow her to take classes in the same classical subjects as her brothers, particularly Latin. Why would they believe girls only needed such classes as embroidery, painting, and playing the harpsichord? It was what had led her, when she was only twelve, to share scripture stories with the children of their slaves on Sunday afternoons. And even though she longed to teach them how to read the stories themselves, she was forbidden by law to do so. It didn't stop her, though, from secretly teaching the young slave, Hetty, how to read—that is, until her father discovered their forbidden nighttime activity and punished the girls.

I took an almost malicious satisfaction in teaching Hetty at night when she was supposed to be occupied in combing and brushing my locks, Sarah thought. The light was put out, the keyhole screened, and flat on their stomachs before the fire, with the spelling book under their eyes, they defied the laws of South Carolina.

And those laws prohibiting teaching the Negroes to read and be educated will never stop me from my firm conviction that all religions, not just those of our Episcopalian faith, should take a more proactive role in improving the lives of those who suffer most, Sarah thought.

At least when her brother, Thomas, was home from Yale, he shared the ideas he was learning about the Enlightenment and the law with his inquisitive sister. It was Sarah's fervent desire to become a lawyer, and at least she had her father's permission to enter his library and read some of his law books. But Sarah was doubtful she would ever be allowed to pursue a law education and career, especially since she was forbidden to study the more difficult subjects. But right now, she needed to do all she could to be a supportive daughter on this trip her father seemed determined to make. They may have had their differences when she was growing up, but Sarah knew she needed to be with her father; she knew he was suffering from an illness, but the Charleston doctors had been unable to find the source of his pain and suggested he travel to Philadelphia to seek a cure.

"All right, Sarah. You win," John Grimké said reluctantly, gazing at this inquisitive daughter who would have been a brilliant lawyer if she had been born a boy rather than the twenty-six-year-old single woman who now stood determinedly beside him. Sarah knew her father wished she had found a husband with whom she might establish a home and then present him with grandchildren, but at least she was free to accompany him on this trip.

Sadly, in less than a year her father was gone—despite leaving Philadelphia for the shores of the Atlantic in a desperate effort to regain his health when his new doctors could still find no cure. Sarah knew she could never in good conscience live in the South again and decided that at least for the time being, she would remain in Philadelphia.

One day Sarah happened to walk by a Quaker Meeting House. Through the open windows, she heard a woman speaking of the evils of slavery and how the faith of the Society of Friends was founded on equality for all humans. Wearing a plain gray dress and bonnet, the woman shared how their work with the secret hiding places for the slaves just seeking their freedom was saving lives, and that there was a higher calling for them to find a way once and for all to put an end to the enslavement of Black men, women, and children.

Sarah was entranced. For many years she had been opposed to the way her father had treated their servants and his refusal to let her teach the children to read. She had come to realize that their grand home, fields, and possessions had all come on the backs of their slaves. *I must know more of the ways these Quakers are helping slaves move to freedom,* she thought, *risking their lives in their efforts.*

Sarah soon began meeting with these newfound members of the Society of Friends, who told story after story of the hardships that the escaped slaves had shared with them. It was after meeting with Israel Morris, a fellow Quaker who shared many of the teachings of John Woolman and the Quaker faith with Sarah, that she more fully understood the need to stand up against the enslavement of her fellow men, women, and children. Each time she heard another story of a slave seeking freedom, her heart broke at the thought of bloodthirsty hounds hunting the fugitives, and how those who were captured often had a hand or foot chopped off to prevent future escapes. She learned of many Quakers hiding those freedom-seeking slaves in cellars and under floorboards to avoid discovery by the men being paid to find and capture them. *I must somehow be a part of this effort and write to my dear sister Angelina to join me in this fight!* Sarah thought.

After only a few months following her father's passing, Sarah was anxious to return to Charleston and share these beliefs with her younger sibling who was so much like herself. *I must persuade her to join me and my now-fellow Quakers in this cause,* she thought. She'd never forget putting pen to paper to cement her thoughts, sharing them with Angelina when she returned once again to the family's plantation:

> *As I left my native state on account of slavery and deserted the home of my fathers to escape the sound of the lash and the shriek of tortured victims, I would gladly bury in oblivion the recollection of those scenes with which I have been familiar. But this cannot be. They come over my memory like gory spectres, and implore me, with resistless power, in the name of a God of mercy, in the name of a crucified Savior, in the name of humanity, for the sake of the slaveholder as well as the slave, to bear witness to the horrors of the Southern prison-house.*

"You must come to Philadelphia and work with me to fight against the immorality of slavery!" Sarah had insisted, hoping the passion of her convictions had become Angelina's as well. And it had! Sarah's continued feelings of repulsion at the South's insistence on owning slaves soon convinced Angelina to join her in the fight to end slavery. Both sisters agreed with the Quakers' stance that the abhorrent practice of using the labors of Negroes in bondage to fill their owners' coffers must end.

The sisters' strong convictions meant they knew their compassion would need to be extended to the slaves purchased by their own father to labor on the Grimkés' vast estates in South Carolina. They concluded that they must set free the slaves they had inherited from their father. They also agreed that they could not live in a state that supported slavery. Plantation owners had continued to insist that these Black men, women, and children were better off working in their fields because they had been given a place to live and work to do, all of which offered them a far better life than living in Africa. The girls agreed that it was simply the landowners' greed, pure and simple, that supported the continued enslavement of these fellow humans.

As soon as they were able to free the slaves and leave the plantation, both sisters moved to Philadelphia where they could volunteer in prisons, hospitals, and institutions for the poor while also joining the Quakers in their fight to abolish slavery. And soon the sisters were traveling around New England, speaking on the abolitionist circuit, at first addressing women only in large parlors and churches, adding women's rights to their cause. The sisters found it invigorating to speak to thousands of women, and eventually men as well.

• • •

Years later as Angelina sat waiting for her sister's funeral service to begin, she hoped many of her fellow Americans would eventually recognize the many wonderful contributions Sarah had made during her time on earth. Angelina thought of the life she and Sarah had shared—a life of passion for the many causes of freedom for both the Negroes and women. Angelina remembered those days when she was a young adult and had felt such a burden for the slaves still in bondage. She had tried to impress upon the northern politicians that they also were indulging the southern practice of slavery through their investment in businesses that depended on slave labor. When she published her booklet, *An Appeal to the Christian Women of the South,* and Sarah published *Epistle to the Clergy of the Southern States,* both arguing against slavery, it was so disheartening to learn of the Southern leaders burning the booklets and warning them they would be arrested if they ever set foot in South Carolina again. Even many of the clergy in the north did not approve of the writings or the speeches that were given in front of men as well as women.

But they kept writing and speaking out against the poor treatment of women and enslaved people. What a sad day it was when even the Quakers expelled Angelina; her husband, Theodore; and Sarah from their Meeting because Theodore was not a Quaker.

After Angelina's booklet had been published, she and Sarah had traveled to New York City and addressed a convention of the American Anti-Slavery Society. Over time they spoke to gatherings of women all over New England, urging women to join them in the movement to abolish slavery and push for equal rights for women. *And to think,* Angelina continued to reminisce, *that I was the very first woman to address a committee in the Massachusetts State Legislature.* She reminded those men that it was both a moral-religious duty to end slavery, as well as a political right to insist on a woman's right to petition. It was not without insults, however. She still remembered the letter she wrote to her friend, Sarah Douglass, describing the abuse that greeted her there:

> *After the bustle was over, I rose to speak and was greeted by hisses from the doorway, tho' profound silence reigned thro' the crowd within. The noise in that direction increased and I was requested by the Chairman to suspend my remarks until order could be restored. Three times was I thus interrupted, until at last one of the Committee came to me and requested I would stand near the Speakers desk. I crossed the Hall and stood on the platform in front of it but was immediately re-quested to occupy the Secretaries desk on one side. I had just fixed my papers on two gentlemen's hats when at last I was invited to stand in the Speaker's desk. This was in the mid-dle, more elevated and far more convenient in every respect. Now my friend, how dost thou think I bore all this? I never*

was favored with greater self–possession. I was perfectly calm—took up the thread of my discourse and by speaking very loud, soon succeeded in hushing down the noise of the people, and was suffered to continue for more than two hours without the least interruption . . .

Angelina's memories continued as she began evaluating the work she and her older sister had done, firmly convinced they were doing God's will. Imagine their surprise when they had learned they had two Black nephews, Archibald and Frances, their brother's sons with his slave, Nancy Weston. It was a way to put into practice their beliefs in the equality of all when they invited the boys into their home to live, eventually even supporting Archibald at Harvard Law School and Francis at Princeton Theological Seminary.

I will always believe that all Americans who do not take a stand against slavery must account for their acceptance of such evil as a God-given right for White men and women, Angelina thought. *And I am still proud of the resolutions that Sarah and I proposed at the anti-slavery convention.* The ones she was most proud of were still fresh in her memory:

Resolved: That we regard the legalized practice of surrendering fugitive slaves to their southern taskmasters as utterly at variance with the principles of liberty professed by us "the freest nation in the world"; and a daring infringement of the divine commands. "Thou shalt not deliver unto his master, the servant that is escaped from his master unto thee."— "Hide the outcast, bewray not him that wandereth. Let my outcast dwell with thee, be thou a covert to them from the face of the spoiler."

Resolved: That as certain rights and duties are common to all moral beings, the time has come for woman to move in that sphere which Providence has assigned her, and no longer remain satisfied in the circumscribed limits with which corrupt custom and a perverted application of scripture have encircled her; therefore, that it is the duty of woman, and the province of woman, to plead the cause of the oppressed in our land, and do all that she can by her voice, and her pen, and her purse, and the influence of her example, to overthrow the horrible system of American slavery.

Resolved: That we must regard slavery in this country as a national sin, so long as it exists in the District of Columbia and the territory of Florida; as long as the northern states surrender the fugitive to his master, refuse to repeal those laws which recognize and secure the usurpation of the master over his slave, and continue pledged to put down servile insurrection at the South; as long as the inter-state slave trade is carried on, and there are governors in our free states, who pronounce the free discussion of the subject of slavery to be "a misdemeanor at common law"; and that we regard slavery to be a national sin, because Congress has the power to abolish it, just so far as it has exercised that power to create and sustain it in our land.

Even though Sarah and Angelina were often threatened for their outspokenness on the need to end slavery and support equality for women, they never gave up their efforts. And how painful it was to receive that hurtful letter banishing them from their home state because abolitionists were not allowed to enter the South Carolina borders. But although they eventually ceased speaking to groups for their own safety, they never stopped fighting for what they knew was right in the sight of God.

After Angelina's marriage to fellow abolitionist and reformer Theodore Weld, the three were determined to continue the work they had begun by founding a progressive school, Eagleswood, in New Jersey. It was their deeply held belief that change would come through the education of youth, and they taught students to think in a different manner about the plight of the Blacks being held in bondage.

Yes, Sarah and I both did whatever work we could endeavor— whether by the spoken or written word—to advocate for the freedom of all humans, Angelina thought. But she wondered now that Sarah's suffering had ended in her eighty-first year and she had gone on to her eternal resting place if she, too, would die, and their work would have been in vain. So many stories continued to pour in from the South where African Americans may have gained their freedom on paper following the Thirteenth Amendment, but many were still forced to work as sharecroppers with little hope of ever having their own land. And those in the North also faced horrible treatment by the many Whites who considered them to be an inferior race. Angelina prayed, *Please, God, continue to show me how I may still use my voice to speak for those lacking the freedoms Sarah and I have been fortunate to have in our lives.*

Chapter 19

September, Present Day
The Club—Nancy's Home

Nancy hummed an old gospel tune while getting the house back in order after the twins spent the night. At least their mom had picked them up for school, saving her precious minutes getting ready for their club meeting. *Ten-year-olds,* she thought with a rueful smile. *When will they stop moving the furniture around, jumping from couch to chair, and leaving food wrappers everywhere? I may have to be a little firmer with them,* she thought, all the while knowing she wouldn't have it any other way. She loved having them in the home she and Allan had lovingly built together.

Allan had done all the electrical work, of course, and a lot of the framing of the ranch-style house. She had helped with the drywalling, painting, and picking out all the hardware. Who would have guessed it would take so many doorknobs and drawer pulls? But the house was their own creation, and she hoped she and Allan could live out their lives there and never have to go to a nursing home like her parents had.

Losing first her dad and then her mom had been some of the hardest days of her life. She was grateful her brother had been the executor of their parents' estate, but she had written all the thank-you notes—and there had been many after their parents had been partners in pastoring so many United Methodist churches over the years.

Glancing at the time, Nancy realized she had to hustle to get the fruit, yogurt, and nuts ready for the women. She imagined they might not be as excited to see the morning's healthier snacks, but she was trying to lose ten pounds to help take the pressure off her knees and their beginning twinges of arthritis. It wasn't easy, and she knew if she baked anything rich and sweet she wouldn't be able to resist eating with the others—and probably the leftovers, too! Plus, Beth was always talking about her desire to lose weight, even though she said she was done trying the latest fad diets.

As she cut up the last of the strawberries and peaches in front of the kitchen window, Nancy noticed Lois's SUV coming up the drive. She was twenty minutes early, and that wasn't like Lois at all. On time? Always. Early? Rarely ever.

"Hey, Nancy! What's happening in your life this fine morning?" Lois bubbled as she came in the back door.

Nancy looked at her quizzically. "What's got you so excited this morning, Lois?"

"Who, me? Oh, nothing, really—sorry I'm early. I just finished reading the paper and downing my first cup of coffee, and I guess I just miscalculated the time."

Nancy persisted, still not convinced there wasn't something more going on. "You and I have been pretty good friends these past couple of years. I think I know when there's something on your mind, and it's time for you to just spit it out!"

Lois looked a bit flustered, but she admitted, "I do have some news, but I'm not ready to share it with everyone."

Intrigued, Nancy smiled and waited, knowing Lois would share when she was ready.

"I may have met someone," Lois finally said, a slight blush coloring her cheeks.

"You mean . . . like . . . a man?" Nancy asked in surprise. "You've been divorced for how many years now—thirty-five? And you've never once mentioned even being interested in someone! So, who is it? Do I know him?"

"I don't think so. His name is Henry Patton, and he moved into one of the condos across the street from my condo a couple of months ago. I happened to see him walking his dog one morning when I was out watering the flowers on my patio, and he stopped to talk. We've gone out to dinner a couple of times, and we have a lot in common. He was a high school teacher in Prairie View, and he decided last year it was time to retire. Eventually he moved to Maple Grove because he was tired of the traffic and college kids roaming the streets at all hours of the night."

"Wow, lady, he sounds great!" Nancy gushed. "Why don't you want to share your news with the others? Does he have a family? Kids? Grandkids? An ex-wife?"

"His wife died almost three years ago from cancer, and he has two kids, one in California, one in Florida, with six grandkids between the ages of six and eighteen. But he doesn't see them very often because none of them live close."

"But you like him?"

"Yeah, I really do!"

"And he has no skeletons in the closet?"

"Not that I know of—not yet, anyway," Lois said with a laugh.

"Then what is it?" Nancy prodded.

"Well, first of all, there's the fact that since I've lived alone for so long I don't think any man would want to put up with my idiosyncrasies. You know, the way I like to eat, the TV shows I like to watch, the restaurants I prefer. And then there's a really big issue we would have to deal with: he's a devout Catholic."

"So?"

"Maybe you don't know the history between Quakers and Catholics," Lois said. "A lot of older Friends don't believe Catholics are saved and going to heaven because they don't live pure lives. They work on Sundays, and some of them drink a lot."

"Are you serious?" Nancy was incredulous. "I know I haven't always been a Quaker, but that doesn't sound like the Maple Grove Friends I've gotten to know since I joined the Meeting after Allan and I got engaged."

Just then the doorbell rang, putting a halt to the conversation. "Please don't say anything," Lois pleaded. "I want to wait and see if anything becomes of the relationship before I tell anyone else."

"Lois, you're early," Beth noted as she and Sylvia walked in. "And you look a little flustered. Is everything okay?"

"Yes, she was early for a change," Nancy said quickly, "and we've just been catching up on what's been going on this past month."

Nancy wasn't sure her observant friend bought her excuse, but Beth didn't pursue it, instead noting the snacks on the table. "Fruit, yogurt, and seeds! Good choice, my friend. I need to start eating healthier."

"Me, too," Sylvia said. "If you all don't mind, let's get started. I have a hair appointment at 11:30. It was the only time she had available, and if I don't get this shaggy mop cut, I'll have to start wearing it in a ponytail!"

As the women sat down with their snacks, Nancy began sharing the story of the Grimké sisters from South Carolina and their passion for the abolition of slavery.

"And they were banned from South Carolina? Really?" Sylvia asked. "That seems a bit extreme."

"Remember, plantation owners relied on slaves to care for their massive acres of cotton and tobacco. It was the thought of having to pay for labor that kept the owners running for government offices in states like South Carolina. They were determined to prevent the abolitionists from ending their massive profits," Nancy said.

"But slavery is a thing of the past thanks to the Civil War and the Civil Rights Act," Lois said. "So, what can we learn from these Quaker sisters?"

"The war and the newly created laws, plus the amendments to the Constitution were important pieces of legislation," Nancy said, "but do you really think a Black man or woman—or any person of color, for that matter—has equality in this country today?"

"Of course!" Lois said.

"See, that's where you're wrong. We live in our lily-white Midwestern towns, and if we see a person who isn't White, we might smile and wave at them, but we never really know what they've experienced in their lives. So I started reading some books by Black authors who've shared what it's like to be Black in America today, and it was shocking to me."

"Like what?" Beth asked. "The only Black family I know is our tax lawyer and his family in Prairie View. It seems to me they're doing very well."

"And that's probably what a lot of us White people think about Blacks and other people of color. But here are some concepts we should probably explore," Nancy said. "Do you know about color blindness? White centering? Tokenism? White apathy? Optical allyship? White exceptionalism?"

"Whoa," Lois interjected. "Slow down! I've never heard of those terms, although I can guess what they mean."

"You probably think you can, but they may not be what you imagine. Next month we have Dr. Ann Preston as our important Quaker woman, so here are some recent books. I suggest we might each choose one to read so we can learn about these experiences. Then we can formulate a plan to address how we might be better able to understand our perceptions of people of color. Once we do that, we can talk about how we might work to make a difference in racial justice today," Nancy finished.

"Okay," Lois said reluctantly, "give us the list; I hope they aren't all hundreds of pages long!"

"No, they aren't!" Nancy began. "The one I read was *Me and Black Supremacy* by Layla Saad, but another great one I just listened to the audio version of is *Caste* by Isabel Wilkerson, plus there's *Becoming* by Michelle Obama, and *White Fragility* by Robin Diangelo, to name a few. Here, I made a list for each of you."

"Thanks for doing all this extra work for us, Nancy. I bet I can get an e-book or audio version and read one of them by next month," Sylvia said. "But since Harriet Tubman is our woman two months from now, do you suppose we could have the extra time to get one of these finished?"

"I like that idea!" came Lois' firm reply.

"Sounds good, Lois—if you're sure your social life won't interfere with your free time," Nancy teased.

Beth and Sylvia looked at each other and then at Lois. "Is there something you want to tell the rest of us?" Beth asked.

"No!" Lois said sharply, giving Nancy a warning look.

"Not to change the subject," Nancy said with a grin, "but there's one more piece of information I found about Sarah. I know we all were kind of upset when Ruth Bader Ginsburg died; if there was any one woman in our more recent history who did more for women's rights than this woman, I'd like to meet her! Anyway, remember in the *RGB* movie, in 1973, Ginsburg quoted Sarah Grimké as saying, 'I ask for no favor for my sex. All I ask of our brethren is that they take their feet off our necks,' when she gave her first oral arguments to the Supreme Court in *Frontiero v. Richardson*. I never realized she was quoting Sarah. And, Sue Monk Kidd based her novel *The Invention of Wings* on Sarah's life."

"I had no clue who Sarah and Angelina even were, and they have just become two of my favorite old Quaker women! But now I'm off to my hair appointment," Sylvia said, glancing at her watch.

"See you next month, ladies, but call me any time if there's news you want to share," Beth added, looking at Lois with a grin.

CHAPTER 20

1977
D.C. LIFE AND SILENT WORSHIP
SYLVIA

"You're a Quaker, aren't you?" Jane asked Sylvia as they sat down to lunch on one of the first days of Sylvia's new internship with their state senator.

Sylvia looked up with surprise, taken aback by the question. How had this woman known she came from a Quaker background?

"I'm sorry," Jane said, "I didn't mean to pry, but I saw you volunteer to work with the Friends Committee on National Legislation when the various lobbying groups were being discussed, so I just assumed that was part of your background."

Jane Streeter, Sylvia's perky, always ready for a good time intern partner who had begun working for their senator ever since her graduation from college, was someone Sylvia thought she would like to get to know better when work in the senator's office wasn't consuming all their hours. Jane had graduated from Columbia University two years before Sylvia and had aspirations of running for office herself someday.

"Yes," Sylvia admitted, relieved there was an easy explanation for Jane's question about her church background. "My family has been attending the Maple Grove Meeting for as long as I can remember, and my grandparents before them."

"The reason I asked was to see if you might be interested in attending the Adelphi Friends Meeting with me some Sunday. My family in Indiana still attends one of the few unprogrammed conservative Meetings remaining in our state. Was Maple Grove a programmed or unprogrammed Meeting?"

Sylvia racked her brain trying to remember the difference between the two. Hopefully her memory was correct in thinking programmed Meetings had pastors whereas unprogrammed Meetings were mostly silent. "Maple Grove is programmed," she said after a pause, "and we have a woman pastor."

"Would you be interested in experiencing an unprogrammed Meeting? I think you would really like the members at Adelphi Friends—there's a bunch of us younger people who attend. I would be happy to pick you up Sunday morning if you're willing to give us a try!" Jane said.

Sylvia had actually been interested in trying out some other denominations since she was on her own and didn't feel the need to necessarily stick to her Quaker roots. But Jane seemed so hopeful that Sylvia didn't have the heart to turn her down.

"That's really nice of you to offer, especially if the meeting house is too far to walk and there are no available buses at that time."

"Great," Jane said with a warm smile. "Write down your address and I'll pick you up around 9:30. We quietly visit a bit as people come into the sanctuary, and then we begin at 10:00 with announcements, and the rest of the service is spent in silent worship."

Soon their lunch break was over and the two hustled back to their desks for the afternoon. Sylvia had met with the senator a couple of times, so he at least recognized her face, she hoped! And she'd met with the FCNL lobbyist, too, but there was so much to learn—way more than any of her poli sci classes had covered. She was beginning to wish she had turned down Jane's offer for Sunday. She knew almost nothing about silent worship meetings and wondered how she would ever manage an hour of sitting in silence!

On the other hand, Jane was cute, bubbly, and someone she could see being friends with outside of work, so she decided it was worth trying.

On Sunday, Jane pulled up right on time in front of the apartment building where Sylvia had been waiting for ten minutes. She hated to be late for anything, let alone the first time attending a new Meeting.

On the short drive to the meeting house, Jane briefed Sylvia on what would be happening. "We believe that in the quiet stillness of meeting for worship, we can hear messages from God. Each of us has direct access to the Divine through the Light of God that is within every person who comes into the world. If we listen, we can be faithful to what we are being called or led to do to help others."

"That sounds the same as at Maple Grove, only instead of sitting in silence for an hour, we only sit for fifteen minutes or so. But I've always wondered, how do we know it's God speaking to us, and not just our own thinking?"

"Here we are," Jane said, looking for a place to park. "There are a bunch of spiritual matters we can discuss when we have more time. For now let's get inside so I can introduce you to some of the other members."

"Okay, sounds good," Sylvia said, hoping her words didn't betray her true feelings. She was never comfortable in new situations and had hoped she and Jane would just go in and sit in silence. At least she could hear voices in conversation already coming through the open windows, which was a bit of a relief.

The service proceeded just as Jane had described. A short time of greeting each other–Sylvia taking note of the kids their age who smiled and welcomed her, wondering if any of them were single– then the announcements and silent worship. Sylvia tried her best to stay engaged in the silence, trying to find the Light of God within, something she had heard mentioned at Maple Grove many times before, but her mind kept wandering to the upcoming week at work, her family and friends who would soon be sitting in their typical programmed worship back home, and the sweet citrus fragrance of Jane's perfume that filled the space between them. Sylvia couldn't help but sneak a glance at the young woman sitting beside her, head bowed, eyes closed. *Yes,* Sylvia thought, *I definitely want to get to know Jane. Maybe we can even start going to the movies or out to dinner on the weekends.*

When the service finished and the clerk rose for dismissal, Jane took Sylvia by the hand and led her around for more introductions, first to the group of elders who had been on the facing bench, then to some of the younger adults who were hanging around outside the meeting house.

"Hey, guys, this is Sylvia," Jane almost gushed. "She just moved here to work in the senator's office with me, and she's a Quaker too!

She hasn't had much experience with silent meetings, but she'll get it figured out if we can get her to keep coming."

After exchanging greetings, several of the young men looked at Sylvia with interest, no doubt wondering if she was also single and someone they might want to date.

"Hey, get your minds out of the gutter. She's all mine!" Jane said, laughing and turning toward Sylvia. "These guys are always looking for cute girls for their fantasies."

Sylvia felt herself blush, even though the guys laughed at Jane's outrageous comments. What did Jane mean with that "she's all mine" comment? But she didn't have time to think about it for long because Jane was pulling her away from the group and telling her they were going out for lunch.

"But—" Sylvia began before Jane interrupted.

"No buts! A girl's gotta eat, and I'm starved!"

Over lunch at a local taco place, Jane patiently answered Sylvia's questions about how to know whether the thoughts a person had in the silence were really from God or just in one's own mind.

"It's not a loud voice or anything—at least that's never happened to me. It's having thoughts of what God might be wanting us to do to make things better for the people we share life with in this world. It's really the center of our beliefs, something we call 'faith in action.'"

"What are some of the things people have felt God calling them to do when they were sitting in the silence?" Sylvia asked.

"One of the things I'm most interested in is donating to local non-profits. There's one in particular we've helped get started. It's a free clinic for people who have very little money and no health insurance. This city might be the center of our country's government, but there are a lot of homeless people and families living in poverty here."

"That's cool," Sylvia admitted. "But how do you keep your mind quiet during the silence? I kept thinking about everything I have to do tomorrow to finalize the senator's schedule for the week!"

"It's not always easy," Jane said with a laugh. "But if I try to focus on my breathing—you know, breathe in, breathe out—it helps for a while, at least. I wasn't great at it this morning, because I kept thinking about this new friend sitting beside me, and all the future fun—and maybe even a little bit of trouble—we might be able to have!"

Sylvia was surprised at Jane's frank sharing of her feelings, and she felt genuine warmth at the thought of what might be in store for them. Funny how the thought of the good-looking guys left her cold.

CHAPTER 21

1813-1872
DR. ANN PRESTON
PENNSYLVANIA

After returning a stack of medical books to the Westtown Boarding School library, fourteen-year-old Ann began her walk back to the dormitory in the crisp autumn air. How fortunate she was to have the opportunity to attend the finest boarding school in Pennsylvania!

"Miss Preston!"

Ann turned to see Headmaster Jones rushing toward her with a concerned look on his face.

"A letter just arrived for thee, and there is a note on the back that says 'urgent.' Please let me know if I may assist thee in any way."

As soon as the headmaster was out of sight, Ann opened the letter. To her distress, she saw it was from her father, insisting she return home immediately to help care for her mother. As the eldest of eight children, Ann had feared something like this might happen due to her mother's frequent bouts with illnesses. *And just as I was learning more and more about the human body,* Ann thought, glancing at the list of medical books for future study that she had written down from her search in the library.

Once Ann had made arrangements to travel the ten miles back to the family home in Westbrook, she began making plans to engage her siblings to help with their mother's care so she might return to school as soon as possible. Once she had her diploma, she vowed, she would apply to medical college and become a doctor.

As Ann entered their sprawling family home, she sensed something was happening. None of her siblings ran out to meet her, and there was an eerie stillness in the farmyard instead of the usual cacophony of sounds. The house, too, was quiet, but Ann could hear voices coming from the upstairs bedrooms. Deciding that perhaps there was a reason for the unusual silence, she refrained from calling out to announce her arrival. As she quietly climbed the stairs, she could hear soft voices coming from her mother's room.

"Greetings, Father and Mother," Ann said quietly, seeing her mother's pale face on the pillow and her father sitting next to her, holding her thin, wrinkled hand.

"Thank thee for returning so quickly from thy studies," Amos Preston said. "Thy mother has been unable to care for thy siblings for a week now, and I am unable to manage our farm without your assistance."

"But where is everyone?" Ann asked.

"Right now the children are in the cellar with the runaways," Amos said.

"How many are there this time?" she asked.

"A family of six—mother, father, and four children," her mother, Margaret, said, her voice weak yet filled with compassion.

"Please take thy belongings to thy room and then stay with my sweet Margaret," Amos requested. "I must see to feeding the animals."

The members in their Quaker community were abolitionists, and their farm, Prestonville, was a safe haven for slaves heading to freedom further north. Ann had always been proud of her family's work as abolitionists, but how was she going to do her part to help care for the slaves' physical needs if she was unable to return to Westtown and then earn a medical degree?

Resigned to the task at hand, caring for her mother and siblings, she vowed to teach her two sisters how to prepare the meals and help her care for their mother. And until her brothers were a few years older and could help their father, they could certainly learn how to sweep the floors and wash the dishes.

As the mundane days dragged on into years, Ann became more and more determined to do what her mother and the other Quaker women her age had never done—meaningful work outside the home. Becoming a doctor was always a part of her nightly prayers, and at last God seemed to provide the answer one day when Dr. Moseley made one of his weekly visits to check on Margaret. He was always interested in Ann's studies and seemed disappointed that she had not been able to remain at the Quaker boarding school.

"So, young lady, what does thee intend to do with thy life's work now that thy sisters seem to be able to care for the housework and for Margaret?" Dr. Moseley inquired.

"I have been teaching some of the younger children in our area, but what I long to do is to become a doctor, Doctor! I am not certain how I can make it happen, but I have always been interested in the differences between male and female bodies, and I'm not certain male doctors always know what is best for their female patients. Please do not be offended," she said with a smile.

"And I believe thee is absolutely correct in that assessment, so perhaps I might be able to help get thee started on this quest," he said. "How would thee like to start as my apprentice, going with me to call on my patients? I would be willing to impart whatever limited knowledge I have, and even let thee assist with some of the easier tasks: setting fractured bones, stitching up deep wounds, those types of injuries. Would that be of interest to thee?"

"That would be wonderful, especially if I might assist thee with things like childbirth and other health issues known only to women!" Ann said eagerly.

"Then I shall speak with thy father, and if he is in agreement, we will begin this arrangement that I have no doubt will benefit us both," he said with a smile.

• • •

Decades later as she lay in bed after the latest attack of the articular rheumatism that now plagued her body, Ann thought of how her work with Dr. Moseley had been the start of a long and fulfilling career in medicine. *Will this disease be the end of my ability to continue teaching at the beloved women's college I worked so hard to help establish?* she wondered. *I am only fifty-seven years of age, but my body is more like that of an eighty-year-old!*

But if my health fails me, at least I will meet my creator knowing I have done everything in my power to strive for equality for women—not only in matters of their health, but also for all the freedoms currently only still enjoyed by men.

Women have come so far in my lifetime, Ann thought. She'd never forget applying to medical colleges only open to men–and being rejected over and over. She was certain that because of her work with Dr. Moseley, she knew as much or maybe even more than many of the men who were granted entrance to the schools. How hopeless she felt, afraid of never reaching her goal of becoming a doctor! But her continued drive led her to the Female College of Medicine founded by her beloved Quakers, Friends who always stood on their testimony of equality for all. Being part of the inaugural class of eight women to graduate from the Female Medical College of Pennsylvania as physicians had just been the beginning of her determination to make a difference when treating some of the unique aspects of the female body, including difficulties with childbirth, lactation, and the aging of hormones.

So many of the women she treated came to her after they were unable to receive proper medical treatment by their male physicians. Ann became determined to secure funding to begin a women's hospital to not only treat women's illnesses but also to train doctors and nurses in the unique aspects of female anatomy.

Later, when she learned the Female Medical College of Pennsylvania had closed due to lack of funds during the war, she was so happy to be able to persuade the college to open again, sharing part of the women's hospital space. What a privilege it was to be appointed as Dean of the college! Not to mention Ann's pride when their institution was the first to graduate African American and Indiginous American women with medical degrees. And how could she forget the importance of organizing social programs teaching hygiene and physiology to some of the poorest women in Philadelphia?

They tried to keep us out of their male-only medical colleges, but even the male students throwing papers, chewed tobacco, and rocks at us women could not stop us from working in their clinics, Ann thought proudly.

She may not have produced a passel of children like her parents, but Ann's home was always open to any and all friends–especially young women who needed encouragement, offering a respite from their struggles to gain equality in the medical field. Her only regret was not being able to remain on this earth to continue the fight for women's rights in all matters, but she was comforted knowing opinions were beginning to change, and women doctors were slowly becoming recognized as being as capable as their male counterparts. *That means I have done my best to carry out the tasks I believe God called me to do.*

Chapter 22

October, Present Day
The Club—Sylvia's
Family Home

Ah, here comes my best friend to help out, Sylvia thought as she saw Beth park her vehicle and come in the back door after a quick knock.

"Hey, friend," was Sylvia's loving greeting as she went to hug Beth. "You're early! Did you think I would need help this morning? Because if you did, you must have read my mind! Dad didn't have a very good night, and I must have shut my alarm off and gone back to sleep. If you want to make the coffee and get the table ready, I'll finish making the fruit salad to have with the yogurt and nuts."

Beth knew Sylvia's father had recently been hospitalized with pneumonia and that Sylvia had spent a lot of time driving her mother back and forth to be with him. Beth had tried to persuade her friend to trade months with her for hosting the club, but Sylvia insisted her dad was home and feeling better, spending most of his time sleeping in his recliner while her mom sat by him, often reading the latest book on the United Society of Friends Women's reading list for the current year. Beth knew Ruth was working on her certificate for being a twenty-five-year reader in the society's literature program, and this was the year she would receive the USFW award at their annual banquet in August.

Sylvia knew she had dark circles under her eyes, and she just hoped Beth didn't notice and say something about how she was working too hard. Beth had offered to trade months hosting with her, but she didn't want any of the women to think she was running out of energy when caring for her parents. And wouldn't you know, she couldn't keep from crying out when the knife slipped and easily slipped through the flesh of her index finger.

"I'm worried about you," Beth said, hurrying over to turn on the water to flush out the cut. "You've been doing too much, and you should have admitted you were really tired when I tried to get you to trade months with me!"

Standing together by the sink as the water continued to flush the wound, Sylvia felt herself lean into Beth, basking in the warmth of Beth's side. *It really almost seems like we are one body . . . almost as if we fit together,* she thought.

"I'm sorry," Sylvia groaned. "That was such a careless thing to do. Who cuts themselves chopping watermelon?"

"Don't feel sorry! I can't think of a single woman our age who hasn't had an accident with a knife sometime in her life—unless she never prepared a meal! I'm going to finish getting the fruit ready while you go find a bandage and check on your parents."

"You're the best!" Sylvia said. "What would I ever do without you?"

Beth was happy she had come early and was able to give her best friend a little extra help.

When the others arrived and the fruit, yogurt, and nuts were on the table, Sylvia stopped them from filling their plates. "Wait a minute—I think there's one more thing for us to enjoy," she said with a smile, returning to the kitchen. And soon a plate of snickerdoodle cookies was in front of them to add to the fruit snack. "I made a batch when my dad got home from the hospital because they're his favorites, and I saved these for us."

"Thank heavens!" Lois exclaimed. "I know we've been trying to offer healthy snacks, but come on! What's one—or maybe two—cookies going to hurt?"

The others just laughed as they each took one—or maybe two—of the sweet treats as a little dessert to go with the fruit parfaits.

Sylvia's admiration for her Quaker woman was obvious to the others the minute she began telling them about Dr. Ann Preston. "She was such a determined woman! If I had half the courage that Ann had to be the person I wanted to be, I wouldn't have any regrets now that I'm almost twenty years older than Ann was when she died."

Looking puzzled, Nancy asked, "What regrets could you possibly have? Who went to work in the Senate right out of college? Who campaigned for all those candidates all those years? You're one of the most well-respected members in our community!"

"Yeah," Beth chimed in, a look of concern on her face, "what do you mean? You've never said anything about things you wish you had done differently."

Before Lois could add her two cents worth to the discussion, Sylvia held up a hand to stop the speculation, wishing she hadn't made that last comment. "Don't you ever wish you had done some things differently in your past? It's not a big deal. I just really admired Ann's tenacity to make her dream of becoming a doctor a reality. It certainly wasn't easy when she had to leave school to help her family and then when her medical school applications were denied."

"But is there anything that we can take from this Quaker woman's life to make a difference in our world today? I don't think there are any barriers to women becoming doctors in this day and age," Lois said doubtfully.

"If you do a little digging," Sylvia replied, "you'll find there are still inequities for women in the healthcare field. For instance, female OBGYNs face barriers in advancing into leadership positions, and they earn around thirty-six thousand dollars less per year than their male counterparts.

"And get this: while men and women begin medical school in similar proportions, when it comes to teaching in those same schools, around thirty-six percent of the women are stuck as entry-level professors, and only one in ten deans in medical schools is a woman. Just think about that for a minute and understand what a brilliant woman Ann must have been to be appointed as dean of her medical school."

"So you're saying that there are still major inequities for women in medicine," Beth asked, pondering this news. "What can we do about that?"

"I suppose we can at least point out these inequalities when we put together all our information, and, hopefully, find a way to share it with the other Friends Meetings," Nancy said.

"Yes, I've been contemplating what we can gain from this pioneering Quaker woman when there is still such a lack of respect for women in medicine today," Sylvia said. "I've been thinking that maybe it's time we addressed the issue starting right here in our own

Yearly Meeting. What if we all signed up to lead one of the workshops during the next annual session? We could at least raise awareness of discrimination against women in the medical field today after sharing a bit about Ann Preston's life."

"I thought our Monthly Meeting just requested we leave the Yearly Meeting," Beth said, remembering Sylvia mentioning that move a few months earlier.

"True," said Sylvia, "but they often bring in speakers to lead the workshops who aren't from the Yearly Meeting, and since a lot of people on the planning committee know us, I think they might be persuaded to allow us to present our findings. When I served on that committee a few years ago, we were always scrambling to find workshop leaders.

"And besides, there are still Meetings right here in our state that continue to insist that women are to be submissive to men! Maybe we could help some of the women start thinking about inequity in their marriages, too. I think that might give them courage to stand up for themselves—and for the all-important Quaker testimony of equality."

There was that idea again about standing up for yourself. The women all wondered what was behind these subtle comments Sylvia was making.

"I can contact the chairperson on the planning committee and at least see if it's a possibility," Sylvia said when the others remained silent, knowing she had been attending annual sessions most of her life and knew a lot of the members on the planning committee.

"It's okay with me," Lois finally agreed, "but don't expect any miracles!"

When the other three began to laugh, Nancy was the one to settle the discussion. "Yes, Lois, we know your opinions on these kinds of changes, but the one thing I'm sure you impressed upon your students was the need to be lifelong learners, right? I don't think it's too late to believe adults can still learn new things, too. I say let's do it! Power to the women in the medical field who continue to persevere in the fight to rise to equal representation in positions of power, and power to Quaker women today to fight for their equality!"

"You're right, as always," Lois admitted. "When you contact the committee, Sylvia, just let them know we will do even more research on gender discrimination in the medical field today. Now, please pass the cookies!"

Chapter 23

1988
Yearly Meeting
Beth

"Are you both ready for Yearly Meeting, and do you have activities in your backpacks to entertain yourselves in the car while I drive?" Beth asked Tyler and Kristy as they gathered the things they would need while camping in the park across from the Yearly Meeting office building and the local Friends Meeting House. They were fortunate that their neighbors, the Joneses, had loaned their small camper for the five days of their Yearly Meeting's annual business sessions, workshops, and worship services, even going so far as to haul it to the campgrounds and set it up for them.

Beth had gotten to know so many of the Friends at their yearly gathering—the young adults, the elders, and every age in between. She was once again a representative from Maple Grove Friends, which meant she had to take notes during the business sessions and give a report during Maple Grove's next Monthly Meeting for business. Thankfully there were activities for kids during the adult sessions, and there was even a nursery for the little ones like Kristy, who was just five and not ready for the structured activities yet. It was August so Bob had too much hay ready to bale right then to be able to get away, but he thought he would be able to make the drive up to enjoy the missionary speaker at the closing banquet on Saturday.

As she drove the hour to the Quaker college where the sessions were held, Beth wondered if there would be any controversies this year. It seemed like there was always some issue that was a bit contentious, often a matter of Quaker beliefs and practice. She secretly hoped there might be a little something to spice up the business sessions.

With the food and bedding unloaded, suitcases stowed under the beds, and clothes changed for the evening's worship service, Beth walked the kids to their activities at the Meeting House across the street and then made her way down the few blocks to the chapel on campus. It was a stately structure, but the wooden folding theater seats weren't the most comfortable, and with no air conditioning, she hoped there would be a breeze streaming through the side windows. *This building could use some updating,* she thought, then reminded herself that this was a Quaker institution, and simplicity was a strong testimony of their faith. She soon found a longtime friend, Margaret, from her days at Twin Pines Camp, and settled in for a rather uninspiring worship service with a speaker who needed a little animation in his voice.

Leaning toward Margaret, Beth couldn't help but whisper, "Why don't they ever have a woman as a guest speaker?" For as long as she could remember, it was always men bringing the messages. She was sure they were given a pretty nice fee for speaking during the four worship sessions, but if Friends really believed in equality, they would have a woman speaking every other year. Margaret just smiled at her and continued listening to the speaker.

When the long, sweaty service was over, Margaret offered to drive Beth back to the Meeting House to pick up the kids, so it wasn't long before she had Tyler and Kristy back in the camper and situated in their beds. As soon as they were both asleep, she joined several of the other camping adults sitting in a circle with their lawn chairs, sharing what had transpired in their lives during the past year. Beth shared stories about the kids and why Bob wasn't with them this time, and she appreciated hearing about the year one of the couples had just spent working in Africa. *This kind of fellowship is one of the best parts of Yearly Meeting,* she thought, and she was sorry Bob wasn't there to enjoy it with her.

The business session the next day started out in the usual manner with the chairpersons of the various Yearly Meeting committees giving somewhat dry reports of their committees' work the past year. Nothing exciting happened during that session or the next. In fact, it wasn't until the last morning of business that things heated up. The topic was the budget, a common concern every year when the money that came in was always less than what they had budgeted. This year it was the line-item budget amounts going to the Friends Committee on National Legislation, American Friends Service Committee, and Friends World Committee for Consultation that became the hot topic. The Yearly Meeting had always sent delegates to these organizations' annual sessions and provided funding to each of them in the budget.

"Clerk, please?" An elderly gentleman rose from a few rows behind Beth.

"Yes, Paul?" the presiding clerk answered, giving him permission to address the representatives.

"I do not believe the money our local meetings are asked to give for our own Yearly Meeting's work should be used to support the budgets of these organizations, especially FCNL. I have studied their work for a number of years, and when I sent a letter asking why they had not taken a stand against abortion and gay marriage, they had no good answer. The Bible clearly states both are sins, but if the people in charge of these groups won't take a stand, I would like to move that we delete their funding from next year's budget."

Whispers and murmurs ran through the room before another man rose and asked permission to speak.

"Go ahead, Lyle," the clerk responded.

"The work of FCNL is to lobby for legislative issues that each of our meetings has been asked to prioritize and send to them. Some of the issues our meeting has sent are economic justice, work with immigrants and refugees, and peace building—especially with the threat of nuclear war right now. Why would we not believe this is important work to continue to support?"

The discussion continued back and forth, agitation evident in the passionate voices on each side of the issue. *For once,* Beth thought, *I don't need to worry about trying to stay awake!*

But it was the last person asking to speak—Paul again—whose words and attitude really angered Beth. Paul was the pastor of a small meeting in the same Quarterly Meeting as Maple Grove.

"I would like to ask the Discipline Committee to insert the words 'homosexuality' and 'abortion' in the list of sins we are admonished to avoid," Paul said. "It needs to be there in black and white so there is no doubt where we stand as a Yearly Meeting on those two issues."

Beth knew she should speak up as she thought about her older cousin, Evelyn, who lived with her partner. Beth had always liked going to their house when she was a kid because the two women were usually laughing at each other's funny sayings, and the looks they gave each other were filled with such love. When she had become a wife and mother herself, Beth had realized the two women were more than just roommates. And they were wonderful women!

She wanted to stand up and say homosexuality was never something they should be listing as sin; in fact, she wanted to remind them that Jesus had said to "judge not lest ye be judged." Just as she was starting to get up the courage to stand and speak on the issue, the clerk rose and said since it was time for lunch, they would table the discussion until the Spring Body of Representatives session in March. He then asked the superintendent to close in prayer.

As the group sat around in the park on the last night of the Yearly Meeting, the main topic of discussion was Paul's request for adding to the list of sins. Beth was relieved to hear no one in their group thought this was the right thing to do. One of the men, a professor at the college, spoke of the current research on sexuality and said that he, like the medical experts, believed a person's sexual and emotional attraction might be toward the opposite sex, or maybe toward a person of the same sex, or maybe somewhere in between. *That's what I believe, too,* Beth thought, but once again she was nervous about sharing her feelings.

"I do hope this doesn't become a major issue," one of the women added. "It just isn't necessary to cut the funding, especially to FCNL. We need them to be working for laws that are just and fair."

Yes, Beth thought, *that's what I believe, too. But will I ever find the courage to say the things I believe when it's in a gathering of nearly a hundred other representatives? That will take some work.* But she knew in her heart there were many such causes worth making her voice heard.

When the banquets were finished and Friends had once again made plans to see one another at the Spring Body of Representatives session in March, Beth and the kids headed home. Beth was upset that Bob hadn't made it to the banquet; no doubt he had found another hay-cutting job that couldn't wait. She wished he would have at least called the Yearly Meeting office to let her know he wasn't coming; but they would soon be home, and eventually her focus turned to all she would need to do to get everything unpacked and ready for work on Monday.

Chapter 24

1820-1925
Araminta ("Minty") Harriet Ross AKA Harriet Tubman Maryland

"Get over here, Minty, and take your punishment!" This was not the first time Minty had forgotten to gather the eggs for breakfast. She knew she was going to get a lashing; she just didn't know how many she would have to endure this time.

"You gonna remember to get them eggs next time?" her owner, Mary Brodess, asked.

"Yes, ma'am, I won't forget again."

"This is the fifth time you have forgotten, Minty, so I believe you will need five lashes to help you remember your task the next time. You know you have my large family to care for, and I will not tolerate disobedience!"

As the small whip came down across her thin back, Minty did her five-year-old best to keep from crying out. She had heard the screams of the other house slaves' punishments on other occasions and had felt the sting of each of their lashes herself.

I will not let them hear me, she thought, determined not to cause others the same fate. *And I'm not going to live the rest of my life being treated like a farm animal, she promised herself. I'm going to be free someday!*

Minty liked her nickname—who would want to be called "Araminta" the rest of her life? But she really loved her middle name, Harriet, because it was also her mother's name. Their whole family had been bought and sold by different White folks, meaning she didn't even know where three of her sisters were now. But at least her momma didn't let them take her little brother, Moses. *I'm going to remember how brave Momma was to stand up to the master when that White man wanted to buy him.*

What do I have to do to be free? Minty wondered when she reached her thirteenth birthday. At least she thought that was how old she was. Momma hadn't known the exact year she was born—nobody kept track of the slaves' ages.

"Minty?" Mary Brodess called out. "Where you at, girl? I need you to get down to the general store and get us our supplies for the week."

"Yes, ma'am," Minty called back from the summer kitchen where she was pitting cherries in preparation for the cherry pies she would bake for the day's noon meal.

Minty always enjoyed going to the store. She loved the sights and smells, all the bolts of cloth, the barrels of sugar and flour, the creak of the old wooden floors. As she approached the store's front porch, an angry White man a little way down the road yelled out to her.

"Hey girl—you grab that boy there by you and you hold him until I can get there! He thinks he can run away from me, but I paid good money for that strappin' healthy buck, and I own him!"

Minty looked at the boy. He appeared to be about her age, and the fear in his eyes sank deep into her soul.

"No sir, I can't help you. I belong to Master Brodess." Minty was afraid to say any more, but she knew this boy was going to be beaten or worse if the White man got a hold of him. "Run!" she whispered in his ear. But the boy seemed to be frozen on the porch's top step.

Minty saw the anger in the man's eyes as he ran toward them both. Too late; she saw the big piece of iron in his hand, and when he threw it at them both, the boy ducked and the heavy weight hit Minty in the head, dropping her to the ground. When she came to and was finally able to sit up, both the man and boy were gone, and she was afraid she was going to bleed to death when she felt the crack in her skull.

No, she thought, *I will not die here; I will return to the house and surely when the Missus sees my head I will not be doubly punished for not getting the supplies on the list.*

• • •

Now ninety-three years of age and living in the Harriet Tubman Home for the Aged, Harriet was so grateful that the land she donated to the African Methodist Episcopal Church had inspired them to build this wonderful place for people like her who were in their final years, and they even named it in her honor! As she sat wrapped in a blanket out on the lawn, feeling the sun's warmth, Harriet's mind was seldom far from her life's memories.

I'll never forget that fateful day on the porch of the general store, she thought, forever bearing the damage that weapon had done to her, even after surgery much later in life to try to alleviate the pain, seizures, and buzzing she had lived with for so many years. Still, that was the day she'd made up her mind once and for all that she would be free if it were the last thing she ever did.

First, though, came the marriage to John Tubman, a free Black man, and the desire to give up the Minty nickname and take her mother's name to indicate her new status as a married woman of twenty-four. Then came her desire to be free herself. When she turned twenty-nine, at least that's how old she guessed she was, she was determined to take her chance at freedom.

Born and raised in Maryland, which had been a slave state for as long as she could remember, Harriet knew that nearby Pennsylvania was a free state, and she had been resolved to flee to Philadelphia by herself when she had heard stories about the Underground Railroad that Quakers and other abolitionists had set up to help slaves navigate their way to freedom. It was a sad day when she was unable to persuade John to go with her; when he chose instead to take another wife to remain with him in Maryland.

But at least eighteen years after John decided to take a more domesticated wife, in '69 she and Nelson Davis had found each other to wed after his time fighting in the war for freedom. And what a blessing they shared with their little adopted daughter, Gertie, until Nelson succumbed to tuberculosis just twelve years later.

What would my life have been like had I not escaped to freedom? If she had not made nineteen trips back and forth from the shores of Maryland to Philly–often in the winter when the nights offered more darkness–to help not only her family members but also over three hundred other enslaved people gain their freedom? *They could not stop us, even when that horrible Fugitive Slave Law was passed that meant freed slaves were never free if they were caught by their masters. Those of us working on the Railroad, though,* she thought with a smile, *we made sure freedom was still available, even if it meant they had to take a little longer journey to Canada where slavery was not allowed.*

Then came the Civil War, when Harriet felt the need to support the Union Army as a cook, then a nurse, and even a spy! It was such a privilege to be a guide at the Combahee River Raid when they were able to liberate more than seven hundred slaves in South Carolina. They called her "The Conductor," and that made all the hard times worth her efforts.

Harriet was never wealthy, but there was more than wealth that made her proud. She did her best to bring freedom to those in bondage. She thought, *I will never forget that day when I crossed the state line into Pennsylvania. I remember looking at my hands to see if I was the same person! There was such a glory over everything; the sun came like gold through the trees, and over the fields, and I felt like I was in Heaven.*

And soon I will be in Heaven. I will see all my relatives who were torn from me and all those who made our work on the Underground Railroad a salvation for so many. And it will be glorious!

CHAPTER 25

NOVEMBER, PRESENT DAY
THE CLUB—LOIS'S CONDO

Lois was humming as she thought about the previous evening she and her neighbor, Henry, had spent together, sharing a pizza and watching a movie on Amazon Prime. It had been a newer movie on the life of Harriet Tubman, and Lois had wanted to watch it to see if there were any more facts on the woman's life as an abolitionist that she might want to share at the upcoming club meeting. She and Henry had been spending several evenings a week together in the past month, but it seemed like they were still both content to take things slowly. They had, however, talked about some of their past lives' major events—and past marriage partners. Of course, Henry's marriage had been much more pleasant than Lois's, but she had openly shared all the misery that had led to her divorce.

Lois remembered the first time she and Mark had held hands–all the way home from that dreadful Four Spiritual Laws conference. How in the world had their younger selves been persuaded to actually knock on doors and intrude on people's daily lives, not to mention their spiritual lives? But at that time in her life, she'd thought it had been worth the pain of talking to strangers just to be able to spend time with her crush. How excited she had been at the prospect of being Mark's new girlfriend.

Mark had been cocky, brash, and unafraid to break the Meeting rules—no drinking, smoking, or sex. He had been almost intoxicating. During the conference, Lois had learned that his parents were divorced, his mom had a love of too much wine, and his dad ruled with his fist. She should have seen the warning signs, as she frequently chided herself after the divorce.

Even though Lois had been deeply in love with Mark at first, over the years his angry outbursts had increased, eventually followed by punches. When he refused to go to counseling, she knew she had to leave for both her sake and Justin's. It hadn't been easy being a single mom and a full-time schoolteacher, but she had loved her job and her son. Her parents and Maple Grove Friends had helped out with childcare when Justin was sick and Lois had to go to work. Justin was like his dad in many ways, and although sometimes she wished he had settled down and started having children, she was grateful he had chosen to channel his aggression in the discipline of the Army.

Yikes, Lois thought, *I'd better leave memory lane and get this quiche in the oven!* A couple of the others in the club had been trying to offer more healthy foods when they were hosting, and quiche was her compromise between something sweet and gooey and carrots and dip.

Sylvia was the first to arrive, this time without Beth by her side. "Good morning, friend!" came her warm greeting. "What's that delicious treat I'm smelling?"

"It's a ham and asparagus quiche with a little pepper jack cheese on top."

"Yum! I can't wait to try it."

"Where's your sidekick?" Lois inquired, grinning at Sylvia.

"Who? Sparky? He's living his dog's life sleeping in front of the east window with dreams of chasing—and catching—squirrels."

"You know who I'm talking about. What's Beth up to this morning since she's not with you?"

"She had a dental checkup at seven, so she should be here anytime now."

Nancy soon joined them with her added excitement at the sight of the bubbling quiche, and as soon as Beth arrived and the quiche was down to a few crumbs, an intense discussion began on the subject of Harriet Tubman.

"She was the bravest woman in American history," Lois gushed, "and definitely the bravest of any of the other Quaker women we've learned about!"

"Wait," Nancy interrupted, "are you sure she was a Quaker? I know she worked with some of the Quakers who were supporting enslaved people trying to seek their freedom, but we were always taught her family was Methodist."

"Does that really matter?" Lois said, a bit of exasperation in her voice. "We are talking about women in history who made a difference in 'being the church,' and she certainly qualifies with the amazing work she did on the Underground Railroad that was supported by so many Friends!"

"Okay, ladies," Nancy said, ever the peacemaker. "Let's think about the purpose of this work we're doing. Yes, we want to celebrate Quaker women who made a difference in people's lives. But we also want to make the point that the move toward more evangelicalism in so many of the Friends Meetings in our region is not what Jesus's life was all about—nor his teachings. So, I believe we should include Harriet Tubman because she was a part of the Friends' work to 'be the church' by leading Black men and children from slavery to freedom."

As usual, Nancy's wise words calmed the simmering disagreement, and Lois began again to share about Harriet Tubman's life.

"Can you believe she took that blow to her head and lived with seizures, pounding migraines, and even some hallucinogenic visions her whole life?" Lois said. "But she didn't let that stop her! Just imagine all those hair-raising trips to help over three hundred slaves to freedom. She used to pretend she was a slave when she was walking those ninety miles from the shores of Maryland to Philadelphia. She would sometimes take cover in some of the Quaker homes and meeting houses on the Railroad, sometimes pretending she was feeding the chickens or cleaning the house when the slave catchers would show up looking for runaways they could capture and return for a reward.

"So back to our work on racial justice," Lois continued. "Did you all have a chance to do your anti-racism reading that we talked about last month?"

"I didn't get the book I chose all read," Beth admitted, "but I promise to finish it, and I think I read enough to know we've all had a massive amount of White privilege in our lives!"

"Yes, it was pretty eye-opening," Sylvia agreed. "There is so much we don't understand because we've never been Black, and we and our ancestors have never been slaves thought of as property, beaten and whipped, or had our children taken from us and sold."

"But slavery was abolished after the Thirteenth Amendment was passed over a hundred and fifty years ago," Nancy reminded them.

"Yes, but there are still so many inequities yet today where Black people are concerned, especially when parents are afraid to let their sons go out at night for fear they'll be questioned and mistreated by aggressive police officers. I think we can continue to meet around the peace pole at the meeting house each week with those of us who are concerned about racial injustice and keep working on the list of actions we generated back in July. I presume you all still have the list Sylvia gave us back then, and if not, I can make copies of mine for you before you leave today. With both our individual actions plus this racial justice group, we can keep looking for solutions to all the things we read about. We definitely have to do something about systemic racism, not only in support of Black people, but also all people of color, including Indigenous people.

"But there's also another kind of slavery that's still going on," Lois said.

"What do you mean?" Beth asked.

"I did some research after remembering one of my student's families lost their fifteen-year-old daughter when she was walking home at night from her shift at McDonald's, just a few blocks from her house. She had been called some names at school that day and had started to cry thinking about it. A man who had been cruising the streets looking for just such a girl saw her and rolled down his window to see if she was hurt—or so he said. She thought he just seemed concerned, and he didn't try to force her to go with him or anything like that.

"But the longer he kept talking to her in that caring voice, the more she opened up to him, telling him about being bullied at school and how her parents were always so mean to her. He was then able to persuade her to go with him by promising he would help her make a lot more money than she'd ever be able to get working at McDonald's. She had been fighting with her parents over her curfew and poor grades, so it wasn't too hard for this john to convince her he would protect her and give her the love she deserved. Her parents said it was like she just disappeared, but she ended up being sold to older men for sex, and she was never allowed to be on her own or have any way to even call her parents. It was like being a modern-day slave. But the good news is that after a year, she was able to escape. She was able to steal a cell phone and call for help."

"It's hard to figure out why this girl decided to go with this man, especially after all the talks we give our kids and students about never going anywhere with strangers," Beth said.

"But it happens way more than you would imagine; there's a multi-billion-dollar sex-trade industry here in the U.S., and seventy-one percent of these modern slaves are female. One in four are just children," Lois said.

"That's horrible!" Sylvia said in disbelief. "But how can we do anything about it here in the Midwest? I thought this was something that happened in places like Las Vegas or New York City."

"I knew you would ask!" Lois said with a smile. "Probably the first thing is just to know more about child trafficking. I learned a lot from organizations that rescue children from these horrible situations, and the places they've set up to offer them help in group homes in some of the bigger cities. But it's happening in rural areas, too, so being informed about the places where kids are apt to be sighted by these traffickers and knowing what signs we should look for in some of these vulnerable kids will be really important. So here are two things I'm thinking we might be able to do to help out.

"First, the last time I drove on the interstate and stopped at one of the truck stops to get coffee and use the rest room, I saw posters with phone numbers for getting help for sex-trafficking taped on the inside on the stall doors. So what if we check with our state organization and see if they might give us more posters to take to gas stations—places where truckers might stop? They seem to be able to recognize kids who might be caught up in this form of slavery.

"Then, what if we work on getting someone from the anti-trafficking organization in our state to come to our Meeting and explain their work and help people be more informed?"

"That's a great idea," Nancy said. "Maybe we can get our Peace and Social Concerns Committee involved in lining up an informational meeting."

"And since you're on the committee," Lois said with a grin, "I nominate you to be our representative to share our concerns. It seems to me that working to end human trafficking—a kind of slavery in our own time—really fits with our Quaker testimony of being active and supportive in our communities. And, I like to think that in a small way, it will be like the work Harriet did to free enslaved people."

"I'll bring it up at our meeting next week," Nancy assured them, "so be prepared to help out with this venture when we bring in an expert to talk about it."

"You're pretty confident you can get the committee to support this, aren't you?" Beth asked.

"I'm going to do my best," Nancy said with modesty.

"Something just occurred to me," Lois said. "Doesn't it seem like every single woman we have researched did something that was highlighting inequality? What about those other Quaker testimonies—you know, peace, integrity, community, simplicity, and stewardship?"

The women were silent for a moment, realizing the truth in Lois's words.

Finally Nancy spoke. "But isn't the equality of all—the equal treatment and equal rights of all people—the underlying basis for peace? And how can you be a person of integrity if you don't treat everyone with equal respect? Isn't the way we spend our incomes to help others by supporting efforts for equality a type of stewardship? And it all is a part of our communities."

"Yes, Nancy's right," Sylvia agreed as Beth also nodded. "And we have a long way to go in a lot of our Meetings when it comes to our views on racism and LGBTQ issues."

"Okay, glad you all got that straightened out for this old teacher!" Lois said with a laugh. "And you're right, Nancy—equality is the basis on which the other testimonies are grounded."

"I have a suggestion about next month," Beth added as the discussion seemed to be finished and they were getting their jackets on to leave. "Since Thanksgiving is only a couple of weeks from now, and then December is always busy, what if we pause our research and gatherings until January? That way I'll have more time to work on my Quaker—Elizabeth Comstock—and we don't have to try to find a time in our schedules to meet."

"Perfect!" Lois agreed. "I'm going to make a trip down to Texas to see Justin at the Army base sometime between Thanksgiving and Christmas. It seems he has a new woman in his life that he'd rather spend Christmas with than coming back home this year."

"Wow! That's great! I think we've all been hoping he'd finally find someone to share his life with—besides his buddies on the base!" Sylvia said.

"Then what will you do on Christmas, Lois?" Nancy asked with a grin. "Any special plans for you that day?"

"Oh, I'll probably just go down to the Catholic Church and help them serve the meal for those who have no one to spend the holiday with. They always have almost a hundred guests to serve that day."

"That's a wonderful, giving thing to do," Sylvia said warmly.

"Yes, there are a lot of fine folks in that church," Nancy said, looking directly at Lois, knowing the new man in her life might also be helping out that day.

"Gotta run, ladies! We can keep in touch via email about the human trafficking work after our committee meets next week," Nancy called as she headed out to meet Allan for lunch.

As Beth and Sylvia walked out together, Beth stopped Sylvia when she reached her SUV. "Do you think you and I might have time to get together sometime after Thanksgiving and before things get crazy closer to Christmas? I'd really like to make some notes on what we've learned from our Quaker ancestors so far and then maybe decide what to do with all the information we're compiling, like maybe putting it all together in a booklet or something. What do you think?"

"That sounds like a great idea," Sylvia said with a smile. "Since it's just the two of us, maybe we can meet for lunch at Ben's Burgers again. I miss those lunches we used to share!"

"It's a date!" Beth said. "I'll be texting you to find a day to get together—maybe even more than one if we need more time."

Sylvia couldn't help the smile that remained on her face and in her heart at the thought of spending more time with Beth. The club meetings had curtailed some of their one-on-one coffee and lunch times together, and she couldn't wait to be with Beth again—just the two of them.

CHAPTER 26

DECEMBER, PRESENT DAY WHERE ARE WE NOW? SYLVIA AND BETH

The enticing aromas of burgers and onion strings hit Beth's senses the minute she stepped through the door at Ben's Burgers. Ben's dad had been a classmate of Sylvia's and Beth's, and the whole town had been so pleased when Ben had returned from culinary school and a big-time internship in New York City to open their now-favorite burger joint.

"Hey, Mrs. Smith," Ben called from the kitchen's order window, "what brings you in today? I haven't seen you and your sidekick in here for a while. I thought maybe you had given up my delicious burgers for tofu and spinach!" he said with a laugh.

"Now Ben, you know I would never turn to tofu and spinach when I could have one of your gourmet burgers. All that delicious aioli smothering those crisp onion strings on that burger with your special seasoning . . . nothing will ever take the place of your cooking!"

Sylvia's entrance was greeted with the same welcoming smile from Ben and a hug from Beth. "Sorry I'm a little late," was Sylvia's breathless greeting. "Dad went out to pick up the mail like he's done every day his entire life, and then when he didn't come right back in, I found him wandering around in the barn, looking for his horse—a horse he hasn't had for forty years!"

"Oh no! Were you scared he might have wandered off?" Beth asked, filled with empathy for her friend.

"I worry about it every single day," came Sylvia's teary reply.

"Will your mom be able to take care of him while you're here? We can meet another day if you need to be back home."

"No, Mom will lock the doors, and as long as she's there to talk to him, he won't try to leave."

"I'm so sorry," Beth added, hugging her again. This time Sylvia's embrace felt fiercer and more clinging than usual.

"I'm sorry," Sylvia said quickly, as if realizing she had been hanging on to a lifeline for too long. "I just sometimes feel overwhelmed with the care my parents need. I've been looking forward to this lunch for weeks, and I'd like to try and give my full attention to you and our discussion—and our food!"

After their burgers and fries were devoured—Beth telling herself it was okay to indulge in these treats once in a while—the women began sharing their thoughts about their club's work.

"Do you think we're really doing anything worthwhile, researching all these ancestral Quakers?" Beth asked.

"You know, I've wondered about that more than a few times," Sylvia admitted. "I think we have to continue to keep our focus on the real purpose in this work. Remember how we agreed that the Meetings in our Yearly Meeting have become too wrapped up in evangelical theology? And how we wanted to emphasize the long-standing Quaker testimonies to help create a new vision for being the church by our actions?"

"Yes, but sometimes I need to remember what evangelical Meetings are about and make sure we agree on why it is important to be doing this work."

"Let's make a list of what the more evangelical Meetings look like," Sylvia suggested, pulling a notebook out of her tote bag. "I knew we'd want to get some of our thoughts down on paper, so I came prepared!" she said with a laugh.

"First of all, their worship services usually focus on interpreting the scripture in a literal way rather than as allegories and metaphors, stories told to make a point. Remember when our pastor at Maple Grove gave a message about Jonah being swallowed by the big fish?"

"No," Sylvia said after thinking for a moment. "I don't think I was there that Sunday, or I would have remembered it."

"It stayed with me because it was the first time I'd heard a pastor talk about this Old Testament story without making it a literal event. When she shared the history of that time and what was happening to the Jews, it became clear that it had more to do with the Jewish temple leaders than about a man named Jonah. This story is now thought by many to be a judgment on the Jewish temple leaders and their practice of killing some of their Jewish followers."

"Why would they kill their own people?" Sylvia asked.

"Simply because they had married Babylonians when the Jews were captured and exiled for years, and they were no longer 'pure' Jews in the eyes of the priests and the other temple leaders. The Jonah allegory was then told to remind these leaders that God's grace was for all."

"Yes, the idea that we should ignore the history of the time when the scriptures were written, and the purpose of the authors, makes it hard to rationalize all the murders in the Old Testament—not to mention the scientific impossibility of some of the miraculous events in both the Old and New Testaments."

"Exactly! Instead of examining progressive authors who have researched the history of the Jews and the new gatherings of believers after Jesus's death, many evangelical pastors—some of whom have only studied at evangelical seminaries—continue to take scriptures at face value. There are so many harmful verses that need to be understood in the context of the times they were written, and the writers who were simply penning their experiences with God as they interpreted them to be."

"But that's just one aspect of evangelical thinking. Thanks to the Moral Majority started by Jerry Falwell Sr. in 1979, a lot of evangelicals are often pro-life, anti-homosexual, pro-gun, anti-liberal, anti-socialist, and pro-police," Sylvia added.

"And, sadly, a lot are pro-White, suspicious of foreigners, anti-science, and open to accepting conspiracy theories," Beth said.

"So, if we want the purpose of our work to suggest a new paradigm for Quakers to 'be the church,' what have we learned from these women?" Sylvia asked.

"Well," Beth said after thinking for a minute, "we know the early Quakers—Margaret Fox, Elizabeth Fry, Mary Dyer—all thought their spirituality was to be experienced by sitting in the silence and waiting for the Spirit of God to speak to their souls, not to be told by the official government church what they should believe."

"Which is basically the opposite of the evangelical belief that there is absolute truth—taking scripture literally—and you should never question what you were taught to believe as a child," Sylvia agreed. "But even more impressive for me was the willingness of these early Quakers to even give up their lives to stay true to their beliefs."

"I'm also impressed by their courage to do the hard work, like Elizabeth Fry going into that prison, and then all the work she did to help those women become whole again," Beth said.

"And then there were all those brave women who fought against slavery," Sylvia continued. "Mott, Douglass, the Grimké sisters, and Harriet Tubman."

"We can't forget the work for women's rights, either," Beth reminded Sylvia. "We wouldn't enjoy the privileges we have today if it hadn't been for so many of the women in this country who persisted in campaigning for the right to vote—something we take for granted that was only accomplished a mere hundred years ago after many long battles. I can't wait until we learn more about Susan B. Anthony, Alice Paul, Elizabeth Comstock, and all the other determined Quaker women coming up."

"And what about Dr. Preston who wanted women to have the opportunities to learn about our unique bodies and become doctors?" Sylvia added.

"We have several more women to explore, and I hope some of them will be more current, because if we want to make changes now, we need some women to emulate who have modeled what it means to be the church," Beth said.

After the women paid their checks and were getting ready to leave, Sylvia said, "Well, I for one am really excited to continue learning about Quaker women who have done such amazing things. But I'm not sure we know how to use these amazing lives to make an impact in our Meetings today."

"I agree, but I think it will come together when we've collected all the stories. I've been thinking maybe we should try to plan some type of retreat next summer to sit in the silence and then see where the Spirit leads us to start making changes in the way we live out our faith today," Beth said.

"I love that idea! Let's suggest that to the others when we meet next month. And on another note, what are you doing for Christmas? Are either of your kids coming home?"

"No, not this year. A long time ago, we established that when Kristy and Tyler had families of their own, we would trade holidays with their spouses' families. So we will be together for Thanksgiving and have our gift exchanges then. I'm not sure yet what I'll do for Christmas."

"Well," Sylvia said hesitantly, "would you want to come for lunch with my parents and me that day? I would love to have you join us, and I think my parents would, too."

Beth looked at the flush in Sylvia's face and wondered if she had been afraid to ask or if her pink cheeks were caused by something else. "I'll let you know a little closer to the twenty-fifth if that's okay with you. Sometimes I like to take some of the goodies I've baked to the elders who don't have big family gatherings that day. But I can probably do that on the twenty-fourth, too."

"Great! I won't tell my parents yet—and my dad wouldn't remember anyway—but I know Mom would love to have the company."

"See you next month, then," Beth called as she headed to her car. "I think the club meets at my place, and I have Elizabeth Comstock to research before then. I've never heard of her, so I hope it won't be too hard to find information about her work. I may have to head over to the university library and their room dedicated to Quaker writings down through history and see what I can find there."

CHAPTER 27

1973

TWIN PINES CAMP DIRECTORS SYLVIA AND BETH

"Are you sure you want to do this?" Beth asked when she and Sylvia were home on spring break. "I mean, direct a camp for elementary kids at Twin Pines? Neither one of us is studying to be teachers, and I don't know what makes little kids tick!"

"Well," her best friend said thoughtfully, "the Young Friends Board did ask us, so they must think we're capable. I know I didn't have a great camping experience the last year my mom made me go, but at least I'm past my 'I don't believe in God' stage of life, and maybe that might help me relate to some of the kids."

"I'm thinking if they asked us, they probably couldn't find anyone else willing to do it!" Beth said, remembering some of the directors who had been recruited to lead camps in the past. "But maybe we could do some fun things with the kids—you know, water balloon fights, scavenger hunts, obstacle races."

"If you're willing to try it, I'm game too!" Sylvia said, looking as excited as a college student getting ready to finish her sophomore year could look.

"So where do we start?" Beth asked. No one had given them a to-do list, and they had no idea what planning was involved in being camp directors.

"Well," Sylvia said, "after they asked my mom if she thought we might be willing to head up the camp, I talked to Leo, the camp board chair, and he said we just needed to line up counselors for the boys' and girls' cabins, plan the morning classes and line up the teachers, and write devotional lessons for each day. Getting those things done will probably be the most work. Then we can do the fun things—

planning the afternoon activities. Leo said the board would find the speaker for the evening chapel services."

"Oh, I see!" Beth said. "So you were already planning for us to tackle this job!"

"Only if you were okay with it," Sylvia said quickly.

"Then I guess we'd better get started!"

Since the girls would be heading back to their colleges in a few short days, they spent as much of their time as possible contacting some of the Yearly Meeting Friends they thought would make good counselors who could also teach classes, dividing up the devotionals they would have to each write in their spare time during the rest of the semester, and generating fun activities for the afternoons—their favorite part of the planning. With only three months before camp was scheduled for the third week in June, it would be challenging to get it all done.

Secretly, Sylvia was pleased that the board had asked her and Beth to be directors, especially knowing how she had treated her counselor that last year she was a camper. She hadn't wanted to be there and made no bones about her doubts.

As Beth and Sylvia headed to Twin Pines the day before camp was to begin, it seemed like only yesterday they had agreed to be camp directors. They were both a little nervous about their responsibilities for keeping all the campers safe, but they were hoping they would feel better after meeting with the staff the next morning before the campers arrived in the afternoon.

"So how nervous are you?" Sylvia asked, looking over at Beth who was driving them the three hours to the camp.

"Only a little," Beth confessed. "I'm sure everything will go well. We've gone over and over the schedule, lined up counselors and teachers for the classes, and we're got some really great activities for the afternoons. Plus we're going to have so much fun staying in the chapel basement and not in one of the cabins full of giggly girls! The only hard part, in my opinion, is sitting through chapel and the altar calls each night. Do we know who the speaker is?"

"It's someone from Indiana who used to be a pastor in our Yearly Meeting. I guess we'll have to wait and see what kind of messages he brings. I'm kind of hoping he won't feel the need to have an altar call every single night," Sylvia admitted. "I hated it when I was a kid—always feeling the pressure to go down in front and kneel at the altar, over and over again."

"Then I say we hang out in the dining lodge in the evenings and eat the leftover desserts while chapel is going on!" Beth said with a laugh.

"I'm willing to sit through the first service, and who knows? Maybe we'll learn something new or feel inspired to be better Christians," Sylvia said.

"Sure!" came Beth's sarcastic reply.

The registration and check-in on the first day seemed to go well, and the little kids—well, ten- and eleven-year-olds—were balls of excitement at the idea of having a fun time away from home for five whole days.

"But what will we do if some of them get homesick and want to go home?" Sylvia asked after dinner was finished and they had escorted the kids to the outdoor vespers chapel where benches nestled into the wooded hillside.

"We'll figure it out," Beth said. "One day at a time."

Sylvia loved Beth's take-charge attitude, and she was so happy to be spending an entire week with her. They had been best friends since junior high, and she had really missed her once they graduated from high school and decided on different careers and colleges—Beth to the two-year junior college, Sylvia to the state university to study political science. Sylvia's uncle had been a state representative from their district when she was in elementary school, and the stories he would share about making laws to help people had been forever ingrained in Sylvia's mind as something she might want to do someday. She didn't think she wanted to run for any offices, but she thought maybe there were jobs behind the scenes of which she could be a part.

As soon as the altar call was finished at the first worship service, everyone headed to the fire ring in the open area where a couple of the counselors had started a fire while the campers went to their cabins to get blankets to sit on. As the song leader led some choruses with his guitar, the warmth of the fire began to take the chill off the night air. It was surprising how cool the evenings could get in June.

Beth and Sylvia were sharing a blanket behind the campers, and since neither had thought to pick up their jackets, they sat shoulder to shoulder for warmth. Sylvia couldn't help the strange feeling that came over her as their bodies connected. *It's just to keep me warm,* she thought . . . *just to keep us both warm.*

When they were back in their room in the chapel basement and sitting on their twin beds, they discussed how the first day had gone. Then they looked at the schedule and all the things they had planned for the first full day with their charges.

"We're going to have to run into town in the morning for some craft supplies," Sylvia said. "One of the teachers is having the kids build and paint birdhouses, and she thought all the paint supplies would already be here."

"I have no idea why she would think there would be paint here," Beth scoffed. "I wish she had just asked us about the supplies she would need before the first day of camp!"

"It'll be okay. The teachers certainly aren't getting paid for their work, and Marilyn did buy all the bird houses herself."

"Oh, I didn't know that. In that case, I guess I can't be too irritated."

"So Marilyn and I can get the paint supplies first thing in the morning if you can handle breakfast and ringing the bell for devotions," Sylvia said. "You're really good at bossing kids around!"

Beth jumped onto Sylvia's bed and tackled her with a light punch on the arm. "Take that back!"

"I would if it weren't true," Sylvia said with a laugh. "You really do have that commanding voice and take-charge manner."

The girls sat on Sylvia's bed for a while, and once again Sylvia felt such warmth for this friend she had missed so much in the two years they had been working on their degrees. She couldn't think of a single time she had ever felt the same way about any of the boys she had occasionally dated. But Beth was dating Bob now, and they seemed to be happy.

What's wrong with me that no boy seems interested in a long-term relationship with me, or that I haven't found a boy who interests me? she wondered as she finally drifted off to sleep.

The rest of the week seemed to fly by, and luckily there were no homesick kids to deal with. Both girls were convinced it was the fun afternoon activities that kept them engaged and wanting to know what was going to happen next. The last day was the most fun of all because Sylvia and Beth let the kids give them shampoos of raw eggs, ketchup, mustard, and any other condiments the kitchen worker let them have. As the goopy mixture ran down their backs and covered their clothes, they both knew they would need long, hot showers to feel clean again.

"That was fun!" Sylvia said as they stood in the bathhouse's communal shower. She tried not to look at Beth, embarrassed. Beth wasn't skinny like Lois; she wasn't really overweight, either. But it was hard not to stare as they helped each other wash the concoctions off their backs. Rubbing the washcloth over Beth's back gave Sylvia that warm, funny feeling again and she wished it would take longer to get clean again.

"Fun?!" Beth retorted. "I hate the smell of eggs, and this just feels so gross!"

"What? You don't like my back scrubs?" Sylvia teased.

"I'm never volunteering for this kind of activity again!" Beth declared.

As the girls dried off and dressed, Sylvia noticed that Beth seemed to have no qualms about being naked in front of her as she chatted about what they needed to do to wrap up the camp session. She seemed fully at ease in a way that made Sylvia feel shy and warm inside.

Sylvia was sad to think that her time with Beth was almost over, not to mention the fun they'd been having with the kids. They'd both enjoyed skipping the evening worship services, and they'd both also felt the Holy Spirit move during vespers and the campfires. It had been a wonderful renewal of Sylvia's enjoyment of the Quaker camping experience. But her awakened feelings for Beth were puzzling, and she had no idea what they meant or what to do with them.

CHAPTER 28
1815-1891
ELIZABETH COMSTOCK
KANSAS

"Wait! Please form a line, one at a time. I promise we'll help all of you," Elizabeth cried as yet another trainload of refugees poured into the headquarters of the Kansas Freedmen's Relief Association, engulfing her.

"Help me! Please!" begged an older woman wearing a ragged dress. "My grandson, Jimmy, and I haven't had food for days after we just barely escaped. Our master said we had to work for him to pay back all the debts we owed—even after Mr. Lincoln said we were free! But we weren't free at all! We had to escape for our freedom just like the others before us. I was afraid we might never make it to catch that train we heard some say would take us to this here promised land. Both Jimmy and me froze the tips of our fingers when that cold snow came. Oh please, miss, help us!"

The woman's plea was just one of the many Elizabeth had heard in her work helping former enslaved people resettle in Topeka more than a decade after the end of the Civil War. *What was the latest count?* Elizabeth wondered. Almost sixty-thousand refugees, she had heard. How could she possibly manage all this relief work?

After her exhausting day, Elizabeth's mind simply would not release her to sleep as she pondered the experiences that had preceded Governor St. John appointing her to her current position in charge of the refugee association.

She'd spent her entire life as a Quaker, attending Quaker schools in England. Then she married her beloved Leslie in her thirties and helped run their shop together, only to lose him to disease after four short years of marriage. *Perhaps I should have sought another man with whom to share life, but when God called me to be a minister, how could I refuse?* she thought.

What would have happened if I had lived out the rest of my life in that English city? she wondered. Instead she'd immigrated to Canada with her sister and young daughter. It would have been easier to have just traveled throughout England, sharing the Quaker message of the power of the Spirit to speak in the silence. But then she wouldn't have been a part of this important mission work in Kansas.

Elizabeth felt it was her highest calling to work with the freed slaves: Exodusters, as everyone called them, just like the Hebrew slaves exodus from Egypt in the Old Testament. And oh, the stories she had heard from so many of the refugees—the inability to live freely because of "debts" owed to their former White owners, being cheated out of their rightful dues, working for a pittance, education thwarted when their schools were burned, and teachers treated brutally.

She'd spent so much time and effort securing supplies for the Exodusters who so often arrived with nothing but the clothes on their backs. All those trips she'd made back to England to gather blankets, clothing, shoes, and other supplies. Anger welled up in her again when she remembered those very supplies being locked up in a New York Custom House because the government was asking for almost fifty-percent duties. They had all those supplies from Meetings in England, had made arrangements for free rail transportation, and then learned that their senators refused to allow them to be released without payment, even deciding to send the supplies to sufferers in Ireland! Elizabeth's thoughts only made her heart ache once again.

Suddenly the still, small voice spoke within, and she knew what she had to do.

I must travel within these United States and raise more funds for our work, she thought. She was sure the governor would help with this appeal for money, clothing, crockery for serving meals, and bedding for comfort in the cold winter nights the Southerners had never before experienced. She thought that she must also write an article for *Friends Review,* Josiah Tatum's periodical, because it had a wide circulation, and John Greenleaf Whittier would surely want to help, too, once he heard of the plight of these thousands of families.

Oh, how I wish Kansas had a temperate climate like England! But I must do this work, she reminded herself. *God has called me to not only find a way to meet the material needs of the Exodusters but also help provide training so they may become employed and earn money to send for their family members left behind.*

Please, God, help me find the aid we need. Help me convince the Yearly Meetings that this is a mission they need to support.

• • •

Less than a year after that sleepless night, sixty-seven-year-old Elizabeth sat in a New York sanatorium recovering from tuberculosis after securing funds for over sixty-thousand refugees who had found their way to Kansas.

I have been blessed to have the opportunity to visit so many Quaker Meetings all over the states, especially in Kansas, Iowa, Indiana, and the West, she thought. In less than a year the supplies began to arrive on the trains.

Elizabeth never forgot hearing the cries of "Glory to God!" when those long-suffering men, women, and children received blankets and clothing. She worked side by side with Laura Haviland in the effort until her health began to fail and she had to return home. And now here she sat as well, halted by this illness, unable to continue with her calling.

Elizabeth still felt the sting of betrayal by her own Yearly Meeting in Kansas, whose representatives had no desire to even consider the needs of the Exodusters pouring into their fair city of Topeka. The good Quaker men and women representatives could spend hours reporting on other mission work yet give scarcely a few minutes for work with the refugees. She supposed they believed that since the War Between the States had been over for thirteen years, the freed slaves were no longer suffering. But if these Quakers were truly intent on participating in mission work, they would surely support their efforts in helping the Exodusters searching for an opportunity to truly be free. And if Friends would put aside petty quarrels about holiness and Inner Light and focus on the starving and needy, what a better world this would be!

If this is to be the end of my work with the freed slaves, I will still do my best to minister to any and all who might be in need, Elizabeth thought. *I was called to be a minister, and I must continue as my calling from God dictates. Eventually I will join my Heavenly Father knowing I have fought the good fight.* Long before her work with the refugees in Kansas, she gave every ounce of energy she had to fight against other injustices. Working in hospitals and prison camps during the War Between the States, as well as pleading for humane treatment of inmates and innocent prisoners were just two of the areas of great need she was blessed to be a part of helping. *Of course, I shall forever feel grateful to have been granted an audience with President Lincoln to request his help improving the conditions in those terrifying prisons!* That in itself had been no small miracle.

Yes, our Quaker testimonies of peace, equality, and temperance were all worth the efforts I gave to help create a better life for others. But I fear there is still much work to be done to assure equality for our Negro citizens. If this disease means the end of my work for justice, I must trust there will be others who will take up the task of making life better for the poor and needy, just like Jesus taught us to do.

CHAPTER 29

JANUARY, PRESENT DAY
THE CLUB—BETH'S HOME

"Brr!" Lois exclaimed as she came through the back door of Beth's farmhouse, closing it quickly to keep out the wind. "I wish I had a condo in Arizona to go to right after Christmas like so many of my retired friends. It sure would be better than this cold northern weather!"

"Come on in!" Beth laughed, knowing she had heard this same lament from Lois every single time the temperatures dropped below freezing. "It's warm in here—I even turned the thermostat up for our meeting today to make sure everyone would be comfortable. And you're early again! What's up with that?"

"I know, I know," Lois said, "I shouldn't complain. I do like the four seasons we get to experience—no, wait! I enjoy three of our four seasons. Winter? Not so much! And I left early this morning because I wasn't sure how your country roads would be after the snow we had yesterday. I actually wondered if maybe you'd reschedule today's gathering."

"I drove home from town last evening after picking up some groceries, and I didn't think the roads were too bad. If you hate winter so much, why don't you try renting one of those nice trailers they have down in Arizona in those senior living parks?" Beth asked. "You could do that for a couple of months and enjoy those warm temperatures."

"I suppose I should look into it, but then I would miss the beauty of the snow, the cardinals and juncos coming to gorge themselves at my two bird feeders. And the snow always reminds me of my students' excitement when they got to roll snowballs for snowmen, make forts with tunnels, and play Fox and Geese. Do you remember playing that game in the snow when we were kids?"

"Sure! It was fun until the circle pattern in the snow got so trampled you couldn't tell where to run. So how was your Christmas? Did you help serve the meals at St. Augustine?"

When Lois didn't answer right away, Beth glanced up from the coffee cake she was slicing and noticed a hint of pink on Lois's cheeks that wasn't from the cold.

"Yes," Lois finally said, "we did help serve the meal. And there were—"

"Wait," Beth demanded, "who is 'we'?"

"Oh . . . uh . . . I went with Henry Patton."

"Who is Henry Patton? I've never heard you mention him before. Does he live in your condo building?"

And with that question, Lois proceeded to fill Beth in on her budding relationship with her new neighbor. "It's nothing serious, really. We just enjoy doing some social things together—you know, movies, dinner, things like that."

"So does Henry go to mass at St. Augustine?"

"Yeah, he usually goes to either the Saturday night mass or the early mass on Sunday mornings."

"I hope that doesn't mean you're going to ditch us Quakers and join the Catholics!" Beth teased, although there was a hint of worry in her question.

"Oh no, we haven't even talked about anything that serious. It's just a friendship right now, and when you consider I've been single since Justin left for the Army, I can't imagine much more developing between the two of us any time in the near future."

"Then I'm happy you've found someone to share a little of your life with," Beth said, feeling a twinge of loneliness. Would she ever meet another man who might be interested in sharing life with her some day? *No,* she thought, *my life really is pretty good, and I do believe I'm perfectly content just spending my leisure time with Sylvia.*

Their conversation came to a halt when first Sylvia and then Nancy joined them, both also complaining about the cold—and the snowy road.

"You should move into Maple Grove," Nancy moaned. "It's kind of scary driving on your gravel road!"

"If I were still working," Beth said, "I would definitely consider selling this place and moving into town. But I love it here, even in the winter. Since I don't have to be anywhere else most days, and it's only a fifteen-minute drive into town when I need to go to the store, I can just wait until the roads are good again. Besides, if I moved into town, Sylvia wouldn't have anyone to call when she needed help with her mom or dad."

"Please don't move until you get too old to drive or until my parents have passed and we can move to the retirement home together!" Sylvia pleaded.

"Shall we get started?" Beth asked quickly, not sure how to respond to Sylvia's request. "There are bowls for the fruit, and you can add lemon or coconut yogurt, some granola, almonds—whatever you'd like. I made a low-calorie coffee cake, too, but I won't be offended if any of you are on your January diets for your New Year's resolutions! There's coffee in the pot, and the water is hot in the kettle on the stove if you want tea. You know my kitchen as well as I do, so make yourselves at home!"

When the discussion turned to Beth's Quaker ancestor, Elizabeth Comstock, Lois was the first to ask why they had never heard of her before.

"It seems like she was pretty amazing," Lois continued, "but we never heard about her in Sunday School growing up, or in youth group, either. She did all that traveling and rounding up support to help freed slaves after the Civil War, yet her name is never even mentioned!"

"I was thinking the same thing," Sylvia said. "We never had any lessons about her in our USFW meetings, either. Seems like her work with the Exodusters would have been a good topic for our group to discuss, especially considering everything going on right now with our immigration policies discouraging people from migrating here from other countries."

"Immigration today is obviously much different from the migration of Blacks from the South to the North after the Civil War," Nancy added, "but there are some similarities, especially when it comes to welcoming people who have left everything they know in search of a better life."

"Okay, Beth, where are we going with this woman?" came Lois's typical question. "How does her life's work influence us today?"

"For one thing, most White people probably think that since the Civil War has been over for more than a hundred and fifty years, things are just fine for Black people. But like we've talked about in previous meetings, the effects of slavery are still being felt today, from the racial wealth gap to the disparities in the justice system. We need to continue our anti-racism work, donating to organizations fighting to make our institutions more equitable and standing up for equal rights. Many are even talking about ways to compensate them for their enslavement—reparations of some sort.

"But Nancy also brought up the important point that we still have some major disagreements right now on how to help the immigrants who are trying any way they can to cross our borders," she continued. "It seems like almost every night on the news we hear stories of undocumented immigrants trying to escape gangs and brutal governments in Mexico and Central America.

"And what about the Dreamers, all those immigrants who were just little kids when their parents crossed our borders? Now they're in high school or college, and some of them even have degrees and good jobs, but some people are saying they should be deported just because they didn't come to the States the legal way, even though this country is all they've ever known," Beth said, the passion rising in her voice.

"Recently I heard there are likely almost ten million undocumented immigrants living here right now, some even in our state, where hundreds are working in meatpacking plants—jobs a lot of American citizens think are beneath them," Sylvia said.

"Are undocumented immigrants the same as illegal immigrants?" Lois asked. "I hear that term used a lot in the news."

"Yes, but saying they're 'illegal immigrants' is a polarizing and dehumanizing way to describe people who want to come to this country," Beth said.

"Especially when all they want is a chance for a better life!" Nancy added.

"I was so disturbed by the policy separating kids—sometimes babies—from their parents and keeping them in unsanitary buildings," Sylvia said. "Now the policy has changed, but I just read there are still hundreds of children whose parents have been deported. The government is still trying to locate the parents and reunite them with their kids. I can only imagine how frightening it would have been if my parents had been taken from me and I had no idea where they were!"

"So, we talked about the legacy of slavery, but what can we learn from Elizabeth Comstock that has anything to do with the current situation with immigrants?" Lois asked.

"There really are quite a few things we can do," Beth said. "First of all, we can learn everything we can about the current situation—there's all kinds of information online. Next, we can contact our current representatives and senators and express our desire that Congress enact immigration reform laws so that anyone who is currently undocumented has an opportunity to become a citizen—especially the Dreamers. And then we can donate to groups who work with the immigrants currently locked up by ICE—you know, Immigration and Customs Enforcement."

"One of the best groups doing this work is our own American Friends Service Committee," Nancy quickly added. "They are doing a lot to help immigrants, like offering legal representation in court when they are arrested and detained by ICE."

"Oh yeah!" Lois said. "I remember that discussion during our Monthly Meeting for business a few months ago, and didn't Maple Grove Friends just donate to the AFSC group in our state capitol working with immigrants there? I bet we could get one of their representatives to come and talk to our youth group. We have to get some of the younger ones involved!"

"Sounds like we have some things we can work on, but don't forget the upcoming election and voting for candidates who support racial justice and immigration reform," Beth reminded them.

"Thanks for sharing all your research on Elizabeth Comstock and ways we can make a difference today, Beth," Sylvia said warmly. "We think we're so much more advanced than they were in the 1800s, but we still have so many issues that require our attention. Great work!"

The warmth of Sylvia's praise washed over Beth, feeling pleased that she had done some of the extra research on the issues surrounding the undocumented folks who risked so much just for the chance at a better life for their families.

Maybe the two of us can get together sometime and watch a movie or share a pizza, she thought, as she watched Sylvia hustle out with the others to their vehicles. They would probably need to hang out at Sylvia's home after her parents had retired for the evening, but it had been too long since they had shared some time together. Besides, they certainly needed something to entertain them on those cold winter days!

CHAPTER 30
1994
VACATION BIBLE SCHOOL
NANCY

"Welcome, everyone, and thanks for volunteering to help out with this time of learning for our kids," Nancy began as she looked at the handful of older women who had probably been a part of their Meeting's annual Vacation Bible School their entire adult lives. Though she couldn't help but note the weariness on some of their faces, she knew they would all do their very best because they believed VBS was an important mission to help children learn more about God and His plan of salvation.

"Let's go over our plans for this year's VBS and see what's left to do," Nancy continued. She still didn't understand why the Christian Education Committee thought she should be the director every year just because she worked from home with Allan. But she couldn't turn the committee down, even though some summers she wanted to. She had been a very successful director for several years, and she really did love seeing how excited the kids were to come each evening for the entire week and learn about God, Jesus, and the Bible.

"I'm pretty excited about this year's theme, Come to the Wonder Fair. The kids are going to love the skits the youth will put on during the opening each evening," Nancy added, trying to generate some enthusiasm in her voice.

"We have five classes: preschool, kids going into kindergarten and first, second and third, fourth and fifth, and junior high. The high school kids who want to come—and don't count on too many!—will meet with the youth sponsors and do their own thing, and then we will have an adult class that Beth will teach for parents and spouses who would like to attend.

"All the teachers' materials are in your classrooms, so you can take them home with you to get started on the lessons. I know we have a month to get everything ready, but it's already the middle of May, and with graduations and Memorial Day, the first day of VBS will be here before we know it," she said with a smile. "During our Sunday School time between now and then, I'll pass around the sign-up sheet for refreshments each evening, and Dorothy's kitchen committee will take care of fixing the drinks and serving the kids.

"Janet will lead the theme song, and then I'll direct the skit that came with the materials. I've recruited some of the youth to help with it each night. They did a great job designing and making the props for the skits last year. We're lucky we have some drama students in our high school group who love doing that sort of thing every year!

"Just like in the past, before I dismiss everyone to go to their classes, I'll select two of the older students to pass an offering plate. All the money we collect plus the offering during the final program on the following Sunday will go toward the Yearly Meeting Missions Board project. This year it's going to help a Friends school in Belize. I'll make a chart for our fundraising goal, including a picture of a thermometer we can color in each night with the amount of the offering. If they 'break the thermometer,' we'll have ice cream sundaes on the last night.

"Janet, I've already given you the recorded tapes for the music classes, and Wilma will take care of the crafts for each group—do you both have everything you need? Those are the two extra activities the kids really look forward to—plus the games and cookies, of course!

"Whew! I feel like I've been talking forever! But I think that's everything. If no one has any questions, why don't you all go to your classrooms to collect your materials and make lists of students you think will be in your class."

This is a lot of work, Nancy thought as she crawled into bed that night, but at least Lois's son, Justin, said he would help with the skit props, even if he refused to be in the skit and probably wouldn't even want to join the high school kids' class since he would be graduating in May. It seemed like he always had a scowl on his face during worship on Sunday mornings.

Nancy knew Lois worried that Justin might regret not going to college. He had already flatly refused Lois's offer to help with tuition, insisting high school was good enough and he could make money right away by just joining the Army. Lois had shared her frustrations about getting Justin motivated to at least go to junior college to learn a trade skill; plumbers and electricians both made good money and he liked doing things with his hands. She was doubly frustrated because Mark had been no help when it came to encouraging his son to continue his education. He rarely spent any time with Justin, especially after remarrying and having younger kids to raise.

Nancy knew Lois was still upset to think how she had been so sure Mark was the right man for her only to discover his antics and anger issues weren't so charming after they were married. And then it had been a bitter revelation to Lois when she learned Mark's new family would include kids. *We tried to warn her,* Nancy thought, *but all she could talk about was how cute and funny Mark was. I'm not sure how I got so lucky to end up with a great guy like Allan!*

Nancy had been right about how the remaining weeks before Bible school would fly by, especially considering everything that went into preparing for their older son's graduation and the party they held for all their relatives and his friends.

Once all the planning and preparations for VBS were completed, though, Nancy enjoyed greeting the kids each day when they arrived at the meeting house. As she praised the youth for their excellent skit work and thanked the adult volunteers for their willingness to be there for the kids, Nancy felt certain all the work she'd put in had been worth it.

She was just finishing straightening up the sanctuary after everyone had left on the next to last night when Beth came in with a concerned look on her face.

"Nancy, can I talk to you for a minute?" she asked after making sure they were the only ones left in the building.

"Sure, what's up? Seems like you've had a pretty good group of adults coming to your classes each night!"

"Yeah, I've been shocked to have almost twenty every night, but if I had known what was going to happen tonight, I would have called in sick and you could have led the discussion!"

"Then give it to me straight!" Nancy laughed. "It can't be that bad!"

"It started with the Bible verse for the adult lesson, the one in John where Jesus says something like 'I am the way, the truth, and the life.

No one comes to the Father except through me.' I know we were always taught that meant unless you were a Christian who believed in Jesus and had accepted Him as your savior, you wouldn't go to heaven."

"Yes, but our pastor has talked about how that's not what that verse really meant, that it has nothing to do with heaven and hell," Nancy reminded her.

"And I thought that's what we all believed," Beth agreed. "But then Ralph started talking about his uncle, John, who was a Mormon, and how he was worried John wouldn't be in heaven when he died. And then Glen spoke up and said that was true, that everyone knew that Mormons were basically just a big cult, and how they didn't believe in Jesus so there was no way John could go to heaven unless he left the Mormons and accepted Jesus as his savior."

"Oh, boy. How did you handle it?"

"Well, you know my nursing friends and I went on that Asian cruise that took us to China, Japan, Taiwan, and the Philippines. We toured all these Hindu and Buddhist temples, and it was so eye-opening, the dedication people had when it came to worship. There was this one Buddhist temple in Hong Kong where a middle-aged man entered the temple and lit a stick of incense and put it in a pot of sand in front of one of a line of small Buddha statues. When I asked our tour guide why he was doing that, he said it was something the man was doing to repent of his sins. And it was so clear to me once again that God is not just a God of Christians, but the God of all," Beth said.

"Did you share that experience with the group?"

"I tried, but the guys started arguing with each other, and quoting scripture—you know, it's that literal interpretation thing we don't really agree with—and finally I just stopped them and said we each had to have our own understanding of God and God's love, and then I changed the subject! But honestly, Nancy, I don't want to do the last lesson tomorrow night because I'm afraid the same discussion is going to come up again."

"Then just remind them you have other topics to discuss, and make sure they're not the least bit controversial!" Nancy said with a smile.

"Easy for you to say! But you agree with me, don't you?"

"Of course! Remember when we did the book study written by the religion teacher who took her students to visit the places of worship for Hindus, Buddhists, Jews, and other religions in Georgia, and how she found things in the other world religions that she wished Christianity would include?"

"Oh, yeah, I forgot about that book, although I'm not sure any of the men actually read it. But maybe I can reread it and bring some of the author's ideas with me tomorrow night in case the topic comes up again."

"You'll do great!" Nancy encouraged her friend. "No one has a better understanding of scripture than you, based on all the books you've read by progressive Biblical scholars, and you can always suggest they visit with our pastor if they still have questions."

"Thanks, dear," Beth said with a smile. "See, this is why you're the one we want to be the director each year!"

"Well, this may be my last year. I've been thinking it's time for someone else with new and fresh ideas to direct."

"But you do such a wonderful job! All the volunteers have told me they always enjoy the week—and that's saying a lot, considering what a handful some of those kids can be when trying to keep them engaged in the Bible lessons! Just wait a while before you make any decisions about next year. We still have the program to get through on Sunday, and you know there are always a lot of parents who come to see their kids sing the new songs, recite what they've learned, and collect the cute crafts they've made."

"One day at a time," Nancy said, secretly wishing the program was already over and everything had definitively been a success. She had big plans for the finale—a "wonder fair" that was going to be bigger than anything she'd ever put together before.

Nancy was pleased that the final program went well, especially when the last offering met their goal and 'broke the thermometer' so the kids—and adults—got to enjoy their promised hot fudge sundaes.

She had asked the pastor if they could have the culminating program on Sunday morning rather than the usual Sunday evening, and that change went really well, too. The kids sang the songs they had learned with gusto, and even though the little kids didn't always remember the verses they were supposed to recite, the last skit by the youth was a great way to wrap up the week's activities. As soon as the program was over, the kids couldn't wait to take their parents downstairs to see the crafts they had made.

But it was the afternoon that provided the most laughs and seemed to bring the community together, especially the parents who didn't normally attend Sunday worship. The "Wonder Fair" she had organized for outside the meeting house following the program was a huge hit. Hot dogs, a dunk tank, balloons, and other carnival games led by the youth had made this year's VBS one of their most memorable.

"Great job, everyone," Nancy said as the volunteers helped clean up after the end of the event. "Thanks for helping to make VBS a huge success this year!"

And it was a success, even though Beth had struggled a bit with the adults. Nancy hoped some of the men would think about what Beth ended up sharing with them from the book on world religions as well as her experiences with Eastern religions. *Either way,* she thought, *it still might be time for a different director next year—someone with new and great ideas!*

CHAPTER 31
1820-1906
SUSAN B. ANTHONY
NEW YORK

"Father," Susan asked, "why was Judge McLean so upset with thee? Isn't he thy business partner making the cotton at the mill?"

"Now, why is a little girl of only ten years wondering about such a tiny disagreement?" her father responded.

"I heard thee arguing with him, and I thought since we are Quakers, we are supposed to be peace-loving people—that's what thee always says."

Daniel had to laugh at his precocious daughter. He would have to remember she was constantly hanging around the adults, anxious to know what was happening with their work.

"It's a simple matter, Susan," he began, knowing her persistence wasn't going to allow the question to disappear. "In the store where we sell the cotton goods we produce, I have refused the judge's desire to sell rum—like they do in many of the other stores in Battenville—and in many other parts of our state. Thee knows Quakers are to refuse all forms of temptation, such as strong drink, and I have insisted we not order any rum. It is my goal to sell the best goods at the fairest prices, and I know we will have all the business we will need."

"Yes," Susan nodded, looking pensive, "I remember when thee and Mother were discussing the evils of strong drink and how it was the cause of poverty, marriages ending, and sometimes children being beaten when their fathers came home drunk."

"My dear Susan, I must entreat thee to refrain from listening to our adult conversations!" Daniel admonished. "But yes, strong drink can certainly be a curse on a family."

"Then as soon as I'm of age, I shall start a temperance movement to spread the word of the evils of alcohol," Susan declared.

Laughter filled her father's voice before speaking, having little doubt that this young girl would no doubt soon start to do her part to advocate for needed societal changes. "Then I shall be very proud of thee," he said genuinely.

"So for now, how old must I be to come to work in the mill?" Susan asked, admiring this father who had stood up to the judge for his beliefs.

"I do not want thee nor thy sisters to work in the mill," Daniel said. "It is too dangerous, and the work is too hard. I need thee to help thy mother with our boarders who work for us, and thee must not neglect thy schoolwork."

"I don't believe that is quite fair, Father," Susan said, then remembered her father's dislike of arguing. "But if there is any illness in the mill and thee is short-handed, perhaps one of us might help thee out," she finished, hoping for a chance to earn a little money to start a secret fund she might one day soon use in her fight for prohibiting the sale of liquor.

"Perhaps," Daniel said with a smile. "For now, thee must focus on thy education before embarking on future crusades."

• • •

Susan was certain education was to become her life's work after her father's business failed when she was only seventeen and finishing her first year of boarding school, she recalled as she rested on her chaise lounge in her bedroom. Now eighty-six years old, she realized her days fighting for the rights of both Negroes and women would soon be ending. *I am so pleased to be able to recall so many of the events of my life,* she mused, trying to put in order all the causes she had fought for.

It began in earnest in '45 when the family business failed and they moved to a farm near Rochester, New York. They soon found a group of Quaker social reformers who had left their congregation because of the restrictions it placed on reform activities. Eventually, in '48, they joined the Quakers to form a new organization, Congregational Friends, and their farmstead became the Sunday afternoon gathering place for local activists. When her father's friends, prominent abolitionists, Fredrick Douglass and William Lloyd Garrison, joined the group, Susan had a deep feeling within her to become an abolitionist. She was just a twenty-eight-year-old girl, giving all those passionate speeches against slavery in spite of the opposition of many who believed a woman should not be doing such work.

Her most important work began when she met Elizabeth Cady Stanton and they joined forces. She was still only twenty-eight when the first women's rights convention was held at Seneca Falls, so she hadn't attended, but when she met Elizabeth three years later, they became fast friends who would continue their friendship and work for fifty more years. *Oh, the speeches the two of us gave, preaching far and wide how slavery was an abomination and that women deserved the right to vote in elections! I do believe my drive and ability to organize made me a successful leader in our efforts for these two inalienable rights,* she thought.

The first organization Susan helped found was the New York Women's State Temperance Society, after she was prevented from speaking at a temperance conference organized by the Sons of Temperance group even though she'd been chosen to attend as a delegate. *I will always be grateful for the lessons my father taught me at a young age when he refused to sell rum in his cotton goods store. And I still believe strong drink has been the cause of many a family tragedy, and temperance a cause worth fighting for.*

Next, in 1863, Elizabeth and Susan founded the Women's Loyal National League and conducted the largest petition drive in United States history up to that time—nearly 400,000 signatures—in support of the abolition of slavery. Meeting Garrison and Douglass was the beginning of her passion for this work, and Elizabeth was in accordance with her desire.

Then there was the American Equal Rights Association, which Elizabeth and Susan together established in 1866. How she loved to work on *The Revolution,* their newspaper that spread the idea of equality for both women and African Americans! But all those speeches she gave throughout the country to raise funds for the newspapers were not always met with support. Susan was heckled more than once by those in opposition to their ideas.

Of course, the passing of the Fifteenth Amendment giving the vote to all men, regardless of race, but not to any women, was a bitter disappointment. Susan was determined that the election of 1872 was the time to right this wrong, and she had the Fourteenth Amendment on her side! After all, it said "all persons born and naturalized in the United States . . . are citizens of the United States, and as citizens were entitled to the 'privileges' of citizens of the United States."

To Susan's way of thinking, those privileges certainly included the right to vote. She had to use a bit of persuasion to get registered—those poor boys at the registration table in the barber shop probably didn't know what hit them when she insisted she had the right to vote, especially after she recited that amendment. So she and her sisters signed up, and they voted. She still had a copy of the letter she wrote to Elizabeth after casting her ballot.

Dear Mrs Stanton

Well I have been & gone & done it!!—positively voted the Republican ticket—strait this a.m. at 7 Oclock—& swore my vote in at that—was registered on Friday . . . then on Sunday others some 20 or thirty other women tried to register, but all save two were refused . . . Amy Post was rejected & she will immediately bring action for that . . . & Hon Henry R. Selden will be our Counsel—he has read up the law & all of our arguments & is satisfied that we are right & ditto the Old Judge Selden—his elder brother. So we are in for a fine agitation in Rochester on the question—I hope the morning's telegrams will tell of many women all over the country trying to vote—It is splendid that without any concert of action so many should have moved here so impromptu—

The Democratic paper is out against us strong & that scared the Dem's on the registry board—How I wish you were here to write up the funny things said & done . . . When the Democrat said my vote should not go in the box—one Republican said to the other—What do you say Marsh?—I say put it in!—So do I said Jones—and "we'll fight it out on this line if it takes all winter" . . . If only now—all the suffrage women would work to this end of enforcing the existing constitution—

supremacy of national law over state law—what strides we
might make this winter—But I'm awful tired—for five days I
have been on the constant run—but to splendid purpose—So
all right—I hope you voted too.
    Affectionately,
    Susan B. Anthony

After her arrest and before the trial, Susan had four months to speak in every town in the twenty-nine districts in the county, and her topic was, "Is It a Crime for a Citizen of the United States to Vote?" She dressed in her best gray silk dress with a white lace color and twisted her hair into a tight knot. She still had her opening speech memorized:

Friends and Fellow-citizens: I stand before you to-night, under indictment for the alleged crime of having voted at the last Presidential election, without having a lawful right to vote. It shall be my work this evening to prove to you that in thus voting, I not only committed no crime, but, instead, simply exercised my citizen's right, guaranteed to me and all United States citizens by the National Constitution, beyond the power of any State to deny.

And then came the trial for her supposed crime—the right to vote!

I will never forget standing up to that judge, even though in the be-ginning I was told I would not be allowed to testify on my own behalf—no doubt because I was a woman! And then, the injustice of hearing the judge declare a guilty verdict he had already determined! At least he asked me if I had anything to say. Well, of course I had something to say—many things, in fact:
    Yes, your honor, I have many things to say; for in your ordered verdict of guilty, you have trampled underfoot every vital principle of our government. My natural rights, my civil rights, my political rights, my judicial rights, are all alike ignored. Robbed of the fundamental privilege of citizenship, I am degraded from the status of a citizen to that of a subject; and not only myself individually, but all of my sex, are, by your honor's verdict, doomed to political subjection under this, so-called, form of government.

But Judge Hunt already had his mind made up and just went right on with his sentence, a fine of one hundred dollars and the costs of the prosecution.

Of course, Susan protested:

May it please your honor, I shall never pay a dollar of your unjust penalty. All the stock in trade I possess is a $10,000 debt, incurred by publishing my paper—The Revolution—four years ago, the sole object of which was to educate all women to do precisely as I have done, rebel against your manmade, unjust, unconstitutional forms of law, that tax, fine, imprison, and hang women, while they deny them the right of representation in the government; and I shall work on with might and main to pay every dollar of that honest debt, but not a penny shall go to this unjust claim. And I shall earnestly and persistently continue to urge all women to the practical recognition of the old revolutionary maxim, that "Resistance to tyranny is obedience to God."

Judge Hunt, in a move calculated to preclude any appeal to a higher court, ended the trial by announcing the court would not order Susan committed until the fine was paid.

But she never paid one dime of that fine; she was willing to take her case all the way to the Supreme Court, if necessary, to preserve the fundamental right to vote that is guaranteed by both the Constitution and the Fourteenth Amendment.

The case was never allowed, but there was a similar case that reached the highest court, and those male justices all determined it was up to each state to decide voting issues. Susan wrote to every woman she had worked with in this battle and told them they would be forced to beg at the feet of each individual male voter in every state! They would need to buckle on their armor and organize wherever the battle for the ballot for women was to be fought.

Over the years, Susan must have given seventy-five to one hundred speeches per year in more than five decades, yet even though they had gotten a bill presented to Congress in '78 for the right of women to vote, it had yet to be ratified by the states, and women still did not have the God-given right to make their choice of leaders known by the simple act of marking a ballot.

Despite the setbacks, Elizabeth and Susan decided they must make a record of their attempts to bring about equality for all, so they worked with a great writer, Matilda Gage, to produce a six-volume history of women's suffrage. *And one day, I believe our work will bear fruit, even if I am no longer alive to see it,* Susan thought.

One thing I know for certain is that we women are strong, we are determined, and we will prevail, no matter how many marches, petitions, and rallies we must continue to hold. My Quaker heritage has taught me that all are equal in God's eyes, and there will be other brave women who will continue with this important work.

Susan hoped she'd be remembered when future women heard her name and the names of those who strived for justice for all women. *Just think of it—I've been striving for over sixty years for a little bit of justice, yet I must surely die without obtaining it. I'm not complaining, for mine is the fate of every pioneer who ever opened up the way for change.* She hoped those she'd spoken with would remember the fear they needed was the fear of not standing by the thing they believe is right and that the right of suffrage would be granted; failure was impossible.

CHAPTER 32

FEBRUARY, PRESENT DAY
THE CLUB—NANCY'S HOME

"I can't wait to hear what you found out about Susan B. Anthony," Sylvia said when everyone was gathered around Nancy's dining room table. "She's been one of my favorite women in history for a long time now, ever since the 1970s when Congress was considering putting her image on that dollar coin."

"Why was she the one they wanted on the coin?" Lois asked.

"It's kind of a long story—and I shouldn't have said anything before Nancy has a chance to tell us what she's found out about her," Sylvia said, looking a bit embarrassed at speaking up so soon.

"Susan B. Anthony was one of the most impressive Quaker women we've had so far!" Nancy said, almost as excited as Sylvia had been. "I know we've said that pretty much every time, but this woman was so passionate about the need for justice for both Black Americans and women, and what she believed was their God-given right to vote in elections."

Nancy went through all the organizations Anthony helped form, as well as her work with Elizabeth Stanton. Everyone was impressed with the courage Anthony had shown in registering to vote and then casting the ballot that led to her arrest and trial.

"Wow! I love all the quotes you found from her trial. But I'm curious to know what you learned about her when Congress decided to put her on the dollar coin, Sylvia. I'm not sure I've ever even seen one!" Beth said.

"Well, I remember all the discussions about why there should be a dollar coin, that it would last a lot longer than paper bills and it would save a lot of money. But they couldn't decide what size the coin should be. If it were too large, people would confuse it with the silver dollar, but too small and it would look like the quarter. Make it gold and it would cost too much. So they finally decided on a small coin that would only cost three cents to make."

"What year was this?" Lois asked. "I kind of remember it coming out, but lots of people didn't like it because it didn't work in vending machines."

"It started in 1995 when Congress paid a nonprofit research company to investigate what kind of dollar coin would be most accepted by the public. They determined it had to be smaller, a different color than the quarter, have a distinctive edge, and be released with a major marketing campaign."

"How do you remember all that stuff?" Lois asked with a laugh. "I can't even remember half the teachers and kids I worked with back then!"

"Well, when I knew Susan B. Anthony was to be our topic this month, I did some quick digging because I wanted to look up a research paper that Jane, one of my friends in D.C., wrote on Anthony for her college honors course," Sylvia said.

"I'm pretty sure they made the coins, right?" Beth asked. "So how did they choose Susan B. Anthony to be on it?"

"That was thanks to a number of women's organizations who wanted a real woman after it was suggested they should just stick with Lady Liberty like the head on a lot of the older silver dollars. When Congress finally decided Anthony would be featured on the new coin, they rejected five drafts of her profile, all for being too pretty! So the artist kept working and made her middle-aged and sterner, which was the one Congress finally accepted."

"Yes, they made the coins, I remember that," Nancy said. "But I never see them around, so what happened?"

"Lois was right," Sylvia said, "the biggest criticisms came from businesses who thought the coin was too often confused with a quarter, and that they didn't have room in their cash registers for all the extra coins. But then a newspaper from Jacksonville, Illinois, published a terrible article. Just a minute, I saved it because it was so shocking," Sylvia said, pulling her phone out of her pocket and scrolling to the article. "Here it is," she said and began reading:

Cynics that we are, we regard the new Susan B. Anthony dollar as mostly a very clever and whopper-reemus campaign for the Equal Rights movement in this country, a last-try effort with a stacked deck to win what most of the public doesn't want—a Constitutional amendment in behalf of the ERA cause. All in the name of a respected pioneer crusader for women's suffrage.

"Obviously, that was written by a man," Lois said sarcastically. "But was that what made people decide not to use the coin?"

"It wasn't only one thing, but articles like that one probably had an effect. There's also one other thing you should know that you probably never read about in your research, Nancy," Sylvia said. "It was pretty well known that Susan had some close relationships with several different women. She never married, and some of the letters she wrote to these women indicated their relationships were more than just friendships."

"So . . . she was a lesbian, is that what you're saying?" Beth asked, closely studying Sylvia's expression.

"Only recently have authors begun to publish articles that list some of those relationships. There was a youthful lesbian orator by the name of Anna Dickinson who some called 'America's Joan of Arc' during the Civil War for rallying the war-weary Union forces to victory with her fiery speeches. Dickinson became the source of Anthony's affections in the 1860s."

"But how would anyone know what their private relationship was really like?" Nancy asked.

"Because Dickinson saved some of the letters Susan wrote to her. Listen to this part of one of her letters to Dickinson," Sylvia said, reading aloud:

I invite you to come to me here and sleep with me in my fourth story bedroom at Mrs. Stanton's ever so many nights to snuggle you darling closer than ever.

"And then there's this one."

Dear Dicky Darling . . . I have plain quarters–double bed—and big enough & good enough to take you in. I do so long for the scolding & pinched ears & everything I know awaits me.

"Wow!" Beth finally managed to break the silence. "This reminds me of some of the books published lately about Eleanor Roosevelt and Lorena Hickok and their relationship."

"That's what I thought," Sylvia said. "I'm happy to hear you've read about them too! But in the 1800s, a woman wanting to change history would have done everything she could to appear as if she just hadn't found the right man to marry. Society wasn't kind to anyone who openly admitted they were attracted to someone of the same sex."

"This is interesting and all, but what are we supposed to learn from Ms. Anthony?" Lois asked, always the one to keep the meeting moving.

"I've been thinking about it ever since I did the research," Nancy admitted, "and I was kind of stumped since we've had the right to vote for a hundred years now. But now that we know Susan was possibly a lesbian, maybe we should see if there are things we can do to support LGBTQ people, especially kids."

"Yes! I was hoping this might be something we could take a look at. I found a couple of facts about these kids that surprised me. Here," Sylvia said, pulling copies of her findings out of her bag for everyone. "Take a look at these statistics."

LGBTQ youth seriously contemplate suicide at almost three times the rate of heterosexual youth.

LGBTQ youth are almost five times as likely to have attempted suicide compared to heterosexual youth.

Suicide attempts by LGBTQ youth and questioning youth are four to six times more likely to require medical treatment than those of heterosexual youth.

In a national study, forty percent of transgender adults reported having made a suicide attempt. Ninety-two percent of these individuals reported having attempted suicide before the age of twenty-five.

Each episode of LGBTQ victimization like physical or verbal harassment or abuse increases the likelihood of self-harming behavior by 2.5 times on average.

"That sounds terrible. But what can we do about any of it?" Beth asked.

"Well, I'm wondering if any of the kids in our Meeting might be questioning their sexuality, and what we would do if they were," Nancy said. "What if we made sure our youth directors have the training they need to work with LGBTQ kids? Every kid needs to know that youth Meetings are safe spaces to bring up anything that might worry them."

"Good idea!" Sylvia said. "I was kind of afraid to bring up the whole issue of Anthony being a lesbian. There are still a lot of churches—and Friends Meetings—that believe being gay, lesbian, or transgendered is a sin. I think we need to come up with some ways to make sure we're doing whatever we can to be open and accepting, especially for our youth."

"Would you be willing to meet with the youth group some night and share some of these statistics, and maybe make sure the kids know we support them and accept them no matter what?" Nancy asked.

"Sure, I'd be happy to," Sylvia beamed. "I have a lot more statistics I could share, but maybe just being open and honest with the kids might make a difference for one of them."

"That's great," Beth said. "I really admire your compassion for young people, Sylvia! Be sure and let us know how it goes when you talk to the group."

Nancy shared a little more about Anthony's life and the many speeches and articles she wrote in an effort to "be the church" and make a difference for all women.

As the conversation ended and the women began discussing their plans for Valentine's Day, Lois finally confessed she and Henry were dating and he was planning some sort of surprise for her.

"About time you admitted you've found someone special," Nancy teased. "When do we get to meet this mystery man, 'Henry'?"

"Yeah, why don't you take a selfie of yourselves on your date and text it to us?" Beth added.

"I keep telling you, he's just someone I enjoy spending time with," Lois insisted, but she couldn't help the smile that crept up her face. "And what are you and Allan doing, Nancy?" she asked in an obvious attempt to change the subject.

"Come on, Beth, let's leave these people with sweethearts to discuss their plans!" Sylvia urged, pulling Beth to her feet and moving toward their coats.

Beth laughed but headed out with Sylvia. "You did a lot of work on Susan B. Anthony, and this wasn't even your month!"

"I know . . . I kind of wanted to have her as my Quaker woman to research, but I knew it was Nancy's turn, so I just did a little extra on my own. Which reminds me, since neither of us has a Valentine, would you want to come over on the fourteenth? I know Mom and Dad would be happy to see you, and they go to bed around eight, so we could watch a sappy movie and pretend we're on a date!"

That was a strange thing to say, Beth thought, but she was also happy to have something to do on the one day of the year when she missed Bob the most. He was such a romantic guy, especially for a farmer, and she missed the past Valentine's Days they'd shared.

"I'd like that," she finally said. "What time?"

"Just come around six and you can eat supper with us. It won't be anything fancy, but I'll whip up something delicious that I think you'll like," she said with a smile.

"Okay, friend, it's a date," Beth said with a smile. "But why don't we just play some cribbage so we can talk about our group work while we play? Then next time maybe we can find a movie on Netflix to watch."

"Sounds great! And if there's snow in the forecast, you can always spend the night rather than drive home on bad roads," Sylvia called back as Beth got in her car, smiling with anticipation of their plans.

CHAPTER 33

1979

DIVORCE

LOIS

"I told you I didn't want kids!" Mark shouted at Lois when she broke the news of her pregnancy. "We talked about this before we got engaged, remember?" His eyes flashed with anger, his face becoming redder by the minute. "So you go ahead and do it anyway! What did you do? Quit taking the pills? You said it was foolproof, so why else would you be pregnant unless you quit taking them?"

Lois knew Mark's anger was only going to get worse; he had punched her more than once. Instinctively, she put her hands over her lower abdomen as if to protect this tiny bit of growing cells. She had always trusted the pill for birth control, understanding the consequences if she opposed Mark's refusal to have children. She had never failed to take the daily pills, but when she had begun to suspect the queasy mornings were a sign of pregnancy despite her efforts, she had waited to make a doctor's appointment until she had hoped it was too late for Mark to insist on an abortion.

When the doctor had revealed there was always a one-percent chance the pill might fail to prevent conception, Lois felt relieved. She'd been faithful in taking her birth control, so clearly she was meant to have this baby if she'd gotten pregnant against those odds. Secretly, Lois wasn't totally unhappy at the news, but she knew Mark would be furious. She just hoped that somehow he might eventually be okay with the idea of becoming a father.

"So when did you forget to take your pills?" Mark demanded.

"I took them every single day," Lois said defensively. "And Dr. Brown said there's always a chance the pills might fail, even if it's a small percentage."

"I don't believe you!" Mark stormed, taking quick steps toward his wife.

Lois saw his raised arm and ducked just in time to avoid the fist that went into the drywall behind her, making a hole.

"Please!" Lois begged. "It won't be that bad! I'll take care of the baby, and I'll make sure he or she doesn't bother you. Wouldn't you like to have a son to work with you or an adorable daughter to make you proud?"

"I told you, no kids!" Mark yelled as he picked up his jacket and headed for the door. "I'm going to The Den for a beer—or ten—and I may or may not come back tonight. I can't stand the sight of you right now."

Lois sat down on the couch, trying to stop her hands from shaking. *I'm a strong woman,* she reminded herself, *and I'm a good teacher. I will be a good mother no matter what, and I don't have to put up with Mark's abuse. I refuse to live in fear, and I must protect this new creation God has given me. But how am I going to do that?*

Lois spent the next few weeks trying to ignore Mark each evening following their almost silent meal. She always had papers to check and lesson plans to go over, so it was a good reason to just go into the office and work at her desk. But because it was winter and there wasn't as much construction to keep Mark working, he seemed to always be waiting for her to come home.

Finally, Lois knew what she had to do. "Mark," she began one evening after they had shared a pizza, once again in silence, "I think we need to talk about our future."

"I don't think there's anything to talk about," he said bitterly. "You've already ruined our lives by getting pregnant."

"I know you aren't happy with this child we've made, but I love him or her. I'm sorry you can't accept the fact that this child has to be a gift from God, especially when you consider there was only a one-percent chance the pills would fail to prevent conception." Lois paused for a moment before plunging into what she knew might lead to yet another angry confrontation.

"Since you can't accept this child, I think it would be best if we separated for a while. I'll go live with my folks and finish out the school year, and then when the baby comes this summer, they'll help me for a few weeks before school starts again. If you want to see how you feel about the child when he or she arrives, maybe you'll want to be a part of our lives again," she finished, looking hopefully at Mark but expecting the worst.

"You know how I feel about this kid—I want nothing to do with it. I should have known better than to marry a goody-two-shoes schoolteacher who'd rather go to church than to our friends' parties or out drinking with us. I'm done with this, and I'm done with you. Go live with Mommy and Daddy, and we'll just call it quits right now. Get your lawyer to draw up the divorce papers and I'll sign them. We don't have much to divide up anyway. It's not like we own this place or have any savings."

Lois couldn't help the sobs that escaped, knowing the marriage was over for sure now. "I'm sorry, Mark," she said between sobs, "I still love you, but I also love this child." Hesitating, she added, "And I think you should get some help for your anger issues."

Mark's swift movement took Lois by surprise as he lunged for her, wrapping his big hands around her throat and squeezing. "You don't know anything!" he shouted. "I should've known you weren't woman enough for me!" As Lois's eyes began to bulge, Mark finally released her and stormed out the back door, grabbing a beer on his way out.

Still shaking, Lois quickly locked all the doors, even though she knew Mark could just use his keys to get back in. Then she grabbed the two suitcases she had already packed in anticipation of leaving, and hurried out to her car. When she got to her folks', Lois called Beth.

"Hi, Beth," she began tearily, "do you have a minute to talk?"

Beth must have heard Lois's voice shake, because she quickly assured her friend she had as much time as Lois needed. As Lois began to reveal things about her marriage that she had never shared with any of her friends, Beth murmured in understanding, giving Lois the strength to continue sharing the stories of Mark's abuse during their short marriage.

"And I don't know what to do," Lois finished, "since in the Bible, Jesus says divorce is allowed only in the case of immorality, and, as far as I know, Mark has never been unfaithful."

"First of all, I don't think we know for sure everything Jesus said word for word since the gospels were written several decades after

His death. And I firmly believe from all His teachings in the gospels that we should never allow physical abuse from a loved one.

"You've only been married now for what—four years?" Beth continued. "How many of those years has Mark been physically abusive?"

"Well," Lois said, "the first year was really great. We were both busy with work, and on the weekends we would go out to eat, see a movie, you know, things most newly married couples do. Then Mark started going to The Den after work for a few drinks. I was okay with that because I knew how hard his construction work was, but it wasn't long before he would come home pretty drunk, and that's when the hitting started. Not every time, of course, but lately it seemed like nothing I did was pleasing to him. He complained about my cooking, said I didn't keep the house clean enough, didn't wash his clothes right—you name it, and he was unhappy about it. I dreaded telling him about the baby because I knew he didn't want kids and would think I got pregnant on purpose, but, you know what? I'm happy about this child, and I will love it even if Mark doesn't want to have anything to do with it."

"Don't let people tell you it's wrong to leave an abusive marriage, honey! And I'm always here to listen to whatever's going on with Mark. I've known him for a long time, too, and there's always been a bit of a dark side to his personality," Beth said.

"I hate to admit it, but I think I kind of liked the way he was always able to speak his mind and not go along with what everyone thought he should do."

"I know, and I know you loved him, Lois, but no one deserves to be punched and choked!" Beth said, her voice rising .

"You're right, but please don't tell anyone about this. I'm still hoping I can talk Mark into counseling to see if we can somehow save our marriage."

After she ended their conversation, Lois thought of her friend's words. She was grateful Mark had left the house before seriously hurting her, and yes, she really did want Mark to go to marriage counseling with her, but she was also relatively certain it was a lost cause. Beth's words about Jesus's teachings had been comforting, but the painful thought of divorce caused another round of free-flowing tears as she pulled into her parent's driveway. She hoped they would welcome her with open arms once they knew about the abuse and heard the news of their upcoming grandchild.

CHAPTER 34

1885-1977
ALICE PAUL
PENNSYLVANIA AND BEYOND

Can we really do this? Alice fretted as she prepared for the biggest project of her entire life, being only twenty-eight years of age. *But we must continue the plan to assure President Wilson knows we women are determined to gain our God-given right to vote.* She had the help of her good friend, Lucy, but she wondered if all the proper plans for their Woman Suffrage Procession down Pennsylvania Avenue on in-auguration day were in place. Once again, Alice went over her notes.

Did all the volunteers I found to contact suffragists from around the nation to come and march get the numbers of women needed to show we are a large force for equality? I certainly hope so. Did I secure the right of our parade to march down Pennsylvania Avenue, ending in front of President Wilson on his inauguration day?

Of course she knew it would be a struggle—and it was—but eventually permission was granted. But that wasn't the end of it! It angered Alice when the city supervisor, Sylvester, claimed women would not be safe marching along the Pennsylvania Avenue route and insisted they change plans and conduct the parade elsewhere. Not being one to give up easily, of course, she just demanded Sylvester provide more police—which, of course, he refused to do. Laughing, Alice thought about how it had taken Congress passing a special resolution ordering Sylvester to prohibit all ordinary traffic along the parade route to allow the plans to proceed and keep the marchers safe.

Alice created the colorful program for the march, and she hoped she had taken care of all the details necessary for success. *We must convince President Wilson of the passion behind this battle we are fighting for equality at the ballot box,* she thought.

As soon as all the women started pouring into D.C., Alice knew they were going to have their parade. *It's here, it's now,* she thought, filled with anticipation. As soon as she and her fellow suffragettes could get the multitude of women lined up to march with Inez Milholland, their famous labor lawyer, ready and waiting to lead the way on a beautiful horse, Alice knew that would be the turning point in their mission.

As she watched the many bands, the women with their banners, the squadrons, chariots, and floats–all representing women's lives, Alice felt a sense of accomplishment. The lead banner with the declaration, "We Demand an Amendment to the United States Constitution Enfranchising the Women of the Country," would surely make a great impression on not just the president, but also all the men in Congress who would need to be convinced of the need for the constitutional amendment.

Soon, many spectators lined the streets. Many of them were cheering, but it looked like trouble might've been coming when a number of men–many coming from the pubs after a morning of drinking–pushed past the ropes and were tripping, shoving, slapping, pinching, and spitting tobacco juice on some of the marchers. *So much for added police protection,* Alice thought with dismay. But she couldn't let the drunken men ruin the march, so they all started shouting, "Girls get your hat pins out," as they marched! Alice could see some of the women were hurt, but it was also gratifying to see some Boy Scouts stepping forward to help the injured women. It angered her to see so many policemen idly standing by doing absolutely nothing to protect the women from the rioters. As they got closer to the inaugural platform, Alice saw some of the Massachusetts and Pennsylvania National Guard members and even some students from the Maryland Agricultural College step forward to form a human barrier to help the women pass.

And then they were there, and Alice's heart swelled with pride as they gathered at the end of the parade route. Now more than ever, Alice believed the march would change the past discrimination, and Congress would finally pass an amendment affording women the right to cast a ballot on election days.

• • •

Ninety-year-old Alice smiled as she sat in her New Jersey home looking through the box of memorabilia she had accumulated through the many years she had dreamed of—and fought for—women's equality. *I would have never guessed as a young girl that I would be one of the leaders in the cause,* she thought, remembering all the events she had been part of—some not so pleasant to recall!

I'm so glad I didn't stop expanding my learning with my degree from Swarthmore College, she thought. *Had I not wanted to study social work in England after earning my master's degree in sociology, I would never have met fellow American, Lucy Burns.* Now there was a woman to admire! Alice was always rather shy, so Lucy's take-charge attitude made them a perfect pair to tackle the rights women deserved.

It was '09 when 108 suffragettes formed a march toward Parliament. They were warned to dress in heavy layers for protection, which was certainly good advice. They were pelted with stones, eggs, rotten fruits, and vegetables while men shouted that voting should be left to them. But they marched with their heads held high and their chins up! "Deeds, not words" became their motto.

And the police? Did they give us any help? Quite the contrary! Instead of protecting our right to free speech and peaceful assembly, we were arrested on one flimsy charge after another. Obstructing traffic? That arrest landed us in a London jail for seven months!

Of course Alice wasn't going to stand for such treatment in a free country, so she organized a hunger strike and simply refused to touch the horrible slop they were insisting they eat. She didn't give in, though, not even when they jammed a tube down her throat to force-feed her! They even threatened to send her to an insane asylum. Alice remembered that experience as though it were yesterday, pulling out the letter she had written to her mother at that time:

Dear Momma, the forcible feeding was terrible. They tied me to a chair because I struggled. One wardress sat astride my knees; two others held my arms and hands while two doctors forced a tube five or six feet long through my nose like driving a stake down into the ground.

Once released from prison, it took an entire month in bed to recover from the ordeal. It was then that Alice decided to return to New

York City, and eventually Lucy followed, joining her in the quest for women's voting rights.

Both engaged in conversations with anyone who could offer ways to get the task done. *Picketing and hunger strikes? Who would have imagined doing such things? I think my Quaker father was proud of all our efforts, although he was probably distressed to learn of the suffering so many of us endured in this important work.*

Alice thought back to that momentous first major event when she returned to the States and joined the National American Woman Suffrage Association. *Yes,* she thought, *with Lucy's help we planned that first important event to take place the day before President-elect Wilson's inauguration.* Of course there were obstacles to obtaining the parade permit, especially when the superintendent of police would not add extra officers for protection until they wrote letters to so many of the congressmen's wives that he finally relented and allowed the parade to proceed.

And that wonderful Inauguration Day—March 3, 1913—will be forever as clear in my mind as this glass of water in my hand. And oh! What a wonderful spectacle we were! Later they learned that somewhere between five and eight thousand women marched to the beat of the nine bands in the parade, waving colorful banners between the twenty-six beautiful floats.

And our efforts were rewarded! Thanks to the persistence of our suffragist leaders, we were finally given an audience with President Wilson, presenting our requests that he support an amendment to the Constitution allowing women the right to vote. I suppose Wilson was trying to maintain his party's support when he simply said it was not yet time for such an amendment, but that didn't stop us. And I, for one, certainly refused to take no for an answer.

Alice knew they would have to take more drastic actions. Thus, her next idea was to organize a demonstration, calling themselves the Congressional Union for Woman Suffrage. The first order of business was to lobby Congress to pass laws for the right of all women of the required age to vote. Of all the marches that followed the first large parade, it was the eighteen months of picketing the White House by over a thousand Silent Sentinels that Alice believed made the largest impression on the president.

They made signs and banners—giant stars on purple, white, and gold flags—and chanted words Alice would never forget, "Mr. President, how long must women wait for liberty?" It wasn't easy; in fact, they endured verbal and physical attacks from spectators, especially after the declaration of war in 1917.

Fortunately, a number of newspapers began writing about the efforts for voting rights, and this led to more and more people supporting the cause. It was a banner day in '18 when Wilson finally announced he was in support of the suffrage movement. Of course, Alice was hoping the president would have the support of Congress to quickly approve an amendment giving the right to vote, but it was two long years before approval was finally granted and the required thirty-six states voted to pass it. Alice named it the Susan B. Anthony Amendment in honor of the pioneering woman who did so much to lay the foundation for their work.

But there were more rights we women deserved beyond that first, basic right to make our selections at the ballot box. There was more work to be done, the main one being the need to end the legal distinctions between men and women in matters of divorce, property, employment, and so on.

So, in 1923, with Crystal Eastman, another powerful suffragette, Alice wrote a draft of what they called the Equal Rights Amendment. They delivered the Lucretia Mott Amendment to Congress in honor of this brave woman's anti-slavery and suffrage activism. It should have been something Congress would have wanted to pass since the wording was simply, "Men and women shall have equal rights throughout the United States and every place subject to its jurisdiction."

Getting something passed in Congress, however, proved to be much more difficult than any of the suffragettes could ever have imagined. It was a full twenty years later before the amendment was reworded to read, "Equality of rights under the law shall not be denied or abridged by the United States or by any state on account of sex," and in spite of its previous failure to be passed, Alice did feel honored to have the amendment renamed the "Alice Paul Amendment." She still believed there were inequalities between men and women, particularly in the workplace, so she continued to advocate for this Equal Rights Amendment.

Sadly, there were women who did not agree with this amendment, most grievously some previous suffragettes who marched in '13. Some of them joined with the League of Women Voters in their opposition to the ERA. Alice never understood why this group felt that sex-based workplace legislation would restrict a woman's ability to compete for jobs with men and earn good wages. Alice felt strongly that only having current protective legislation in the workplace hurts women wage earners because some employers simply fire them rather than implement protections on working conditions that safeguard women. Women were still paid less than men, lost jobs that required them to work late nights, and were blocked from joining labor unions on par with men. Alice was convinced that the ERA was the most efficient way to ensure legal equality in all areas, and she never understood why working women were hesitant to support the amendment.

Alice refused to give up the fight, and when the women's movement gained steam when she was in her seventies, her hopes for passage of the ERA seemed imminent, and imagine how happy she was when Congress finally passed the bill in '72. This time there was no problem gaining Congress's approval, but sadly, in order to get enough votes to pass, there was a stipulation put on the ratification of the amendment by the states: it had to be completed in seven years. Getting it approved by the necessary thirty-eight states became a major stumbling block. It grieved Alice to think that all their work on this major effort for equal rights for women failed to gain that necessary approval.

I still wonder if states would have ratified the amendment with ease had it not been for Phyllis Schlafly's STOP ERA crusade against us in the '70s, Alice thought. Schlafly argued that women should have the right to be in the home as a wife and mother, that courts would interpret such an amendment as abortion on demand, that same-sex marriage would be allowed, and that women would certainly be drafted to serve in the military. All scare tactics . . . it was so hard to understand why one woman would revolt against securing the rights for all other women.

Alice took heart in knowing she played a role in getting some protections for women added with the addition of Title VII in the Civil Rights Amendment in '64, thanks to the support of her good friend House Representative Howard Smith. He was one of the ERA's biggest supporters and was able to secure the prohibition of sex discrimination for women in the workplace through the amendment.

Most people would assume I was satisfied with my work as one of the women who had tirelessly given so many years to bring about equality for all. Equality was so much a part of my Quaker heritage, and it demanded my lifelong devoted efforts. But until there are guaranteed equal rights for all women by a ratified amendment to the Constitution, our work will not be done. It is my fervent hope that there will soon come a time when the Equal Rights Amendment will once again come before the states to be ratified and become law.

CHAPTER 35

MARCH, PRESENT DAY
THE CLUB—LOIS'S CONDO

Lois couldn't help but think about all the work Alice Paul had done to secure the right to vote for women, and how she even wrote the Equal Rights Amendment, which was still not a part of their constitutional guarantee of equality. She knew they were nearly finished with all the women their club had identified as Quakers from the past who could help them navigate the changes they thought should be a part of the Society of Friends in the twenty-first century. But would anyone even care about all the decades of work these brave women had done to make the world a better place?

As she put the homemade cinnamon rolls in the oven to bake, knowing the sweet aroma of cinnamon and butter would linger in the kitchen when the others arrived, Lois's thoughts drifted to the previous night she had spent with Henry.

They had shared a wonderful meal at a classy restaurant in Prairie View to celebrate their six-month anniversary. At first she thought it was premature to be celebrating an anniversary, but Henry had been so sweet when he insisted that any time a man and woman their ages enjoyed spending time together, it should be celebrated.

And she had been shocked when Henry surprised her with a beautiful ruby necklace, and although she wasn't sure it meant they were destined for a more permanent relationship, she was still so happy to be spending time with him. She had not wanted another relationship for years after the abusive marriage with Mark ended, focusing her energies on her son and her students. But she was beginning to realize how much she missed having a man to share the simple things in life with . . . movies, restaurant meals, performances at the university's theater, or just sharing a Netflix show and popcorn with each other.

As the intercom buzzer interrupted her thoughts, Lois pressed the button to unlock the condo's exterior door, knowing she'd better get the smug look off her face before the person requesting entrance walked through the door.

"Hi!" came Beth's cheerful greeting after a few moments. "Yum! This doesn't smell like fruit and yogurt to me!"

"I'm getting tired of healthy snacks and decided it was a cinnamon roll kind of morning," Lois declared with a grin. "The rolls are just about ready to take out and frost."

"Works for me," Beth said happily. "And now that the March sun is finally bringing some warmth, I've been able to do more walking outside."

"So true. I just love seeing the new buds on the trees. They remind me that one of the best things about living in the Midwest is the seasons," Lois said.

After the others arrived and they all devoured the warm, sticky cinnamon rolls without a word about them not being healthy, Lois began filling them in on Alice Paul's work.

"Can you imagine organizing a march for eight thousand women with no social media back then?" she finished.

"Well," Nancy observed, "you did say she had a doctorate in political science, which is not something most women would have done back then, so I'm guessing she was a very smart and capable woman."

"Yeah, she really was," Lois agreed. "Interestingly, like many of the other women we've talked about, she closely partnered with another woman, Lucy Burns, and together they did so many great things to gather support for women's suffrage—parades, mailing pamphlets and letters to women all over the country, anything they could think of to get their message to as many women as possible. It's fascinating to think how many of these powerful women partnered with other women, not men, to accomplish the work they thought needed to be done."

"I agree!" Sylvia said. "They're a powerful example of what two women working together can do. I know Jane and I were a great team when we worked together in the senator's office. We put together some really important pieces of legislation for the senator to propose. They weren't always passed out of committees, but we felt like we had done everything in our power to make the proposed bills easy to understand so they would have the support needed to get them sent on to the full Senate."

"I remember you talking about your work with Jane and how close you were," Beth said. She studied Sylvia for a moment, and then said, "And here we are again, trying to figure out what difference this makes in our day and age. Like we decided before, it seems like so many of these women were fighting for equality. Don't you think we already have gender equality in most things now?"

"Are you serious?" Lois asked. "Think about it! We just talked about inequality between women and men when we discussed Ann Preston. And remember that article Sylvia shared at one of our other club meetings—the one from the Yearly Meeting newsletter about the importance of women being submissive to their husbands? And then there's that whole problem of some pastors in Friends Meetings using scripture passages literally to call LGBTQ people sinners without any historical basis for how the ancient languages were translated into today's English. What kind of equality is it when LGBTQ Friends are being shunned in our own Quaker churches? I sure don't think that's equality!"

"Yes, of course you're right, Lois," Nancy said, "but where does that leave us for our work to 'be the church' this month? We've already been working on issues around equality for several months. What else should we be looking at?"

"Maybe we should take a look at the United Church of Christ's list of things they consider 'being the church' that their denomination has agreed to support," Sylvia suggested. "Here—I have the list in my bag."

As always, Sylvia had the needed information at hand. "Here's what it says," she began. "Being the church includes protecting the environment, caring for the poor, forgiving often, rejecting racism, fighting for the powerless, sharing earthly and spiritual resources, embracing diversity, loving God, and enjoying life. Now, what if we aligned these ideas with our ancestral Quaker testimonies of simplicity, peace, integrity, community, equality, and stewardship?"

"Yeah, I've been thinking about protecting the environment," Lois admitted, "and it seems to me that doing what we can for the environment is also a part of stewardship. My school always planned activities for Earth Day to get the kids involved at a young age, so I dug up some of my old lesson plans and made a list of things we might each encourage our families to do to help climate change."

"I guess it definitely pays to have a teacher in the group," Nancy said, laughing. "What are some of the things on the list?"

"Here are a few of the ones I think are really important," Lois said, handing a detailed list to each of the others.

> *Replace old light bulbs with LED ones when they burn out.*
> *Look for Energy Star appliances that save electricity.*
> *Get your insulation checked by an expert and see if it needs an upgrade.*
> *See if you can set your thermostat for lower temps in the winter and a little warmer ones in the summer.*
> *Grow a garden.*
> *Explore where your power comes from and consider solar panels.*
> *Reduce, reuse, recycle.*

"That last one was always our focus with the kids–you wouldn't believe how much paper and food they waste! And there's a lot of other ideas on the list with more details on ways to go about doing the various suggestions."

"I think Allan and I have already done a lot of these things, but it's worth talking to our kids and grandkids about," Nancy admitted. Sylvia and Beth nodded in agreement.

Together the friends got to work aligning more of the ways they wanted to pursue being the church as they fit with the testimonies the previous Quaker women had worked so hard to uphold.

As they finished their lists, Beth said, "I sense our exploration of influential women is nearly finished. We'll have to synthesize all our research and thoughts together if our work is to have any impact on any of the Society of Friends Meetings."

"I agree," Sylvia said. "But I've been thinking, we may be doing a disservice to women today if we don't add one or two more women who are still living, women who are 'being the church' and have been inspirations for Friends today. Surely there are some modern-day women who might also be considered a type of pioneer in their efforts to move away from so much of the evangelical thinking. Would learning about them take away from the work of all the ancestors we've been highlighting?"

"Do you have someone in mind?" Lois asked. "I'm not opposed to adding a living inspiration, but I'm not sure how we would pick someone when there are probably a lot of women who might qualify."

Beth glanced at Sylvia. "Do you have someone in mind since you've been thinking about this?"

"Kind of," Sylvia said sheepishly. "Do you remember several years ago when I went on one of the African work teams Karen Bauer organized to spend three weeks working with the widows and orphans in Kenya through Friends Bringing Hope, the nonprofit she founded?"

"Of course!" Nancy quickly answered, "and I think she would be the perfect current woman to add to our group of influential Quaker role models! I remember that Sunday when she came and shared a slideshow of her organization and how you felt like you wanted to be part of her work there."

"Would you be okay if we added her, Lois?" Beth asked.

"Sure," Lois agreed. "I hadn't thought about Karen's work, but I know we were all impressed with everything that Friends Bringing Hope has been able to do for the widows and orphans. Since it's your turn to feature one of the women, Sylvia, I say go for it!"

"Thanks!" Sylvia smiled in relief. "I'll email Karen for permission to use her organization and start putting together some of the details about the work she's been doing in Kenya. Oh, and by the way . . . I've been noticing that stunning necklace all morning, Lois. Is it a gift from Justin?"

"No, Henry gave it to me."

All three women turned to Lois in anticipation of an explanation.

"What?" Lois grinned. "Henry and I have been seeing each other for six months now and he just wanted to thank me for doing things with him."

"So this is kind of like a promise ring—er, necklace?" Nancy asked.

"No! This isn't college, ladies," Lois retorted. "Henry and I are just friends."

"With benefits?" Beth joked.

"If going out to dinner and to the movies is 'with benefits,' then yes. And that's all I'm going to say," Lois said.

Sylvia grinned at Beth and Nancy. "'With benefits,' for sure—I would call a ruby necklace a pretty nice benefit!"

"Don't you have to go home and start working on this assignment?" Lois said as she walked to open the condo door. "Quit trying to make something out of my relationship with Henry that just isn't there."

"Sure, Lois, whatever you say!" Beth teased.

"Goodbye, friends. Now get out there and enjoy the warm spring weather!" Lois said, closing the door on their laughter.

CHAPTER 36

1980
NEW RELATIONSHIPS
SYLVIA

Over the past year, Sylvia had often thought back to that momentous conversation she and Jane had had that night at the pizza place and what might have happened if she hadn't finally agreed to move in with her work partner. Would she have ever found out who she really was and what kind of life she hoped to have?

"So what do you think?" Jane had asked as she and Sylvia were waiting for their pizza with the works to arrive.

"I think it's been a long week and I just want our food to hurry up and get here," Sylvia had said. She'd been working for the senator for a couple of years by then and she and Jane had become good friends.

"Come on, Sylvia, you still haven't answered my question. Will you consider sharing my apartment with me? There's plenty of room in addition to the two bedrooms, and it'll save us both a lot of rent money. Think about it: we could share groceries, plan some meals together, split the utilities, and I already have all the furniture we would need since you're still living in a furnished apartment."

"Well," Sylvia said slowly, "I'm still not sure you would want to live with me all the time. I don't sleep very well some nights, I often spend my evenings working on things for the next day—and if I'm not working, I'm talking with family and friends from back home. But it would definitely help with my budget, though."

In the end, she'd said yes, and that one little word had changed everything. Not long after Sylvia moved in, Jane had shared her true feelings.

"Hey, Sylv, do you have time for a chat?" Jane had called from her room one evening.

"Sure. Hang on—I'm just finishing with the dinner cleanup."

Drying her hands as she headed to Jane's room, she was surprised to see her new roommate sitting on her bed rather than on the love seat under her window.

"Come and sit," Jane suggested, patting the bed beside her.

"Okay," Sylvia said slowly, wondering what Jane wanted to talk about.

"Have you ever wondered why neither of us ever go on dates?" Jane began.

"Well, I'm guessing it's because no one has asked us!" Sylvia said with a laugh. "Do you have some handsome man you want to set me up with on a blind date?"

Jane was serious as she replied, "No. I'm not sure about you, but I have no interest in dating a handsome young man," she said.

"What do you mean?"

"Have you not figured out yet that I'm only interested in women? I've always known my attractions were different from the time I felt my first infatuation with some of the girls in my high school, although I never let anyone know that it was other girls, not guys, I wanted to be with. And then in college, I had my first real relationship with another girl in our dorm. I thought we were in love, but she ended it when we both graduated and moved to different parts of the country. Since then I've never found anyone I really wanted to be with . . . at least not until now."

Sylvia wasn't sure where this conversation was headed, but she was beginning to have an idea. It was exciting while also making her a bit nervous.

"So what was it like? With your college roommate?" she finally asked.

"It was just casual at first—a little flirting, a little teasing, and the feeling that we couldn't stand being away from each other. We ate all our meals together, studied together, and hung out on the weekends."

"And then? How did you become more than friends?"

"Eventually we began hugging each other for any little reason, snuggling on the couch, things like that, and then one night I just decided to kiss her and see if she was interested in taking our relationship a step further," Jane finished.

"So it was physical, then? Is that what makes it a lesbian relationship?" Sylvia couldn't help being a little intrigued about this revelation, and there was the new thought that maybe Jane's reason for wanting to have this talk was to see if she might be interested in a relationship with her, and what that might be like.

"It seems to me that sexuality lies on somewhat of a spectrum," Jane began. "There are some women—and men—who are totally heterosexual. They have absolutely no desire for intimate relationships with anyone other than the opposite sex. And at the other end of the spectrum, there are some of us who have no desire for relationships with the opposite sex, and I think a lot of people are somewhere in between. For me, new relationships almost always start slowly, first with that emotional connection."

"Have you had other relationships with women?" Sylvia asked, her curiosity growing.

"Yes, I've had a few, but none have had that deep soulmate connection," Jane said with a shrug.

Sylvia thought she knew where this conversation was going, but she still wasn't sure. Yes, there were things about Jane that she adored, like her refusal to back down when confronted, making sure she was a person of integrity in all her responses. And she had been enamored with the sweet citrus aroma of Jane's perfume from that first day in worship with her. And then she was always teasing Jane about the clothes she would and wouldn't wear. Jane hated dresses, but her pantsuits were always accented with matching blouses and a few nice pieces of jewelry.

But did she want to be with Jane in a romantic way? Sylvia had never thought about it, but she had always looked forward to seeing her roommate and work partner first thing every morning. And now leaving the apartment together and grabbing a drink and scone at the nearby coffee shop actually did kind of feel like they were special partners.

"You're awfully quiet," Jane said, looking anxiously at Sylvia.

"Why haven't you ever shared any of this with me before?" Sylvia finally asked.

Jane reached over and took Sylvia's hand in hers. "I've been attracted to you since that first Sunday you agreed to go to the silent meeting with me," she confessed. "And, if I'm totally honest, I think I've fallen in love with you—well, actually, I've been in love with you for a long time, but I wasn't ever sure it would work out. You used to talk a lot about finding a nice Quaker guy to date and marry, so it didn't seem like you were going to be interested in anything more than friendship with me."

"So what changed your mind?" Sylvia asked. "You know I've gone on several dates with a couple of guys since we've met."

"I don't know, really. I suppose since we've been sharing this apartment it seems like you've quit looking for men to date, and there are times when we've been working together in the kitchen, and you lean toward me and our bodies connect. But maybe you haven't had the same feelings I've had. I just wanted to be honest with you and let you know what I've been thinking about."

There was a new feeling of excitement growing within Sylvia that she had never felt before, and even her heart began beating faster. As she looked at Jane, considering this new aspect of their friendship, she felt a desire to see where their relationship might be going. She knew there were strong disagreements among some of the Friends Meetings on the whole subject of being open and accepting of gay and lesbian Friends, but Jane was one of the most devout members of their Meeting, and she didn't think Jane would want to be in a same-sex relationship unless she felt it was acceptable in her Meeting—and in God's eyes.

"You keep throwing these new things at me," Sylvia said, playfully pushing Jane back on the bed. They wrestled a bit, laughing, until they ended up lying there, just holding each other. "I have a lot to learn about this whole idea of the spectrum of sexuality, but I'm open to exploring it with you—if that's what you're suggesting."

As she lay in her own bed that night, pondering everything Jane had revealed about falling in love with her, Sylvia couldn't help but think back on all the times she had had crushes on other girls and women without even realizing it. Sometimes it was admiring some of the women her mom's age in their Meeting, but there were also the times she felt almost intoxicated by some of the women she hung out with in her dorm. And now, this evening, if she were honest with herself, she would have to admit the feelings she'd had lying next to Jane were way deeper than anything she had ever felt with any of the guys she had dated. *Am I ready to take this relationship to the next level?* she wondered. Would it mean giving up her wish to have a family and kids someday? Questions continued to fill her mind until much later in the night when she finally succumbed to the sleep her mind and body needed.

Yes, Sylvia thought as once again she and Jane sat in the silence of worship, *what an eye-opening, life-changing year this has been. I have discovered a love with a woman I would never have dreamed possible, and I can only wonder what it will mean for my future.* Of course she knew she needed to center down in worship and let these thoughts go, but it would be a challenge as she felt the warmth of Jane sitting close, and that still intoxicating citrus perfume she had come to love filling the small space between them.

CHAPTER 37
1956-PRESENT
KAREN BAUER
WISCONSIN AND KENYA

"I was really excited but also a little nervous when we decided to take on the interim position as principals at Friends Theological College a couple of years ago," Karen admitted to her husband, Stanley, as they drove up the road to their farm in Wisconsin. It was 2004, and they had just gotten home from their second trip to Kenya at the invitation of their friend, Mary Juma.

"The College in Kaimosi was so rural!" she said. "All those dirt roads were so treacherous in the rainy seasons, and widows living in thatched-roofed huts that leaked rain that ran down the hard, mud-packed walls. But I know we made the right decision to accept that interim position. Little did we know that was only the beginning and we would be returning just a couple of years later!"

"Lots of water over the dam since then," Stan agreed. "But God has been faithful to provide for our safety and the resources we've needed to help the widows and children over the past few years. And it was a great challenge for this old farmer to begin to restore the dairy project at the college when we were first there," he added. "There were several acres for cows to graze, and we soon understood the cultural importance of having animals. We were only there for two semesters that first time, but the dairy project is still profitable for the college."

"It was Mary Juma coming with the African women's delegation from Kenya to the USFW Triennial Conference a couple of years later that was really the beginning of our work to develop a program to help sustain life for the widows and orphans," Karen reminded him. "Having Mary stay in our home for a few days, hearing her share the great need of the women and children in her community, was the impetus for starting a new type of mission work. And that's how Friends Bringing Hope came into being."

"I'm so glad we returned to explore Mary's invitation. What an amazing feeling to step on Kenyan soil once again," Stan said.

"Of course!" Karen said. "It was such a powerful experience. I'll have to write about it before the memories fade."

That night Karen got out her journal and recorded everything she could remember about their arrival during their most recent trip:

I first knew I was in Kenya when I felt the warmth . . . stepping off the plane at 11 pm on a late December evening and being warm. We looked forward to spending the next 18 days of "midwinter" without being cold. Of course, the real warmth we anticipated was not so much physical but emotional, the reuniting with old friends. Our first such experience came at the airport as we met our friend, Alex, and his beautiful young family. They had delivered the vehicle that we would be using.

I could smell Kenya, it has a fresh earthy smell, difficult to identify but impossible to forget. Then the quiet of the Mennonite guest house in Nairobi and being awakened by birds of Kenya. These birds gave me a secure feeling of being welcomed back. The busy streets and many people talking in many languages, English, Swahili, and the Kenyan "mother tongue"—the beautiful sound of wonderful people. As we traveled from Nairobi to Kaimosi, many other sights and sounds welcomed us back: the rough roads, the green lush land, the dry barren areas stricken by drought, the baboons, zebras, gazelle, and warthogs grazing alongside the road. Then the many people we saw walking, the small mini-buses they call matatus, the driving on the left side of the road, the dodging cows, goats, sheep, donkeys and carts, trucks, and bicycles while driving. And I'll never forget the ceremonial dress of the boys who just became circumcised, the music of Kenya, the wonderful warm sunshine, and, of course, the beautiful people. I was home in Kenya.

So many emotions started to swell in me. I became so excited that we would soon be seeing friends with whom we had prayed, sung, and worshiped for several months two years ago. At the Kaimosi intersection from the tarmac road to the dirt road we saw Alex's new red duka, his small kiosk. It has improved so much that he even has a refrigerator to keep sodas cold!

Entering the Friends Theological College compound, we were greeted by the night staff. We had missed our friends so much. There waiting for us to arrive were Rueben and Linet, friends that we have kept in touch with since last leaving and we were so happy to see them again. Mary Juma greeted us and offered a prayer of thanksgiving for our safe travels and the blessing of our future work. We were back in Kaimosi and happy.

Karen closed her journal, knowing those were memories she would never forget.

• • •

As Karen made notes for another work trip to Kenya almost two decades later, Stan checked in to see how the planning was going.

"Kenya has truly become your home away from home," he mused. "How many work teams have you taken since you created Friends Bringing Hope?" Stan hadn't always been able to go with Karen once they were back on the farm in Wisconsin and he was still pastoring in Iowa.

"There have been twenty work teams so far, with forty-five people joining me on these trips," Karen said. "The work is always there, and it's always on my mind. When we pull up the lane of the dirt road and the women and children of the widows' groups start singing and dancing, it fills me with joy to hear them call out 'Momma Karen! Momma Karen! You came back!'

"But I haven't done it all myself," she added. "We wouldn't be able to do much of our work without the Kenyan Quakers who work for the Rural Service Programme, one of the best organizations started by Quaker missionaries. They have the Kenyan field staff who live in the rural communities and identify the widows' groups and the individuals most in need. The ability to build houses for the neediest of the widows, plus helping provide some of the widows' groups with income-producing products, were both ideas that have created such long-lasting relationships with so many Kenyans. And because you were going to be pastoring in Iowa, I had soon realized the long-term work would mainly be something I would need to create and oversee."

"It's amazing that you worked with them to build houses for over one hundred displaced widows and orphans," Stan said. "It's quite a sight to see the Americans on the work teams pushing handfuls of mud between the sapling walls of the frames for the new homes RSP has put up with funds from Friends Bringing Hope. Those photos are so fun to look back on."

"And don't forget the other important part of the work of the non-profit," Karen reminded him, "all those varieties of income-producing projects we've supplied for the widows."

Her thoughts drifted to the many women who had been left homeless and without school funds when the AIDS epidemic hit, killing so many of the men. *At first,* she thought, *I didn't understand the culture and could not wrap my head around how mistreated the widows were. I could not imagine family treating family that way.* The cultural customs of wife inheritance, stigma, and superstitions were mind-boggling. They had to find ways to help these women live lives free from the oppression so prevalent in their male-dominated societies.

The patriarchal social customs in Kenya made it so very difficult for a widow to be able to live alone if she chose not to become another wife to one of her brothers-in-law. Polygamy was still prevalent in rural areas, and a man having more than one wife was just one of the many tribal customs and laws that made it imperative for Friends Bringing Hope to do everything possible to help the women and their children in the widows' groups live sustainable lives.

"It's been challenging," she said, "but I do feel good about the way our work has also elevated the status of the widows in their rural communities. In many ways, their lives are more sustainable, they are safer, and they are no longer ostracized. Some even find good employment, and then they can pay their children's school fees and buy food and medicine."

"You're so right, and I've always enjoyed helping find those income projects for the widows' groups," Stan said, laughing. "Goats?

Great fun! Chickens, calves, pigs, sheep? All my favorites. But of course, the firewood and fire briquettes for cooking are invaluable for allowing the women to avoid the danger of being attacked by men when they have to go into the wooded areas to find fuel."

"And then there are the sewing machines and cloth to create a variety of clothing and toys, and the soap projects we've helped with, too," Karen added.

"But you're still working full time, and we have twelve grandchildren and lots of events to go to," Stan reminded her. "How many more trips do you think we have in us—especially in you when I'm not able to go with you?"

"Only time will tell, but the need is still great. We are making such a difference for these women, and, most importantly, we save lives and give them days of safety and joy. Plus there are all the scholarships we've given to orphans so they can attend high school. That's the future for so many of these children, a future where they can go to college if they score high enough on their exams, and that gives them a chance for a life out of poverty.

"Remember when we had just come back from Kenya after that first visit with the leaders in the Rural Service Programme? One morning, the Sunday School discussion centered on the story of Jesus feeding the five thousand. The last verse said, 'There were about five thousand men who ate, not counting the women and children,' and it hit me: Jesus valued and counted and fed the women and children—something radical for the patriarchal society Jesus lived in. He had elevated those members of society in much the same way our work helps elevate the Kenyan women who are the ones making and serving the food in their culture, too. And Jesus also had compassion for the sick and healed everyone who came to him. The widows and orphans are not unlike the lepers in Jesus's day, and they need Friends Bringing Hope to respond to their needs the best ways we can.

"I hope we've done justice to our mission to impact people's lives in such a way that they're able to fulfill their God-given potential, freed from stigma, oppression, and violence," she continued. "The faith of these Kenyans is strong—we see that every Sunday when we worship with them on these trips. But it's their everyday lives that need whatever help we can give them.

"I really hope there will be another Quaker group or the Kenyan Church who will take up the challenge of 'being the church' to these women and children when we're no longer able to continue," Karen told Stan.

The passion for this work was still so clear in all the reminiscing she and Stan were doing that morning as they sat in their century-old farmhouse. *There will be as many more mission trips as my health and the finances of Friends Bringing Hope will allow,* Karen vowed to herself. *This is what missions should be about: making life better for the most vulnerable, no matter where they might live. Through it all, I will keep Philippians 1:11 in mind, the scripture that is the foundation of the work of Friends Bringing Hope:* "May you always be filled with the fruit of your salvation—the righteous character produced in your life by Jesus Christ—for this will bring much glory and praise to God."

CHAPTER 38

APRIL, PRESENT DAY
THE CLUB—SYLVIA'S
FAMILY HOME

Would Beth ever feel the same way about her? Sylvia wondered, the very same way she felt when she was with Beth? That thought had been in the back of her mind for months now, especially after the Valentine's Day meal they had shared together with her folks. They had decided to cook the dinner together, laughing as the gravy they made for the mashed potatoes turned out lumpy and the pork roast a little overcooked. But it was the time after her parents had retired for the evening that the two women had begun to share more of their past from the many years they had lived and worked apart.

Maybe I shouldn't have told her about my relationship with Jane, Sylvia fretted, remembering the puzzled look on Beth's face and her questions about how her past love with Jane had all come about. *Too late now,* she thought, hoping she hadn't ruined the chance of a future relationship.

Sylvia had asked Beth to come early to their club meeting that morning so Beth could visit with her parents while she fixed the morning's snack. Her dad had been especially restless and confused the past several weeks, and Sylvia knew her mom needed a distraction. She also knew her mother was almost to the breaking point of caring for her dad, even with Sylvia's help, and their decisions about the future of his care were looming large.

As Beth's laughter rang out from the living room, once again Sylvia felt that warmth that Beth always seemed to radiate. Realizing she had barely begun mixing up the cranberry-orange-walnut muffin batter, Sylvia quickly added the remaining ingredients, spooned them into the tins, and then popped them in the oven to bake.

When the muffins had baked and cooled enough to handle, she arranged them on one of her mother's crystal platters with the fresh blueberries, blackberries, and raspberries sitting in bowls around the table. S he was pleased with how everything looked when the others began to arrive.

"Where's Beth? I saw her car parked by the barn, so I figured she was already here," Lois asked, always the most observant one

"She's with Mom and Dad. I'm sure Mom would enjoy saying hi to you and the others, too," Sylvia suggested. She led Lois to the living room, saying "Look who's here, Mom."

"Oh, Lois!" Ruth beamed at the sight of this woman who had once been a part of their Meeting's youth group when Ruth and John had been the leaders. "I do believe I see a bright smile on that face of yours! Is Justin coming home for a visit?"

"No, not until next Thanksgiving," Lois said cheerfully.

"But there is a reason for that grin," Beth said with a sly look on her face. "Lois has a new 'friend'—of the male variety!"

"Oh, my dear! That is just wonderful," Ruth said. "I always thought someone would come along after your divorce from Mark and sweep you off your feet. I just didn't think it would take quite so long! Is it anyone I might know?"

"His name is Henry Patton, and he just moved to Maple Grove about a year ago. He lives across the street from me now, and we've enjoyed spending a little time together."

"Well, you just enjoy this new relationship, and someday you need to bring him here to meet me," Ruth said warmly. "It's been many years since I was a youth leader, but all of you in that group will always have a special place in my heart."

When Lois didn't immediately respond, Sylvia thought she saw a few tears in Lois's eyes. She quickly added that she would be sure to remind Lois to do just that.

Soon Nancy joined them, and even though she hadn't been in the youth group with the others, she had worked with Ruth on several meeting committees and was happy to have the chance to see her again. It had been several months since Ruth had been able to attend worship at Maple Grove because John could no longer sit through a service without becoming agitated.

"Are you all ready?" Sylvia asked after the women had visited with Ruth for a while. "Would you and Dad like one of the muffins you've been smelling?" she asked her mother with a smile.

"That would be lovely. Now you girls go on with your big meeting," Ruth said with a shooing motion.

"This muffin is yummy, and your mom is so nice!" Nancy said, devouring one of the breakfast treats. "I miss my parents every single day. And I know your dad struggles with dementia, but at least he's still here with you."

"Yes," Sylvia said slowly, "but before long, I don't think Mom and I will be able to give Dad the care he needs without additional help. We're planning to visit some care centers with dementia wings so Dad can be cared for by professionals and Mom can have a more normal life. We looked into twenty-four-hour care here at home, but the cost was just too high, and if I know Mom, even if we hired the help, she would still be doing some of his care."

The other three women murmured sympathetically. They'd all dealt with the challenges of aging parents and knew how stressful it could be.

"Thanks, friends," Sylvia said. "I appreciate your support. But enough of my home life! Let's get going on today's Quaker woman. So, even though I was there for worship the Sunday Karen presented her work with the widows' groups in Kenya, I didn't really know much about the history of how Karen—and her husband Stan, too—got started working with the widows and orphans and created their nonprofit, Friends Bringing Hope. When I called Karen to get some of the details of how the work got started and how many trips she had organized, I was blown away by everything Friends Bringing Hope has done for widows and orphans in Kenya. The stories she told me about some of their experiences during the mission trips they've sponsored is really the story of what the compassion of Jesus is all about—and what the focus of mission trips should be."

"Tell us one of those stories," Lois begged. "I'd love to hear more."

"Okay. The first time Karen and Stan went to western Kenya—a really poor area—they were interim directors of a Quaker theological college. The college is in the middle of a compound with several buildings, and the college hires Kenyans to do some of the upkeep on the grounds. They also hire housekeepers because there aren't a lot of job opportunities in that area, and these jobs give the women a little income.

"So one day, Karen was talking to one of the older groundskeepers, who was always cheerful in spite of having to do the tedious job of slashing the grass with a blade and then raking it. When Karen noticed he was using a tool made from sticks that required him to stoop over to rake up the cut grass, she began to wonder why the workers didn't have real rakes.

"Then on another day, Karen returned from her work at the college and noticed their housekeeper, Rachel, who had been hired to clean the guest house where they were living, was washing the floor on her hands and knees. Karen asked her if she had a mop she could use to make the work easier, and when she said no, Karen asked her if she'd like one, and she said she would. Then Karen noticed the broom Rachel had been using was also handmade from grass. So the next time Karen was able to go to the nearest more modern city, she took Rachel with her and let her pick out all the things she needed to help with the housework, plus rakes for the groundskeepers.

"Karen said a lot of Americans would just assume the use of handmade rakes and brooms was part of the Kenyan culture instead of asking if they would like store bought tools—actions that cause Americans to continue to perpetuate the oppression of the poorer Kenyans."

"Wow!" Nancy said. "That makes sense. But Sylvia, what I want to know is, what was it like for you when you went on one of the mission trips with the Bauers?"

"Honestly? It was life-changing!" Sylvia said. "When we would go to pack mud into the walls of one of the new houses, it was heart wrenching yet humbling to hear the prayers of gratitude from widows who were no longer trying to keep the rain out of their thatched-roofed huts with old newspapers. The new houses had metal roofs and even occasionally a second room. We would always take a few gifts for the new homes, like thin foam mattresses from the local outdoor market, tin cups, cooking pots, and a bag of sugar for their tea. No appliances, no furniture, just a dirt floor, but now with a real roof over their heads.

"And get this, Lois," Sylvia continued, looking at the retired schoolteacher. "At one of the widows' groups we visited, we were led into a one-room hut that was being used as a primary school. There were a few simple wooden desks, but the bulletin board on one of the mud walls was just a piece of cardboard! I was literally in tears as I looked around that room and thought of our classrooms and the modern equipment we have here. But those kids? They were so proud of what they had learned and the things they wanted to recite for us. I just wish every parent who complains about our educational system here could visit these rural African schools for even one day!"

"That sounds like an amazing experience," Lois said, "and an amazing modern Quaker woman who is making a huge difference! I had assumed we'd only be researching Quaker women from the past, but Sylvia's suggestion to feature the Bauers and their work with Kenyan widows and orphans was fantastic. Friends Bringing Hope should be a model for all Meetings' approach to missions."

"I do have one more suggestion," Sylvia said tentatively. "What if we also featured a modern-day African woman from Kenya I learned about when working with Karen. Her name is Margaret Amadavi, and her work is something we should all aspire to."

"And here I thought we were ready to wrap up this project," Lois teased, although there was a hint of displeasure in her voice at the prospect of yet another month of gathering information. "Whose turn is it if we do another month? Not mine, I hope."

"It's mine, and Sylvia has already asked me about doing it—so no worries, Lois!" Beth said, laughing.

"Then will that be the last one?" Nancy asked. "There really are a lot of other women still living that we could feature."

"I'm not sure we need to add more women," Beth said slowly. "Yes, I know there are a lot of current Quakers who have done work to 'be the church,' but I can't think of anyone who has had the magnitude of impact that the women we've learned about so far have had."

"I agree!" Lois said firmly. "The work we've done has been really eye-opening, and there has to be an endpoint. Besides, if we start naming women still living, we'd be sure to leave out some because we just wouldn't know about them."

"Lois has a point," Nancy said. "Let's have Beth research Margaret Amadavi and then see what we need to do to finish the project."

"I agree," Beth added. "If all our efforts are to have any impact in the work of the church today, we have to share our findings and all the ways we think it's possible to continue to honor our long-held Quaker testimonies. I know we've been so disappointed in some of the Yearly Meetings these past few years. Remember that time a pastor's wife stood up during the Spring Body of Representatives meeting and shouted that she would never accept anyone from another religion sharing a display of their work during the annual sessions? She was so angry, and no one disputed what she was saying. Or remember when someone contacted FCNL and told them our Yearly Meeting was not one of their supporters?" Beth added.

"Let's focus on the future and stay away from what's happened in the past," Sylvia implored.

"So what are we going to do with all this research we've accumulated?" Lois asked. "We had a purpose when we started this project over a year ago. We need a plan if we want to make sure we haven't wasted our time doing all this work!"

"Sylvia and I have been talking about this, and we have an idea we want to throw out to see what you all think," Beth said, pausing to look at Sylvia.

"I'm game," Nancy said.

"You haven't even heard it yet," came Lois's quick response.

"Have any of you been to one of the retreats they occasionally have out at Prairie Woods?" Sylvia asked.

"My high school youth group used to have a weekend retreat there every year," Nancy said. "But that was a long time ago! I didn't know the retreat center was even still open."

"It is, and their weekends are all booked, but they have openings during the week. We thought it might be fun to spend a few days in the middle of some week and see if we can create some type of document out of our notes—a pamphlet, or maybe even a small booklet if we have enough material. Something we can then share with other Friends Meetings, and especially the USFW groups," Beth finished.

"I think it's a great idea!" Nancy said. "Do you have some dates that might work?"

"Wait—what about your parents, Sylvia? Can you get away for that long?" Lois asked.

"Actually, I've already talked to my brother to see if he and his wife might be able to come and spend a few days with the folks since they're both retired now. I told them about our project, and they were both excited about it and said they'd be happy to help out. And we need to make some family decisions about Dad's care anyway, so hopefully we can do that while they're here."

"Great! Are you on board, Lois? Can you give up a couple of nights with Henry to be with us ladies?" Beth asked with a laugh.

"Of course! I didn't do all this work to quit now!"

"The retreat center has openings in the middle of June. That lets us meet in May to learn about Margaret Amadavi and then get our notes together for a retreat in June. We thought that would be a great time since hopefully there will be enough nice days for walks in the woods between our writing sessions. Can you both check your calendars right now and see if June fifteenth, sixteenth, and seventeenth are open? That's a Tuesday, Wednesday, Thursday," Sylvia finished, looking at Lois and Nancy.

As the dates were confirmed and plans were made, there was an air of excitement at the prospect of actually making a difference in helping Friends Meetings "be the church" after learning all the ways Quaker women had influenced society in the past—and were continuing to do so.

CHAPTER 39

1998

SO MANY QUESTIONS

BETH

As soon as Tyler and Kristy were both settled in for his junior year and her freshman year in college, Beth knew she wanted to use some of her free time to do more scholarly reading in the area of theology. Those long-ago questions about whether God actually existed that had so plagued her and many of her friends in their early teens continued to enter her mind, especially now that her kids were out of the house and their activities didn't require so much of her time.

What had sparked this new interest was a recent lunch date she had enjoyed with one of the few Quaker women pastors in their Yearly Meeting. Beth knew this young pastor, Lisa, was someone she wanted to get to know better after hearing her speak out against including homosexuality in the list of sins in the Yearly Meeting Book of Discipline. Lisa was so fervent and so willing to take a stand on the issue that Beth couldn't help but admire her.

When Beth had decided to invite Lisa to join her for lunch during their Yearly Meeting sessions that August, little did she know what a journey she would be embarking on in her quest to answer some of those nagging theological questions. It was Lisa's first query to her that got the ball rolling: Did Beth really believe it was Jesus's blood that would save people from their sins?

When Beth responded that they'd been singing "There's Power in the Blood" and "Whiter Than Snow" in worship for years, Lisa suggested she read a book by a more progressive author, feeling confident Beth would find a new answer to the question of Jesus's death and the shedding of blood for sins.

For so many years, I was so sure I had all the answers to every-thing there was to know about God: salvation, heaven, hell, scripture, Beth mused. *I rarely questioned anything in scripture and simply believed everything I was taught during all those years of Sunday School classes, including the ones I taught in my thirties and forties. And now I'm not even sure what I actually believe! Every time I read yet another book about progressive Christianity, it makes so much sense to me,* Beth thought as once again she considered the list of questions she still pondered about her beliefs.

The first and main question she wanted to answer was exactly what it meant to say you were a Christian. Was it believing the things she had been taught in Sunday School and in all those sermons she had tried to pay attention to? Or was it something totally different? It had taken time, but every day Beth was more and more convinced that being a Christian had to include the actions Jesus highlighted in his teachings: feeding the poor, caring for the sick and imprisoned, fighting against oppression and injustices, and taking care of the environment.

Another of the questions Beth now struggled with was how to read scripture. Was a person supposed to believe every word written and take all the events in scripture literally? The more Beth read about the history and times when the authors of the books of the Bible were writing about their experiences with God, including the years of passing down oral stories before they were ever recorded, it became clear to her that there were big problems in taking the Bible literally rather than figuratively. When she read about the importance of remembering that the historical Jesus was a Jew, she realized that, rather than worshipping the man Jesus was, being a twenty-first-century Christian required believers to follow his teachings from passages like Matthew's Sermon on the Mount as important guidelines for living.

Beth was also beginning to understand that when she followed those teachings, they could lead to healing and wholeness, even providing mystical connections with a loving Spirit God. Beth liked to think of those experiences when she felt so close to the reality of God's Spirit as "thin places." Sometimes she experienced them in worship, but even more often she felt them when she was in nature and absorbing the magnitude of God's marvelous creations.

And what about people who lived in other countries and worshipped other gods? She had been taught that unless a person was a Christian, they had no hope of eternal life. Was that really why people should give up their lives to be a missionary in a foreign country? To save people? It made no sense, especially when she thought of her cruise to several Asian countries and her visits to both Buddhist and Hindu temples. She had experienced the way the non-Christian worshippers were connecting with the divine in their own ways, and there was little doubt in her mind that their connection to the God of Spirit was just as authentic as hers was in Christianity. And then there was the Indiginous American approach to the Divine. Their ways of understanding God certainly involved approaches that would be condemned by some evangelical Christians. The whole idea of dualism—I'm saved, you're not; I'm going to heaven, you're not—was never Jesus's message.

One of the biggest questions Beth had been challenged by was the role of gays and lesbians in the church. So many Quaker Meetings were adamant that you could love the sinner but hate the sin. But how was that possible? If you hated the sin, then you were certainly judging the person to be a sinner—another of Jesus's admonitions to avoid. There were those few verses that certainly called homosexuality a sin. What was a person supposed to do with that? Reading books by Christian writers who had battled their same-sex attractions and even attempted to end their lives because of the impossibility of living in a celibate or even heterosexual world when they were living a lie only made Beth more certain that homosexuality wasn't a sin. But she wanted to know what those ancient words originally written in other languages really referred to when centuries later they were translated to mean homosexuality.

Once again, a thorough study of the Bible's history, the ways scriptures had been copied and changed, and the late interpretation of ancient Greek and Latin to add the word "homosexual" to the Bible helped Beth answer this question. Down through the years, the questionable meanings of some of the ancient words were often debated, and the English word "homosexuality" was deemed correct in the eyes of the male church leaders. But Beth had become convinced that to be a follower of Jesus's teachings had to include accepting all who might come through their meeting house doors—evangelical believers and questioning agnostics; women and men as equal in God's sight; lesbian, gay, bisexual, transgendered, queer believers; all those of other nationalities; and those of all races, societal classes, and abilities. All were to be accepted as the creation of a loving God.

Another area that didn't seem to be a concern for a lot of twenty-first-century Christians was caring for the earth. Why was this even an issue? She could not, as some professed, believe there was no need to care about the earth because Jesus would soon be coming back to take all the Christians to heaven. Beth totally disagreed with that idea, especially since Jesus spent his entire short life advocating for "heaven on earth" with radical inclusion and fighting against the injustices of the Roman occupation and the synagogue leaders.

But the last question she had struggled with had probably been the one that had made the biggest change in Beth's religious life: the relationship between God and Jesus. She had read several scholarly works on the history of the times Jesus walked the earth and had been astonished to learn that it was decades after His death when church leaders changed the purpose of Jesus's life.

In reality, Jesus' life's work focused on fighting against the Roman domination of the common villagers with the goal of overthrowing the government to create a new way of living for all. If that were true, it meant Jesus had simply been killed for daring to stand up to those in authority. After thorough research and study, many theologians now agreed that it wasn't until several centuries later that the purpose of Jesus's life and death somehow became a way for God to save the lives of sinners.

What kind of God would this be, a divine father requiring the death of a divine son because humans are sinful? Beth would never accept this idea of atonement theology—that a loving God would require a supposed son's death as a sacrifice. What parent would ever do that to a child? Especially an all-powerful deity?

One of the most important things Beth now understood was the necessity of asking questions about one's beliefs. When she had been able to set aside some of those teachings from her childhood, she felt she was now free to live a life of action to help create that "heaven on earth" that Jesus taught and strove to do in his life.

It seemed to Beth that to bear the label of being a Progressive Christian, she needed to be vigilant with both her words and her actions. Jesus never minced words when he saw injustice, particularly with the faith leaders of his day. But he was also entirely compassionate when it came to the most vulnerable. *I don't think we can do anything less if our foremost desire is to follow Jesus's teachings,* she thought.

I've read almost all of progressive author John Shelby Spong's books, and I have to agree with him that if God is the source of all life, then the only way to worship God is to live so fully it makes God visible to others; and if God is the source of love, then the only way to worship God is to love wastefully; and we must always strive to be all we can be to make life better for others—that is the very best way to worship God.

Even the Old Testament prophet, Micah, had written one of Beth's go-to verses she had posted on her refrigerator: "And what doth God require of thee but to do justly, and to love mercy, and to walk humbly with thy God."

I'll always have questions, Beth mused, knowing her ideas and understandings would continue to evolve during her lifetime, but there would always be that mystery of God to explore; a God who was not another male human, but a spirit that had to be worshipped as Jesus told the Samaritan woman at the well: They that worship God must worship him in Spirit and in truth.

CHAPTER 40

1968-PRESENT
MARGARET AMADAVI
KENYA, AFRICA

E-mail message from Beth to Lois, Sylvia, and Nancy:

Subject: Margaret Amadavi

Hey, friends! I am so excited to share the latest on Margaret Amadavi and the important work she's doing in Kenya. Since it's a little hard to talk back and forth with someone in Africa, I decided I would present her work in an interview format. I wrote several questions for her input, and she was gracious enough to respond in detail, giving great insights into her work as an educator at Friends Theological College (FTC) and her life growing up in a large Quaker Kenyan family. Happy reading!

Please tell me a little about your years growing up in Kenya—your family, the Friends Meeting you attended—anything that helped you become the woman you are today.

I was born in a Quaker family of ten, five boys and five girls. I'm number nine and the youngest daughter. Growing up in a large family of not only ten siblings but also with six stepsiblings and many other extended family members, life was both a struggle, but also fun. Fun because I was never lonely, and a struggle because it was survival of the fittest when it came to feeding and sleeping.

The greatest joy was when we went to Sunday school where we were famous because of our family choir. My mum tells me that I was a very funny youngest choir conductor in our family and that I was loved by many. I loved singing, though my older siblings were always cross with me for trying to out-sing everyone else (being loudest in the group).

The church services were long but at the same time fun. I learned many Bible stories that became a strong foundation for my theological studies later in life. Quakers then were more passionate about the gospel of Jesus than what I see in the current Friends churches. Hymns that were sung in the church were rich with theological content that focused on glorifying God. My mother at 92+ often remarks that if Jesus had returned in those days, we would all be in heaven with him now. But she also notices that today's worship is fake, utilitarian, and mechanical in most cases. I agree with her that church worship today is utilitarian in nature, especially the fact that most charismatic churches preach prosperity gospels, and gospel music is but business in my country. They contain very low percentages of theological content. This has affected even Quaker worshippers.

Please tell me about your education and how you chose your career as an educator. What was hard about getting to be a teacher? Did you always want to teach?

I went to a Quaker school at primary (elementary) level. But I studied in Catholic schools for both my secondary school certificate and Advanced Level Certificate of Secondary School Education (KCSC).

Thereafter I started to do odd jobs for survival. I met my boyfriend after staying at home for two years after high school. Due to his father's involvement in politics being considered anti-government, the government at that time threatened to punish him severely, so he fled the country and arranged for some of his older children, including my boyfriend, to travel to the United Kingdom and America as students.

When my boyfriend returned for a visit in Kenya, we connected, and he left without knowing I became pregnant. I never found a way to let him know I was pregnant with his baby, and when he finally returned, the boy was two years old, and he refused to believe the child was his. So being proud as I was, I didn't want to beg him, and I worked hard doing some odd jobs to raise my son. My parents have been very supportive, but paying his tuition was an uphill task, and so his schooling has taken a little bit longer than usual. I thank God he is writing his college final exam in Textile Fashion and Design this February.

It's been a tough journey, but God's grace has been sufficient all through. I tried two more relationships and when they didn't work, I stopped trying and just focused on my education, raising my boy, and ministry. I have been single since then, dedicating my life to serving God in both the church and Friends Theological ministry.

What have been some of your challenges in pursuing higher degrees since you've told me you're now working on your PhD?

After being at home for over ten years, I went to college at Friends Theological College (FTC) from 2000 to 2003 to study for a diploma in Theology. Going to FTC was the beginning of my breakthrough in life. There I worked with the principals of FTC, Patrick Nugent and Mary Kay, homeschooling their two daughters so they could focus on administering their duties as principals at the college.

I graduated with a degree in Development Studies, majoring in Organizational Development, and I continued teaching development courses at FTC for over eleven years where I also served as chaplain. Thereafter, I enrolled at Kenya Highlands Bible College, now Kenya Highlands Evangelical University, for my bachelor's degree. During this time I was offered the chaplaincy services at Kaimosi Boys High School for two years. Ministering to almost a thousand boys was both challenging and exciting. I loved playing the role of mother to orphaned boys. For two years I never experienced rude behaviour from any of the boys! We built a very good rapport and even their performance improved. And the principal and teachers were also all very loving and cooperative. I was able to complete my undergraduate studies at Kenya Highlands in Christian Education, which I finished in 2017.

I then took a six-month sabbatical leave to visit the U.S. But my plans came to a halt when I was deported upon my return to Houston from Mexico where I had joined my cousin and her friend on a one-week holiday at Cancun Beach. I was sent home with nothing but a small bag of beach clothes and 70 dollars. With a 3,000-dollar bank loan and my son's college tuition to pay, and also no job, it seemed like my life had come to an abrupt end. To make matters worse, my visa had been canceled and all my clothes were back in the U.S. My dreams of studying and becoming the first black woman principal of FTC now seemed unthinkable. My world became bleak, and I didn't want to face my family and friends back home. I couldn't eat or sleep for months.

How I survived the ordeal, only God knows. That's why I can now confidently share the sentiments from somebody who said, "I'm not waiting for proof that God exists, because I'm proof that God exists." When God is not finished with you, not even the mightiest in the universe can destroy you. I remembered a verse in Joshua 1:5 which reads, "Be strong and courageous . . . for nothing shall stand against you all the days of your life."

And as I started reflecting on those promises, I decided to call my mother's sister and share my dilemmas. She encouraged me not to give up, and after a few days, I received a call from my very aunt letting me know I had been invited by Kamusinga Yearly Meeting to be their main speaker during their United Society of Friends Women's annual conference. I was like, are you out of your mind?! If I'm this broken, how will I ever speak to people? And what message will I deliver to them? Believe you me, that theme was for me more than it was for those people I was to minister to. It read, "In this world, you will face many troubles, but take heart, I have overcome the world!" The text was from John 16:33, but I shared the entire chapter. This chapter spoke to my condition and people were very blessed throughout the session. I was so full of the Holy Spirit that sometimes it felt like it was not me speaking. I spoke to both men and women and I blended my testimony with the message of the day.

After the conference I returned to FTC with renewed Spirit to face my colleagues and students as an adjunct professor. God had touched a kind-hearted lady mama, Georgia Fuller, who was willing to pay my tuition to graduate school. This was a welcome move for I needed something to take my mind off my deportation. It was like history repeating itself, for God did it again by intervening in my life at just the right time. Previously, kind-hearted people like Karen Nash Bauer, Sandy Davis, Jody Richmond, Patricia Downs Shrock, and

Mary Kay Rehard had been instrumental in shaping my early ministry and education life. As missionaries in Kenya, these good people contributed a lot to what I am today. I will forever be grateful to each one of them in a special way. As I write now, I'm in my second year of studying for my PhD.

What is your current work at FTC?

I started teaching at FTC in August 2017. I began teaching introductory courses before I specialized in the area of Development Studies, which focus on the role of the church's social responsibility. This was covered in units titled Theology of Development and Community Based Development (CBD). I also teach Administration and Management, Christian Education, and Christian Worship.

I also joined the FTC students on an outreach ministry through creative singing, scriptural teaching, art, and talent. "Friends Witness Team" was the name given to this group of students I was in charge of. This team's role was to reach out to young people with the gospel message in a unique manner as well as recruit students for FTC. Young people embraced Christian faith and practice, as the approach was appealing to them. One of the fruits of this ministry was an increase in enrollment at FTC.

Becoming an Academic Dean

During the era of FTC Director Dr. Robert J. Wafula, I was appointed Dean of Academics in 2014, the post I held until 2018, when I resigned to enroll for a PhD in the United States. I traveled to the US at the end of October 2018 and started the admissions process for Education Leadership Management at Houston Baptist University. But I had to travel back to Kenya to apply for the student visa and renew my travel visa, which was due to expire in three weeks. And that was when returning from Mexico and being detained at the security check in Houston I was given the choice to be taken to a detention camp or be deported! I was so afraid of detention camp that I chose the latter. It was the most traumatizing experience of my life, but by the grace of God I survived the ordeal.

Current Work

I'm currently studying for my PhD in Development Studies at St. Paul's University Limuru in Kenya. Teaching Community and Theology of Development courses gave an opportunity to partner with the Friends Bringing Hope team led by Karen Nash Bauer and her family from the USA, along with the Kaimosi Rural Service Programme team in their mission to build houses for the poor widows and orphans.

I usually join Karen and the RSP team and have CBD and TOD students join the two teams to offer free labour in the process of creating the mud and using it to mud the walls of the houses. In this process the students learn lessons about the practical aspects of helping others. That's the power of transferring the theories they learn in class to real-life situations. They also learn about Christian service as an expression of worshiping God.

And finally, what challenges are still present for Quakers in Kenya that you are trying to address? Patriarchy? Polygamy? AIDS? Anything that you see as areas where you are striving to make a difference. What are your future goals that will help the Kenyan Society of Friends be better able to do the work needed to make life better for Kenyans, especially the poor, the widows, the orphans?

There are many challenges in the Quaker church today. First, there are issues with church management structures, which have for a long time been the source of conflicts between the lay leaders (presiding clerks) and the trained pastors. The problem arises with the question: Who is better placed to lead the church? Church structures lack clear provisions for remunerating trained ministers, causing pastors to live in poverty and give substandard pastoral services, while trying to find other sources of income to supplement the handouts from their workstations.

Secondly, there is a lack of contextual theology that would address the many sociocultural and economic issues of the church.

Third, there are many challenges when looking at modernization of the church, which demands use of technology; this is especially a big challenge among Quakers in the rural areas.

Fourth, there are external forces from other church denominations that threaten to dilute Quaker values through psychological appeals such as healing miracles and prosperity gospel. This is a competition that lures Quakers to abandon their original values and try to adjust to these pulling forces. Gospel healing miracles are particularly appealing to many Quakers during this time of AIDS, increased blood pressure, and cancer.

Fifth, gender disparities in Quaker church leadership pose many challenges. Although women make up the majority of members in the African Quaker church, men dominate in leadership and decision-making, even those decisions that have a direct impact on women. This has been an impediment for Quaker women to participate meaningfully in the growth of the Quaker church. A large number of women have resigned themselves to simply accepting the status quo and then joining together to oppress their fellow women. For example, a young woman is widowed, and the senior women advise her not to get married or love another man but to commit her life to Christ. On the other hand, an older man is widowed, and the same women join hand-in-hand to find a suitable woman for him. This is just one example of some of the women hindering those of us seeking to be "the church," but there are many. Women in the African churches are subjected to more of the traditional rituals, such as funeral preparation, than men. When it comes to land, business, or property ownership, it is ten times harder for women than men to secure them.

And finally, the issue of polygamy is still very rife in the African Quaker Church. Even worse is infidelity among some church leaders. One young woman student of the Bible shared with me that a very powerful church leader made sexual advances on her when she went to ask for help from him. The good thing, though, was that even though the young woman was desperate, she didn't submit to his selfish desires. Other women have said that they were forced to marry a man in order for them to qualify as ministers.

What I'm Doing to Make a Difference

I'm rethinking my PhD research topic, which earlier was titled "Effects of Financial Insecurity Among Retirees, Focusing on Teachers," and changing it to "Deconstruction and Reconstruction of Contextual Theology in the African Quaker Church." I'm looking for more partners to help finance my research. This I believe will contribute to addressing most of the challenges mentioned above.

I am using my teaching platform to educate both male and female students on the importance of an engendered approach to leadership and development. I'm grateful that FTC gives equal opportunities to students when it comes to work study. Those from families where all household chores belong to women learn to appreciate that cleaning the kitchen and washing utensils doesn't make them less of men than they already are.

I counsel many women students who feel discriminated against by using my own example. I encourage them to read the constitution of Kenya about the rights of women so they can use it against men with selfish intentions.

Last year, for example, I took in a Samburu lady with her two daughters and a nephew who had been suspended from the church. Although I didn't have anything to offer in terms of money and material things, I offered her a family and the love of Christ. My mother and siblings became her family, and from my home she was able to find her footing, a church to serve, and a home of her own. Today I bumped into her when travelling from Nairobi and she shared with me good news that both her daughters who are in different grades secured position 1 in their new boarding school. That's what I call God's blessings and a living testimony!

My dream has been to establish an assisted living facility to help the most vulnerable senior citizens just to get food and have a place to sleep. When we do house-to-house visitations, many times we encounter the elderly living in appalling conditions. In the whole of my county, there's not one facility to care for the seniors. Kenyan women have always been on the forefront to help. We have taken clothes to the churches so they may be taken to places like Turkana where living is difficult. Currently I'm looking for partners to help me support the prison ministry around Kakamega, where one of the FTC graduates is serving as chaplain. This will help children whose parents are in prison. There are children born and staying with their mothers in prison or living with relatives who can't take them to school because they are poor. Some of these children are on the streets and so there's much we can do as women, but resources are scarce.

There is much work to be done to "be the church" in Kenya, and with God's help, I will continue to do all I can to see that it happens.

CHAPTER 41

MAY, PRESENT DAY
THE CLUB—BEN'S BURGERS

"I'm so glad you all decided our last monthly gathering could be here to support Ben and his business," Beth said warmly as the four were gathering on the patio outside their favorite burger joint. "I'm sure Ben is happy to have our business since he seemed pretty excited to see us again."

"Seriously, Beth," Lois admonished, "did you really think any of us would object after months of eating mostly nutritious brunch foods?!"

"No," Beth admitted, "but I do think we were trying to uphold the Quaker testimonies of simplicity and community by just sharing our homes with each other rather than spending money on foods that we love but aren't always nutritious!"

"And I have really missed Ben's onion strings," Sylvia admitted.

"And I've missed his famous cherry pie—and that's definitely not low calorie, but oh so good!" Nancy added.

"So I presume you got–and read through–all the interview materials I was able to acquire from Margaret Amadavi?"

"Oh my word!" Sylvia said. "What a woman! And what a life she's lived so far."

"She has had so many different educational experiences that I had trouble keeping track of all of them," Lois said, laughing. "I know how hard being a teacher is here in the U.S., but I had no idea Kenya would be such a misogynist society! I thought Kenya was one of the more progressive countries in Africa, but between what Karen Bauer shared, and now Margaret's experiences, I think I really didn't have nearly as many things to complain about in my schools."

"And then to be deported with only a few beach clothes and seventy dollars!" Sylvia added. "The big cities like Nairobi are definitely more modern, but when I was there with the Bauer's work team, I was shocked at the rural areas. It was almost like stepping back to the 1800s! And that's what makes it all the more impressive that Margaret has continued to persevere with the pursuit of her PhD, and the way she aspires to work to make things better for the women, the elderly, and the poor in the Quaker churches."

"Yes, she really is a wonderful current Quaker woman who is doing so many things to 'be the church.' But once again, ladies, what are we to take from Margaret's work to make a difference for our Friends meetings today?" came Lois' usual question. "We certainly don't have much in common with the Kenyan Quaker meetings."

"And we knew you'd ask!" all three women said almost simultaneously, laughing at their friend who always wanted to cut to the chase and proceed with the action steps.

"That's what I've been pondering ever since I read Margaret's life story," Beth said with a frown. "It seems the rural Kenyan society doesn't do much for women, but it's not like we haven't focused on equality with a lot of our ancestral Quakers."

"One thing the African Quakers do well," Sylvia remembered, "is knowing the importance of community. While our work team was there, a wife of one of the night guards was in the hospital and we went to see her. She was diabetic and it was fairly obvious that her life was in peril. And, I have to tell you, if any of us were taken to a hospital like that one in Kaimosi, we might never heal, either. And, sadly, a few days later the woman died. It was then that I got to experience a Kenyan Quaker funeral."

"What was it like?" Nancy asked.

"First, it's a time of families and loved ones gathering together. It's very expensive for the family of the deceased because they are expected to feed family and visitors whenever they arrive–and often stay for many days. And then there's the purchase of a casket, and those are on display and sold outside on the ground right along the roads."

"So what was the funeral like?" Beth wanted to know.

"Stan Bauer was the only one who went the day of the actual funeral service because we were on a schedule for working with the widows' groups, but the night before we all went to the woman's house. Stan had bought a forty- or fifty-pound bag of rice to take to the family, and when we got there, the woman's body was laid in an open casket outside the house. There was a long path that led to the casket, and there was a lot of family sitting on couches and chairs lining the dirt path down to the house. We all walked past the body, then sat down, and Stan and Karen visited with some of the family. It was the week-long event with extended family that made the biggest impression on me!"

"So how does that fit with any of our Meetings?" Lois asked. "There's nothing that comes close to what you experienced in Kenya, Sylvia."

"No, but the way the Friends meeting members in the community gathered around to support the family says a lot about the Quaker testimony of community. What are we lacking in our own Meeting communities?" Nancy asked.

"That's a great question," Beth added, "and remember how Margaret invited the woman and her children to come and live with her huge family when the woman just needed some help? How many of us would have done that? So now I'm wondering what we can do to support the services in our communities that help the homeless and the families without enough food? And it just occurred to me that maybe we could be involved in the free lunch they serve down at the community center every day. My friend says her church supplies the food for one meal a month and members sign up to bring casseroles or fruit, cookies, bread and butter, etc. to their church the Sunday before their day to supply the meal, and then volunteers take it to the center and make the final preparations for everything there. What if we asked our Meeting to consider providing one of those meals one day a month? And if they don't need any more organizations to donate and prepare the food, maybe we can just do a fundraiser for the meals since I'm sure they have extra expenses like providing drinks, clean-up work–whatever they need help with."

"It's a good start!" Sylvia said. "Can you get the contact information from your friend and see what our options are?"

"Sure. And . . ."

"Oh boy! Here we go again!" Lois jumped in.

Giving Lois a disapproving look, Beth continued. "That's just one thing we might try. But now I'm wondering what we are doing in our own Meeting to encourage community. We meet on Sundays for worship, and that's about it!"

"But we're all really busy, Beth!" Lois objected.

"Then what if we just do some small gatherings, maybe once every two months or so, where we have a movie night, or a cookout at a city park, or maybe even a mystery supper, or some other Sunday evening gathering just to offer a time to bring in Friends and not have it be anything to do with religion!"

"I think it's worth exploring," Sylvia said. "I remember my mom talking about some of the things the meeting used to do when she and Dad were younger."

"Times have changed!" came Lois' stubborn lack of interest.

"What if Justin came back to live here, and he wanted to see all of his old Meeting Friends who are still here attending our meeting? Would he come to worship on Sunday?"

"Probably not!"

"But would he come if we were having a hot dog roast and games at the park?"

"He might. Okay, I get your point," Lois relented. "I'm sorry. I guess I'm just getting old, and my energy level isn't what it used to be. But if it would help our younger families feel more a part of the community, then it's worth a try."

"And," Nancy said excitedly, "maybe we could get some of the others interested in all these things we've been doing this past year to be the church."

"Thanks, you guys!" Beth said with a deep sigh. "I was afraid to even suggest these things, but then I thought–if Margaret Amadavi could do all the work in her country to make a little bit of heaven on earth, what are we waiting for?"

As the four friends began sketching out ideas for ways to build their community, there was a feeling that the original Quaker testimonies were still important and worth their focus.

Chapter 42

June, Present Day
The Club Retreat at
Prairie Woods

Sylvia had asked Beth if she wanted to go to Prairie Woods with her ahead of time to get things set up in the meeting room where they would have their group discussions. Excited at the prospect of culminating this year-long project, Beth said she'd be happy to go early with Sylvia. Since they lived within a few miles of each other, they had agreed to make the plans for meals and do the general pre-retreat work for the group.

The two women had been meeting once a week in person, not to mention all the emails and text messages that had flown back and forth between the two of them. They had joked that it reminded them a little of their days as camp directors at Twin Pines all those years ago.

Sylvia was happy with her deepening relationship with Beth, especially since her parents were now in an assisted living retirement center. Ruth had been reluctant to leave the farm she had so lovingly cared for all her married life, from the large garden to the many colorful flower beds and yard decorations she had created. But she also knew she could no longer care for her husband, who had sunk deeper into his dementia. When both of their children had issued the ultimatum that they make the move, Sylvia knew her mother had been secretly relieved.

"Are you sure we have everything we need?" Sylvia asked as they unloaded their supplies at the retreat center.

"Will you quit worrying?" Beth teased. "You do remember all those times you were responsible for scheduling the senator's meetings and trips, don't you? Lois and Nancy know what food they're supposed to bring, you and I planned the topics for discussion and ideas for sharing our research, and all that's left is deciding who's sleeping where!"

"Well," Sylvia said hesitantly, "it would be nice if you and I could share one of the two private rooms, and Nancy and Lois the other. One of the rooms has a bunk bed, and the other one has two twin beds. I think we should be the ones to take the bunk beds. More than once I've heard Lois complain about the pain in her arthritic knees."

"Works for me—I claim the top bunk!" Beth declared.

As soon as they had unloaded all their supplies, made up their beds, and got a few snacks and drinks set out in the meeting room, first Lois and then Nancy arrived.

"Perfect timing!" Sylvia said. "We just finished getting everything ready."

"Nice work, ladies! I see you've got everything we might need for good brain power! So where do we start?" Lois asked, always adamant about not wasting time.

As soon as they were settled at the large round table, Sylvia got the retreat started. "First, I wanted to share this quotation by Madeleine L'Engle that I came across the other day. I think it will help us stay focused on our purpose: 'We draw people to Christ not by loudly discrediting what they believe, by telling them how wrong they are and how right we are, but by showing them a light that is so lovely that they want with all their hearts to know the source of it.'"

"That's the perfect way to begin," Nancy said. "I know we want to share what we've learned from these amazing Quaker women and the actions we need to take to 'be the church' today, but we have to do it in a loving way if it is to have any chance of making an impact on a hurting world."

"Exactly," Beth agreed. "And that will be the challenge. So let's start by making a list of all of the Quaker women we talked about and how their lives and work can still motivate our local meetings today."

Soon the women all had their notes out as Lois began writing all their ideas on the big flip chart she had kept when her teaching career was finished. The more they each shared, the more their excitement grew as they began to believe their work might truly challenge the Society of Friends to focus on actions that embodied Jesus's teachings of bringing "heaven on earth" for all who were suffering.

"So now we have lots of lists and lots of ideas. How do we present them to other Meetings in our Yearly Meeting and maybe even beyond to Friends' Meetings in the United States and even further to Friends in other countries?" Sylvia asked.

"I say we table this discussion for today and go for a walk," Beth suggested. "When we were doing a little exploring before you other two arrived, Sylvia and I found a really cool trail that leads to a small waterfall. My brain has had about all the thinking it can handle for one day!"

After the hike and a meal of sandwiches and chips, the women moved to the screened porch to enjoy the cooler evening watching the wildlife that came into the yard. Catching up on their lives since their last club meeting kept the conversation going well past sunset.

Once they were settled in their rooms, Beth and Sylvia began talking about how things had gone that afternoon and what they wanted to accomplish the next day—the only full day they would be at the retreat center. It wasn't long before they both decided they had better get some sleep if they wanted to be in good shape for the big day ahead.

"Night, Beth," Sylvia said sleepily, "Thanks for all your work today. I love you!"

"You, too," Beth said after a pause, and then all was silent but for the frogs and crickets making music outside in the summer night.

• • •

The morning sun shone brightly through their rooms' curtainless windows, waking Beth naturally with no need for an alarm. She stretched, surprised she had slept so well on the somewhat hard bunk bed. As she fully awakened, Sylvia's words last night echoed in her mind. Surely she had just meant "I love you" like good friends love each other. Or had she meant more than that?

She didn't have time to ruminate on it for long, though. Breakfast for four wouldn't get made by itself! When she got out to the communal area, she found Nancy was in the small kitchen getting a big pot of coffee started.

"Thanks for getting that started, Nancy. I'll get breakfast ready. I'm sure the others will be up soon—I don't know how anyone can sleep through that bright morning light!"

229

Sylvia joined them soon after, and when the food was ready and they were all sipping their coffee, they began to wonder why Lois wasn't up yet.

"I'll go check on her," Beth volunteered.

As she got close to Lois and Nancy's room, she could hear Lois talking.

"I'm sorry, honey," Lois said. "I forgot all about our plans for tonight. I should have looked at my calendar when you asked me if I wanted to go to the baseball game. It was so long ago, and the retreat was somewhere in the back of my mind. I promise I'll make it up to you!"

Beth left without knocking on the door, returning to the kitchen to fill the others in on the conversation she had just overheard. "Seems like Lois and Henry are still an item, even though she hardly said anything last night when we asked her about their romance!"

"We have one more night we can grill her for details," Nancy said with a laugh, "but we'd better pretend you didn't hear her conversation, Beth."

Their work continued throughout the day, and once they had gathered and organized all their information, the discussion centered on how to disseminate their findings.

"I think we should put everything in a booklet, including some photos of the various women," Sylvia suggested.

"And then what?" Nancy asked. "We would have to find a publisher and figure out how to market it."

"I've been thinking about this," Lois said, "and when I mentioned it to Henry, he said he had a friend in Prairie View with a print shop who would probably be willing to make something up for us for a small fee."

All three grinned at Lois, realizing she had just given them new information about her love interest.

"That sounds great, Lois," Sylvia said. "And we are all expecting a thorough update this evening on this relationship with Henry that you seem reluctant to share with us!"

It had been a long time since Lois had blushed such a deep scarlet color, but she just smiled and for once didn't say anything.

"Well, I think we should celebrate," Beth said. "We've accomplished everything we set out to do to get this little project to its final stage, and we even have a plan for printing, thanks to Lois's beau."

"I thought we might want to celebrate our hard work, so I brought a bottle of wine for our last evening," Nancy said.

"If only our Quaker ancestors could see us now," Sylvia joked, knowing how many of their grandparents were teetotalers, as was common among the older generations of Friends.

As they once again sat together enjoying the evening and sipping their wine, Beth was the first to prod Lois about her relationship with Henry.

"So, Lois, spill it! What's going on with you and Henry?"

Once again Lois seemed flustered as she reached into her pocket and took out her phone. Scanning through her photos, she found one of the two of them enjoying a cozy dinner in a restaurant, passing it around to show the others.

"Wow, he's really good looking. You both look pretty serious in this photo! When's the wedding?" Nancy asked, grinning.

"Well," Lois confessed, "we've actually been discussing our futures, and for now we're happy just living across the street from each other and enjoying each other's company."

"But wouldn't you want to spend every day with each other?" Nancy asked, thinking about her many years living and working with Allan.

"Maybe, but we've both lived alone long enough that we would need to spend a lot more time with each other to know if it might work to be together all the time. We do have an Alaskan cruise planned for this August, so that will probably be a learning experience for both of us!"

"Lois, this is way more serious than you've ever let on to us, your very best friends and working partners!" Sylvia admonished, smiling. "I know I would be totally excited if I had someone I was falling in love with. I would be jumping at the chance for a life together with someone I loved—maybe even thinking about marriage."

Beth couldn't help but notice the look of longing on Sylvia's face as she shared her feelings—and the way she had glanced at Beth as she shared them.

"Time will tell," Lois said, shrugging her shoulders. "Which reminds me, it's time for me to go inside and give Henry a call and apologize once again for canceling our date tonight." She filled the others in on missing the ballgame, and no one was willing to admit they already knew all about it.

"I'm going to call it a night too. Wine always makes me sleepy," Nancy said with a yawn.

Then Sylvia and Beth were alone on the porch, listening to the sounds of nighttime in the woods. For the first time, Beth felt awkward sitting alone next to Sylvia. She knew she had to ask her friend about the things she had shared both the night before and in their conversations with Lois.

When she finally worked up the nerve, she said, "Can I ask you a question?"

"Sure, you can ask me anything! I hope you know that."

"Well . . . when we were talking about Lois and Henry, you told us you would like to be sharing life with someone you were in love with, too. Do you really feel that way?"

Sylvia took a deep breath before answering. "Yes, I really would. Even though I've been in love before—you know about my relationship with Jane—I've never been married. Of course, for a long time same-sex marriage wasn't possible. Now I often wonder how it would feel to be with the person I loved each day, sharing our lives, going to bed together each night, and rehashing the events of our days."

"That makes sense," Beth said. "There are times when I feel the same way. Bob's been gone for so long now that sometimes I can hardly remember what it was like to have someone to share my life with, especially now that the kids have families of their own." She paused before continuing. "So, do you ever try those online dating sites? I think they have those for same-sex couples."

"I've thought about it, but I have always believed if it were meant to be, I would find the woman I would want to share my life with. And then, marriage could be a part of our conversation," Sylvia said.

The air between the two women felt electric, giving Beth the courage to ask the question she had been pondering for months. "And have you ever found that person since you were with Jane?"

"I think I may have," Sylvia said slowly, "but it has to be a two-way street, and I'm not sure you feel the same way I do."

Beth felt frozen, and when she didn't respond, Sylvia finally added, "And it's okay if you don't feel the same way. I just hope this won't hurt our friendship."

Again, silence permeated the space between them. Finally Beth found her voice.

"I'm sorry. I just don't know what to say. This is such a totally new experience for me. I know I feel something for you that's different from what I had with Bob, but I'm not sure it's beyond friendship."

"That's okay," Sylvia said. "I wasn't sure how you would respond to the things I've been sharing with you, and I think you have to have known from some of our times together this past year that I've felt this way about you for a long time. And really, ever since we were in high school I've felt this special connection with you. But it was evident that you were going to be with Bob, and I was happy for you."

"So do you think a person can be in love with both a man and a woman? You've only been with women," Beth said.

"I am certainly not an expert on love," Sylvia began, "but yes, I think our relationships begin with an emotional connection, and I think there is a spectrum that spans from strictly opposite-sex attractions to strictly same-sex attractions, and most of us are somewhere in between."

"That makes sense," Beth said after thinking about it for a minute. "I guess I have felt a little something special between us for a while now, but it never occurred to me that there was ever anything more than just friendship between us."

"What do you think now?" Sylvia asked.

"I honestly don't know," Beth admitted. "But now that you've shared your feelings so openly, I'm willing to explore the idea of becoming more than just a good friend."

"That's all I could have hoped for," Sylvia said with a sigh of relief. "I've wanted to admit my love for you for a really long time, but I was so afraid of how you would respond. I'm happy to let time determine where our relationship might go."

• • •

It had been a wonderful year of learning for each of the women.

"This just proves to me that reaching an age beyond retirement doesn't have to mean your life will no longer involve work that can make a difference for others," Nancy said the next morning as they were packing up after cleaning the kitchen and the rooms they had shared.

"Yes, I just figured when I retired from teaching I would spend all my time reading books. I had no idea I would get so into this project and find it so rewarding," Lois said.

"I bet you didn't figure you'd find another man to share your life with, either," Beth teased her.

"I can't wait to share some of these stories of amazing Quaker women with the twins," Nancy agreed. "And I've loved working with each of you. We've made a great team, and I hope we can find other ways to work together in the future!"

"We will," Sylvia said emphatically. "There are so many areas of need for us to explore and ways to learn how we can do a better job being the church. Systemic racism is alive and well in this country, the environment is in desperate need of attention, and exploring ways to make life better for others should give us plenty of areas where we can keep working."

Each woman's step was a bit lighter as they headed to their cars, their thoughts mingled with past accomplishments and future goals.

"Let's keep meeting each month and working on all those ideas we came up with to let God's light shine wherever there is darkness," Beth said, almost prayerfully.

"Exactly," Sylvia said, smiling at Beth.

"Why don't you all come over for dinner some evening," Lois called out with a glint in her eye. "I'll invite Henry to join us so you can all get to know him and quit asking me questions."

"Deal!" Nancy said. "Let's set a date now."

Beth and Sylvia had carpooled, and as Sylvia drove them home, Beth turned to her best friend–a woman who might become something more in the future.

"You know the one big idea I think I learned this past year?"

"What?"

"Being the church by the actions we do is what it really means to call ourselves Christians; following Jesus's teachings to bring a little bit of heaven on earth," Beth said. "I've had so many questions about what I should believe, when I should have been asking what I should be doing instead!"

"I think you've just summarized Jesus's teachings in a nutshell!" Sylvia said.

Beth watched the beauty of the countryside pass by her window with a secret smile. She was grateful to be part of an amazing group of friends who were committed to doing justly, loving mercy, and walking humbly with God, doing the work to be the church thanks to the lessons they had gleaned from the lives of the Quaker women they'd studied. Perhaps their work would someday be considered a model for future Quakers to help guide their work when following Jesus's teachings to love God and love their neighbors, creating heaven right here on earth.

Author's Note

First, a note of extreme gratitude for my daughter Alisha's many editing comments and helpful revisions. Everyone should have a professional editor in their family! She was so gracious to plow through my first (and subsequent) writings to come up with all the needed changes. She's been an absolutely invaluable editor (and loving daughter)!

And now for my own experiences which led to this novel. Growing up in an orthodox Friends Meeting in the Midwest with a variety of pastors over the years, many of the experiences the four women share in this book are my own experiences, especially through my time as a child and young adult. My Friends Meetings—and later, our Yearly Meeting—were focal points of our family, and we seldom missed the two Sunday services, Thursday evening Bible Studies, and annual revival meetings. During those years I thought I had all the answers to life's questions through the teachings I had absorbed in the two major meetings I had been a part of. It wasn't until my children were raised and on their own that I began to question and explore some of those early beliefs that became harder to accept.

Through the various writings of progressive theologians who have done massive amounts of research, especially on the historical aspects of scripture, my spiritual journey became one of questioning and seeking. I will forever be indebted to Bishop John Shelby Spong, Marcus Borg, Diana Butler Bass, Brian McClaren, Phyllis Tickle, and Quaker pastor, Phillip Gulley, for their insights into what it means to bear the label of "Christian" in 2021.

And please note—if you've wondered which woman's life represents mine, there isn't one. Each of the women's stories from the past contains bits and pieces of my story. But it's the underlying theme that is most important to me—that to "be the church" must involve more than sitting in a pew on Sunday and believing a never ending, unchanging set of doctrines. It must include the actions that correspond with Jesus's teachings, especially those found in the Sermon on the Mount in the book of Matthew.

My challenge is to continue to question, explore, and find ways to live out my faith.

ABOUT THE AUTHOR

Susan McCracken's heritage began on an Iowa farm with a family who could be found sitting in the Indianola Friends Meeting House for various worship services several times a week. In addition, there were summer camp sessions at Camp Quaker Heights, Quaker retreats, and many, many youth group meetings. After high school graduation, her career choice was education, and after five years in the classroom, marriage took her to Southeast Iowa where she spent twelve years farming with her husband and raising four children. Susan then returned to the classroom and eventually the principal's office to finish out her career. When their children were teenagers, their local Meeting was unable to secure a pastor and Susan became the interim pastor at Pleasant Plain Friends for two years while still working as a principal. Upon retirement from both positions, Susan continued to focus on supporting a strong education for future students by supervising student teachers for the University of Iowa. During this time, she also accepted the position of part-time pastor at West Branch Friends Meeting. After serving there for four years and fully retiring, she saw an opportunity to do some writing once again. Susan has four previously published historical fiction novels based on Quakers settling in Iowa in the 1800s: *For the Love of a Friend, For the Gift of a Friend, For the Call of a Friend,* and *For the Blessing of a Friend.* She has been blessed with a loving family and eight wonderful grandchildren!

Printed in the USA
CPSIA information can be obtained
at www.ICGtesting.com
LVHW092257230324
775354LV00008B/399